THE POETIC EDDA

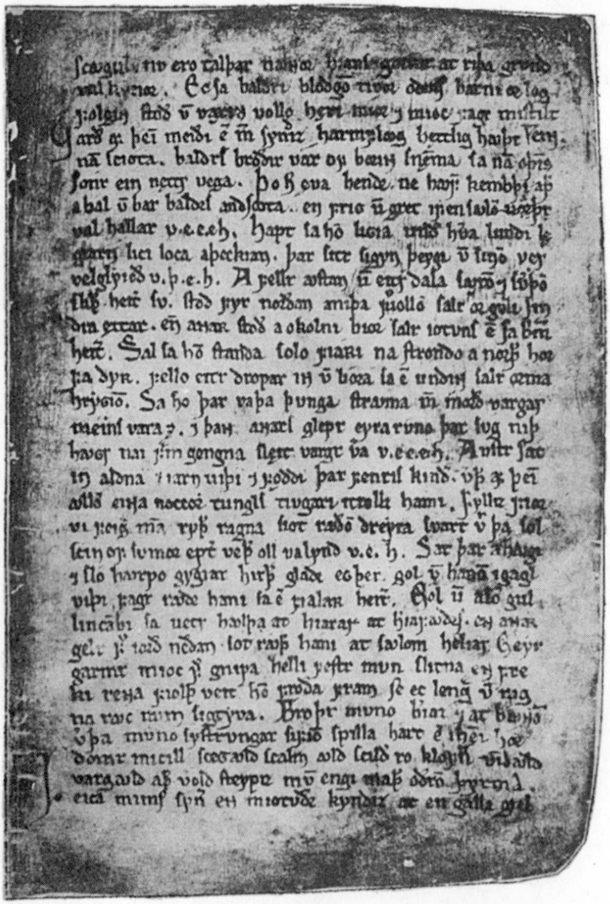

A PAGE FROM THE CODEX REGIUS COMPRISING VERSES 31 TO 45 OF THE VOLUSPO

THE POETIC EDDA

THE MYTHOLOGICAL POEMS

Translated from the Icelandic with an Introduction and Notes by
Henry Adams Bellows

DOVER PUBLICATIONS, INC.
Mineola, New York

Bibliographical Note

This Dover edition, first published in 2004, is an unabridged republication of the first part (including the General Introduction and the Lays of the Gods, but leaving out Lays of the Heroes and the Pronouncing Index) of *The Poetic Edda,* originally published as volumes XXI and XXII of the Scandinavian Classics series by the American-Scandinavian Foundation, New York, and Oxford University Press, London, in 1923.

Library of Congress Cataloging-in-Publication Data

Edda Sæmundar. English. Selections

The poetic Eddas : the mythological poems / translated from the Icelandic with an introduction and notes by Henry Adams Bellows.

p. cm.

Unabridged republication of the first part of: The poetic Edda; originally published: New York : American Scandinavian Foundation, 1923.

ISBN 0-486-43710-8 (pbk.)

1. Edda Sæmundar—Translations into English. I. Bellows, Henry Adams, 1885-1939. II. Title.

PT7234.E5B5 2004
839.6'1—dc22

2004047807

Manufactured in the United States of America
Dover Publications, Inc., 31 East 2nd Street, Mineola, N.Y. 11501

To George Lyman Kittredge

CONTENTS

NOTE TO THE DOVER EDITION

This edition reprints only the first half (comprising the General Introduction and the Lays of the Gods) of the book that was first published in 1923. The Lays of the Heroes are not included in this edition. Readers should keep this in mind when, in the General Introduction on the following pages, Bellows mentions (at the bottom of page xviii, for example) "the heroic lays," or when (on page xv) he speaks of "thirty-four poems."

ACKNOWLEDGEMENT

The General Introduction mentions many of the scholars to whose work this translation owes a special debt. Particular reference, however, should here be made to the late William Henry Schofield, Professor of Comparative Literature in Harvard University and President of The American-Scandinavian Foundation, under whose guidance this translation was begun; to Henry Goddard Leach, for many years Secretary of The American-Scandinavian Foundation, and to William Witherle Lawrence, Professor of English in Columbia University and Chairman of the Foundation's Committee on Publications, for their assistance with the manuscript and the proofs; and to Hanna Astrup Larsen, the Foundation's literary secretary, for her efficient management of the complex details of publication.

GENERAL INTRODUCTION

THERE is scarcely any literary work of great importance which has been less readily available for the general reader, or even for the serious student of literature, than the *Poetic Edda.* Translations have been far from numerous, and only in Germany has the complete work of translation been done in the full light of recent scholarship. In English the only versions were long the conspicuously inadequate one made by Thorpe, and published about half a century ago, and the unsatisfactory prose translations in Vigfusson and Powell's *Corpus Poeticum Boreale,* reprinted in the Norrœna collection. An excellent translation of the poems dealing with the gods, in verse and with critical and explanatory notes, made by Olive Bray, was, however, published by the Viking Club of London in 1908. In French there exist only partial translations, chief among them being those made by Bergmann many years ago. Among the seven or eight German versions, those by the Brothers Grimm and by Karl Simrock, which had considerable historical importance because of their influence on nineteenth century German literature and art, and particularly on the work of Richard Wagner, have been largely superseded by Hugo Gering's admirable translation, published in 1892, and by the recent two-volume rendering by Genzmer, with excellent notes by Andreas Heusler, 1914-1920. There are competent translations in both Norwegian and Swedish. The lack of any complete and adequately annotated English rendering in metrical form, based on a critical text, and profiting by the cumulative labors of such scholars as Mogk, Vigfusson,

Finnur Jonsson, Grundtvig, Bugge, Gislason, Hildebrand, Lüning, Sweet, Niedner, Ettmüller, Müllenhoff, Edzardi, B. M. Olsen, Sievers, Sijmons, Detter, Heinzel, Falk, Neckel, Heusler, and Gering, has kept this extraordinary work practically out of the reach of those who have had neither time nor inclination to master the intricacies of the original Old Norse.

On the importance of the material contained in the *Poetic Edda* it is here needless to dwell at any length. We have inherited the Germanic traditions in our very speech, and the *Poetic Edda* is the original storehouse of Germanic mythology. It is, indeed, in many ways the greatest literary monument preserved to us out of the antiquity of the kindred races which we call Germanic. Moreover, it has a literary value altogether apart from its historical significance. The mythological poems include, in the *Voluspo,* one of the vastest conceptions of the creation and ultimate destruction of the world ever crystallized in literary form; in parts of the *Hovamol,* a collection of wise counsels that can bear comparison with most of the Biblical Book of Proverbs; in the *Lokasenna,* a comedy none the less full of vivid characterization because its humor is often broad; and in the *Thrymskvitha,* one of the finest ballads in the world. The hero poems give us, in its oldest and most vivid extant form, the story of Sigurth, Brynhild, and Atli, the Norse parallel to the German *Nibelungenlied.* The *Poetic Edda* is not only of great interest to the student of antiquity; it is a collection including some of the most remarkable poems which have been preserved to us from the period before the pen and the printing-press replaced the poet-singer and oral tradition. It is above all else the desire to make better known the dramatic force, the vivid and often tremendous imagery, and the superb conceptions embodied in these poems which has called forth the present translation.

WHAT IS THE POETIC EDDA?

Even if the poems of the so-called *Edda* were not so significant and intrinsically so valuable, the long series of scholarly struggles which have been going on over them for the better part of three centuries would in itself give them a peculiar interest. Their history is strangely mysterious. We do not know who composed them, or when or where they were composed; we are by no means sure who collected them or when he did so; finally, we are not absolutely certain as to what an "Edda" is, and the best guess at the meaning of the word renders its application to this collection of poems more or less misleading.

A brief review of the chief facts in the history of the *Poetic Edda* will explain why this uncertainty has persisted. Preserved in various manuscripts of the thirteenth and early fourteenth centuries is a prose work consisting of a very extensive collection of mythological stories, an explanation of the important figures and tropes of Norse poetic diction,—the poetry of the Icelandic and Norwegian skalds was appallingly complex in this respect,—and a treatise on metrics. This work, clearly a handbook for poets, was commonly known as the "Edda" of Snorri Sturluson, for at the head of the copy of it in the *Uppsalabok*, a manuscript written presumably some fifty or sixty years after Snorri's death, which was in 1241, we find: "This book is called Edda, which Snorri Sturluson composed." This work, well known as the *Prose Edda*, Snorri's *Edda* or the

Younger Edda, has recently been made available to readers of English in the admirable translation by Arthur G. Brodeur, published by the American-Scandinavian Foundation in 1916.

Icelandic tradition, however, persisted in ascribing either this *Edda* or one resembling it to Snorri's much earlier compatriot, Sæmund the Wise (1056-1133). When, early in the seventeenth century, the learned Arngrimur Jonsson proved to everyone's satisfaction that Snorri and nobody else must have been responsible for the work in question, the next thing to determine was what, if anything, Sæmund had done of the same kind. The nature of Snorri's book gave a clue. In the mythological stories related a number of poems were quoted, and as these and other poems were to all appearances Snorri's chief sources of information, it was assumed that Sæmund must have written or compiled a verse *Edda*—whatever an "Edda" might be—on which Snorri's work was largely based.

So matters stood when, in 1643, Brynjolfur Sveinsson, Bishop of Skalholt, discovered a manuscript, clearly written as early as 1300, containing twenty-nine poems, complete or fragmentary, and some of them with the very lines and stanzas used by Snorri. Great was the joy of the scholars, for here, of course, must be at least a part of the long-sought *Edda* of Sæmund the Wise. Thus the good bishop promptly labeled his find, and as Sæmund's *Edda,* the *Elder Edda* or the *Poetic Edda* it has been known to this day.

This precious manuscript, now in the Royal Library in Copenhagen, and known as the *Codex Regius* (R2365), has been the basis for all published editions of the Eddic poems. A few poems of similar character found elsewhere have subsequently been added to the collection, until now most editions include, as in this translation, a total of thirty-four. A shorter manuscript now in the Arnamagnæan collection in Copenhagen (AM748), contains fragmentary or complete versions of six of the poems in the *Codex Regius,* and one other, *Baldrs Draumar,* not found in that collection. Four other poems (*Rigsthula, Hyndluljoth, Grougaldr* and *Fjolsvinnsmol,* the last two here combined under the title of *Svipdagsmol*), from various manuscripts, so closely resemble in subject-matter and style the poems in the *Codex Regius* that they have been included by most editors in the collection. Finally, Snorri's *Edda* contains one complete poem, the *Grottasongr,* which many editors have added to the poetic collection; it is, however, not included in this translation, as an admirable English version of it is available in Mr. Brodeur's rendering of Snorri's work.

From all this it is evident that the *Poetic Edda,* as we now know it, is no definite and plainly limited work, but rather a more or less haphazard collection of separate poems, dealing either with Norse mythology or with hero-cycles unrelated to the traditional history of greater Scandinavia or Iceland. How many other similar poems, now lost, may have existed in such collections as were current in Iceland in the later twelfth and thirteenth centuries we cannot know, though it is evident that some poems of this type are missing. We can say only that thirty-four poems have been preserved, twenty-nine of them in a single manuscript collection, which differ considerably in subject-matter and style from all the rest of extant Old Norse poetry, and these we group together as the *Poetic Edda.*

But what does the word "Edda" mean? Various guesses have been made. An early assumption was that the word somehow meant "Poetics," which fitted Snorri's treatise to a nicety, but which, in addition to the lack of philological evidence to support this interpretation, could by no stretch of scholarly subtlety be made appropriate to the collection of poems. Jacob Grimm ingeniously identified the word with the word "edda" used in one of the poems, the *Rigsthula,* where, rather conjecturally, it means "great-grandmother." The word exists in this sense nowhere else in Norse literature, and Grimm's suggestion of "Tales of a Grandmother," though at one time it found wide acceptance, was grotesquely inappropriate to either the prose or the verse work.

At last Eirikr Magnusson hit on what appears the likeliest solution of the puzzle: that "Edda" is simply the genitive form of the proper name "Oddi." Oddi was a settlement in the southwest of Iceland, certainly the home of Snorri Sturluson for many years, and, traditionally at least, also the home of Sæmund the Wise. That Snorri's work should have been called "The Book of Oddi" is altogether reasonable, for such a method of naming books was common—witness the "Book of the Flat Island" and other early manuscripts. That Sæmund may also have written or compiled another "Oddi-Book" is perfectly possible, and that tradition should have said he did so is entirely natural.

It is, however, an open question whether or not Sæmund had anything to do with making the collection, or any part of it, now known as the *Poetic Edda,* for of course the seventeenth-century assignment of the work to him is negligible. We can say only that he may have made some such compilation, for he was a diligent student of Icelandic tradition and history, and was famed throughout the North for his learning. But otherwise no trace of his works survives, and as he was educated in Paris, it is probable that he wrote rather in Latin than in the vernacular.

All that is reasonably certain is that by the middle or last of the twelfth century there existed in Iceland one or more written collections of Old Norse mythological and heroic poems, that the *Codex Regius,* a copy made a hundred years or so later, represents at least a considerable part of one of these, and that the collection of thirty-four poems which we now know as the *Poetic* or *Elder Edda* is practically all that has come down to us of Old Norse poetry of this type. Anything more is largely guesswork, and both the name of the compiler and the meaning of the title "Edda" are conjectural.

THE ORIGIN OF THE EDDIC POEMS

There is even less agreement about the birthplace, authorship and date of the Eddic poems themselves than about the nature of the existing collection. Clearly the poems were the work of many different men, living in different periods; clearly, too, most of them existed in oral tradition for generations before they were first committed to writing. In general the mythological poems are strongly heathen in character, and as Christianity became generally accepted throughout Norway and Iceland early in the eleventh century, it is altogether likely that most of the poems dealing with the Norse gods antedate the year 1000. On the other hand, Hoffory, Finnur Jonsson and others have shown pretty conclusively from linguistic evidence that these poems cannot have assumed anything like their present form before the ninth century. As for the poems belonging to the hero cycles, one or two of them appear to be as late as 1100, but most of them clearly belong to the hundred years following 950. It is a fairly safe guess that the years between 900 and 1050 saw the majority of the Eddic poems put into shape, but it must be remembered that many changes took place during the long subsequent period of oral transmission, and also that many of the legends, both mythological and heroic, on which the poems were based, certainly existed in Norway, and quite possibly in verse form, long before the year 900. In considering such poems it is essential to forget the present mode of composition, whereby a poet at once fixes his thought and his style by means of writing, and to remember that for at least two centuries, and possibly much longer, the correct transmission of many of the Eddic poems depended solely on accurate hearing and retentive memory.

As to the origin of the legends on which the poems are based, the whole question, at least so far as the stories of the gods are concerned, is much too complex for discussion here. How much of the actual narrative material of the mythological lays is properly to be called Scandinavian is a matter for students of comparative mythology to guess at. The tales underlying the heroic lays are clearly of foreign origin: the Helgi story comes from Denmark, and that of Völund from Germany, as also the great mass of traditions centering around Sigurth (Siegfried), Brynhild, the sons of Gjuki, Atli (Attila), and Jormunrek (Ermanarich). The introductory notes to the various poems deal with the more important of these questions of origin.

Introduction

Of the men who composed these poems,—"wrote" is obviously the wrong word,—we know absolutely nothing, save that some of them must have been literary artists with a high degree of conscious skill. The Eddic poems are "folk-poetry,"—whatever that may be,—only in the sense that some of them strongly reflect racial feelings and beliefs; they are anything but crude or primitive in workmanship, and they show that not only the poets themselves, but also many of their hearers, must have made a careful study of the art of poetry.

Where the poems were composed is almost equally uncertain. The claims of Norway have been extensively advanced, but the great literary activity of Iceland after the settlement of the island by Norwegian emigrants late in the ninth century makes the theory of an Icelandic source for most of the poems plausible. The two Atli lays, with what authority we do not know, bear in the *Codex Regius* the superscription "the Greenland poem," and internal evidence indicates that this statement is correct. Certainly in one poem, the *Rigsthula,* and probably in several others, there are marks of Celtic influence. During a considerable part of the ninth and tenth centuries, Scandinavians were active in Ireland and in most of the western islands inhabited by branches of the Celtic race. Some scholars claim nearly all the Eddic poems for these "Western Isles," in sharp distinction from Iceland; their arguments are commented on in the introductory note to the *Rigsthula.* However, as Iceland early came to be the true center of this Scandinavian island world, it may be said that most of the evidence concerning the birthplace of the Eddic poems in anything like their present form points in that direction, and certainly it was in Iceland that they were chiefly preserved.

THE EDDA AND OLD NORSE LITERATURE

Within the proper limits of an introduction it would be impossible to give any adequate summary of the history and literature with which the Eddic poems are indissolubly connected, but a mere mention of a few of the salient facts may be of some service to those who are unfamiliar with the subject. Old Norse literature covers approximately the period between 850 and 1300. During the first part of that period occurred the great wanderings of the Scandinavian peoples, and particularly the Norwegians. A convenient date to remember is that of the sea-fight of Hafrsfjord, 872, when Harald the Fair-Haired broke the power of the independent Norwegian nobles, and made himself overlord of nearly all the country. Many of the defeated nobles fled overseas, where inviting refuges had been found for them by earlier wanderers and plunder-seeking raiders. This was the time of the inroads of the dreaded Northmen in France, and in 885 Hrolf Gangr (Rollo) laid siege to Paris itself. Many Norwegians went to Ireland, where their compatriots had already built Dublin, and where they remained in control of most of the island till Brian Boru shattered their power at the battle of Clontarf in 1014.

Of all the migrations, however, the most important were those to Iceland. Here grew up an active civilization, fostered by absolute independence and by remoteness from the wars which wracked Norway, yet kept from degenerating into provincialism by the roving life of the people, which brought them constantly in contact with the culture of the South. Christianity, introduced throughout the Norse world about the year 1000, brought with it the stability of learning, and the Icelanders became not only the makers but also the students and recorders of history.

The years between 875 and 1100 were the great spontaneous period of oral literature. Most of the military and political leaders were also poets, and they composed a mass of lyric poetry concerning the authorship of which we know a good deal, and much of which has been preserved. Narrative prose also flourished, for the Icelander had a passion for story-telling and story-hearing. After 1100 came the day of the writers. These sagamen collected the material that for generations had passed from mouth to mouth, and gave it permanent form in writing. The greatest bulk of what we now have of Old Norse literature,—and the published part of it makes a formidable library,—originated thus in the earlier period before the introduction of writing, and was put into final shape by the scholars, most of them Icelanders, of the hundred years following 1150.

After 1250 came a rapid and tragic decline. Iceland lost its independence, becoming a Norwegian province. Later Norway too fell under alien rule, a Swede ascending the Norwegian throne in 1320. Pestilence and famine laid waste the whole North; volcanic disturbances worked havoc in Iceland. Literature did not quite die, but it fell upon evil days; for the vigorous native narratives and heroic poems of the older period were substituted translations of French romances. The poets wrote mostly doggerel; the prose writers were devoid of national or racial inspiration.

The mass of literature thus collected and written down

largely between 1150 and 1250 may be roughly divided into four groups. The greatest in volume is made up of the sagas: narratives mainly in prose, ranging all the way from authentic history of the Norwegian kings and the early Icelandic settlements to fairy-tales. Embodied in the sagas is found the material composing the second group: the skaldic poetry, a vast collection of songs of praise, triumph, love, lamentation, and so on, almost uniformly characterized by an appalling complexity of figurative language. There is no absolute line to be drawn between the poetry of the skalds and the poems of the *Edda,* which we may call the third group; but in addition to the remarkable artificiality of style which marks the skaldic poetry, and which is seldom found in the poems of the *Edda,* the skalds dealt almost exclusively with their own emotions, whereas the Eddic poems are quite impersonal. Finally, there is the fourth group, made up of didactic works, religious and legal treatises, and so on, studies which originated chiefly in the later period of learned activity.

PRESERVATION OF THE EDDIC POEMS

Most of the poems of the *Poetic Edda* have unquestionably reached us in rather bad shape. During the long period of oral transmission they suffered all sorts of interpolations, omissions and changes, and some of them, as they now stand, are a bewildering hodge-podge of little-related fragments. To some extent the diligent twelfth century compiler to whom we owe the *Codex Regius*—Sæmund or another—was himself doubtless responsible for the patchwork process, often supplemented by narrative prose notes of his own; but in the days before written records existed, it was easy to lose stanzas and longer passages from their context, and equally easy to interpolate them where they did not by any means belong. Some few of the poems, however, appear to be virtually complete and unified as we now have them.

Under such circumstances it is clear that the establishment of a satisfactory text is a matter of the utmost difficulty. As the basis for this translation I have used the text prepared by Karl Hildebrand (1876) and revised by Hugo Gering (1904). Textual emendation has, however, been so extensive in every edition of the *Edda,* and has depended so much on the theories of the editor, that I have also made extensive use of many other editions, notably those by Finnur Jonsson, Neckel, Sijmons, and Detter and Heinzel, together with numerous commentaries. The condition of the text in both the principal codices is such that no great reliance can be placed on the accuracy of the copyists, and frequently two editions will differ fundamentally as to their readings of a given passage or even of an entire poem. For this reason, and because guesswork necessarily plays so large a part in any edition or translation of the Eddic poems, I have risked overloading the pages with textual notes in order to show, as nearly as possible, the exact state of the original together with all the more significant emendations. I have done this particularly in the case of transpositions, many of which appear absolutely necessary, and in the indication of passages which appear to be interpolations.

THE VERSE-FORMS OF THE EDDIC POEMS

The many problems connected with the verse-forms found in the Eddic poems have been analyzed in great detail by Sievers, Neckel, and others. The three verse-forms exemplified in the poems need only a brief comment here, however, in order to make clear the method used in this translation. All of these forms group the lines normally in four-line stanzas. In the so-called Fornyrthislag ("Old Verse"), for convenience sometimes referred to in the notes as four-four measure, these lines have all the same structure, each line being sharply divided by a cæsural pause into two half-lines, and each half-line having two accented syllables and two (sometimes three) unaccented ones. The two half-lines forming a complete line are bound together by the alliteration, or more properly initial-rhyme, of three (or two) of the accented syllables. The following is an example of the Fornyrthislag stanza, the accented syllables being in italics:

Vreiþr vas *Ving*þórr, es *vakna*þi
ok *síns hamars* of *sakna*þi;
skegg nam *hris*ta, *skǫr* nam *dý*ja,
réþ *Jarþar burr* *umb* at *þreif*ask.

In the second form, the Ljothahattr ("Song Measure"), the first and third line of each stanza are as just described, but the second and fourth are shorter, have no cæsural pause, have three accented syllables, and regularly two initial-rhymed accented syllables, for which reason I have occasionally referred to Ljothahattr as four-three measure. The following is an example:

Ar skal *rísa* sás *an*nars *vill*
fé eþa *fjǫr hafa*;
*ligg*jandi *ulfr* sjaldan *láer* of *getr*
né *sof*andi *maþr sigr*.

In the third and least commonly used form, the Malahattr ("Speech Measure"), a younger verse-form than either of the other two, each line of the four-line stanza is divided into two half-lines by a cæsural pause, each half-line having two accented syllables and three (sometimes four) unaccented ones; the initial rhyme is as in the Fornyrthislag. The following is an example:

Horsk vas *hús*freyja, *hug*þi at *mann*viti,
lag heyrþi *orþ*a, hvat á *laun máel*tu;
þá vas *vant vit*ri, *vil*di þeim *hjalþ*a:
skyldu of *sáe sig*la, en *sjǫlf* né *kvamsk*at.

A poem in Fornyrthislag is normally entitled *-kvitha* (*Thrymskvitha, Guthrunarkvitha,* etc.), which for convenience I have rendered as "lay," while a poem in Ljothahattr is entitled *-mol* (*Grimnismol, Skirnismol,* etc.), which I have rendered as "ballad." It is difficult to find any distinction other than metrical between the two terms, although it is clear that one originally existed.

Variations frequently appear in all three kinds of verse, and these I have attempted to indicate through the rhythm of the translation. In order to preserve so far as possible the effect of the Eddic verse, I have adhered, in making the English version, to certain of the fundamental rules governing the Norse line and stanza formations. The number of lines to each stanza conforms to what seems the best guess as to the original, and I have consistently retained the number of accented syllables. In translating from a highly inflected language into one depending largely on the use of subsidiary words, it has, however, been necessary to employ considerable freedom as to the number of unaccented syllables in a line. The initial-rhyme is generally confined to two accented syllables in each line. As in the original, all initial vowels are allowed to rhyme interchangeably, but I have disregarded the rule which lets certain groups of consonants rhyme only with themselves (*e. g.,* I have allowed initial *s* or *st* to rhyme with *sk* or *sl*). In general, I have sought to preserve the effect of the original form whenever possible without an undue sacrifice of accuracy. For purposes of comparison, the translations of the three stanzas just given are here included:

Fornyrthislag:

Wild was *Ving*thor *when* he a*woke,*
And *when* his *mighty* *ham*mer he *missed;*
He *shook* his *beard,* his *hair* was *brist*ling,
To *groping set* the *son* of *Jorth.*

Ljothahattr:

He must *ear*ly go *forth* who *fain* the *blood*
Or the *goods* of ano*th*er would *get;*
The *wolf* that lies *id*le shall *win* little *meat,*
Or the *sleep*ing *man* success.

Malahattr:

Wise was the *wom*an, she *fain* would use *wis*dom,
She *saw* well what *meant* all they *said* in *sec*ret;
From her *heart* it was *hid* how *help* she might *ren*der,
The *sea* they should *sail,* while her*self* she should *go* not.

PROPER NAMES

The forms in which the proper names appear in this translation will undoubtedly perplex and annoy those who have become accustomed to one or another of the current methods of anglicising old Norse names. The nominative ending -r it has seemed best to omit after consonants, although it has been retained after vowels; in Baldr the final -r is a part of the stem and is of course retained. I have rendered the Norse þ by "th" throughout, instead of spasmodically by "d," as in many texts: *e. g.,* Othin instead of Odin. For the Norse ø I have used its equivalent, "ö," *e. g.,* Völund; for the ǫ I have used "o" and not "a," *e. g.,* Voluspo, not Valuspa or Voluspa. To avoid confusion with accents the long vowel marks of the Icelandic are consistently omitted, as likewise in modern Icelandic proper names. The index at the end of the book indicates the pronunciation in each case.

CONCLUSION

That this translation may be of some value to those who can read the poems of the *Edda* in the original language I earnestly hope. Still more do I wish that it may lead a few who hitherto have given little thought to the Old Norse language and literature to master the tongue for themselves. But far above either of these I place the hope that this English version may give to some, who have known little of the ancient traditions of what is after all their own race, a clearer insight into the glories of that extraordinary past, and that I may through this medium be able to bring to others a small part of the delight which I myself have found in the poems of the *Poetic Edda.*

THE POETIC EDDA

VOLUSPO

The Wise-Woman's Prophecy

Introductory Note

At the beginning of the collection in the *Codex Regius* stands the *Voluspo,* the most famous and important, as it is likewise the most debated, of all the Eddic poems. Another version of it is found in a huge miscellaneous compilation of about the year 1300, the *Hauksbok,* and many stanzas are included in the *Prose Edda* of Snorri Sturluson. The order of the stanzas in the *Hauksbok* version differs materially from that in the *Codex Regius,* and in the published editions many experiments have been attempted in further rearrangements. On the whole, however, and allowing for certain interpolations, the order of the stanzas in the *Codex Regius* seems more logical than any of the wholesale "improvements" which have been undertaken.

The genera' plan of the *Voluspo* is fairly clear. Othin, chief of the gods, always conscious of impending disaster and eager for knowledge, calls on a certain "Volva," or wise-woman, presumably bidding her rise from the grave. She first tells him of the past, of the creation of the world, the beginning of years, the origin of the dwarfs (at this point there is a clearly interpolated catalogue of dwarfs' names, stanzas 10-16), of the first man and woman, of the world-ash Yggdrasil, and of the first war, between the gods and the Vanir, or, in Anglicized form, the Wanes. Then, in stanzas 27-29, as a further proof of her wisdom, she discloses some of Othin's own secrets and the details of his search for knowledge. Rewarded by Othin for what she has thus far told (stanza 30), she then turns to the real prophesy, the disclosure of the final destruction of the gods. This final battle, in which fire and flood overwhelm heaven and earth as the gods fight with their enemies, is the great fact in Norse mythology; the phrase describing it, *ragna rök,* "the fate of the gods," has become familiar, by confusion with the word *rökkr,* "twilight," in the German *Götterdämmerung.* The wise-woman tells of the Valkyries who bring the slain warriors to support Othin and the other gods in the battle, of the slaying of Baldr, best and fairest of the gods, through the wiles of Loki, of the enemies of the gods, of the summons to battle on both sides, and of the mighty struggle, till Othin is slain, and "fire leaps high about heaven itself" (stanzas 31-58). But this is not all. A new and beautiful world is to rise on the ruins of the old; Baldr comes back, and "fields unsowed bear ripened fruit" (stanzas 59-66).

This final passage, in particular, has caused wide differences of opinion as to the date and character of the poem. That the poet was heathen and not Christian seems almost beyond dispute; there is an intensity and vividness in almost every stanza which no archaizing Christian could possibly have achieved. On the other hand, the evidences of Christian influence are sufficiently striking to outweigh the arguments of Finnur Jonsson, Müllenhoff and others who maintain that the *Voluspo* is purely a product of heathendom. The roving Norsemen of the tenth century, very few of whom had as yet accepted Christianity, were nevertheless in close contact with Celtic races which had already been converted, and in many ways the Celtic influence was strongly felt. It seems likely, then, that the *Voluspo* was the work of a poet living chiefly in Iceland, though possibly in the "Western Isles," in the middle of the tenth century, a vigorous believer in the old gods, and yet with an imagination active enough to be touched by the vague tales of a different religion emanating from his neighbor Celts.

How much the poem was altered during the two hundred years between its composition and its first being committed to writing is largely a matter of guesswork, but, allowing for such an obvious interpolation as the catalogue of dwarfs, and for occasional lesser errors, it seems quite needless to assume such great changes as many editors do. The poem was certainly not composed to tell a story with which its early hearers were quite familiar; the lack of continuity which baffles modern readers presumably did not trouble them in the least. It is, in effect, a series of gigantic pictures, put into words with a directness and sureness which bespeak the poet of genius. It is only after the reader, with the help of the many notes, has familiarized himself with the names and incidents involved that he can begin to understand the effect which this magnificent poem must have produced on those who not only understood but believed it.

Voluspo

1. Hearing I ask from the holy races,
From Heimdall's sons, both high and low;
Thou wilt, Valfather, that well I relate
Old tales I remember of men long ago.

2. I remember yet the giants of yore,
Who gave me bread in the days gone by;
Nine worlds I knew, the nine in the tree
With mighty roots beneath the mold.

---

1. A few editors, following Bugge, in an effort to clarify the poem, place stanzas 22, 28 and 30 before stanzas 1-20, but the arrangement in both manuscripts, followed here, seems logical. In stanza 1 the Volva, or wise-woman, called upon by Othin, answers him and demands a hearing. Evidently she belongs to the race of the giants (cf. stanza 2), and thus speaks to Othin unwillingly, being compelled to do so by his magic power. *Holy:* omitted in *Regius;* the phrase "holy races" probably means little more than mankind in general. *Heimdall:* the watchman of the gods; cf. stanza 46 and note. Why mankind should be referred to as Heimdall's sons is uncertain, and the phrase has caused much perplexity. Heimdall seems to have had various attributes, and in the *Rigsthula,* wherein a certain Rig appears as the ancestor of the three great classes of men, a fourteenth century annotator identifies Rig with Heimdall, on what authority we do not know, for the Rig of the poem seems much more like Othin (cf. *Rigsthula,* introductory prose and note). *Valfather* ("Father of the Slain"): Othin, chief of the gods, so called because the slain warriors were brought to him at Valhall ("Hall of the Slain") by the Valkyries ("Choosers of the Slain").

2. *Nine worlds*: the worlds of the gods (Asgarth), of the Wanes (Vanaheim, cf. stanza 21 and note), of the elves (Alfheim), of men (Mithgarth), of the giants (Jotunheim), of fire (Muspellsheim, cf. stanza 47 and note), of the dark elves (Svartalfaheim), of the dead (Niflheim), and presumably of the dwarfs (perhaps Nithavellir, cf. stanza 37 and note, but the ninth world is uncertain). *The tree*: the world-ash Yggdrasil,

3. Of old was the age when Ymir lived;
Sea nor cool waves nor sand there were;
Earth had not been, nor heaven above,
But a yawning gap, and grass nowhere.

4. Then Bur's sons lifted the level land,
Mithgarth the mighty there they made;
The sun from the south warmed the stones of earth,
And green was the ground with growing leeks.

5. The sun, the sister of the moon, from the south
Her right hand cast over heaven's rim;
No knowledge she had where her home should be,
The moon knew not what might was his,
The stars knew not where their stations were.

---

symbolizing the universe; cf. *Grimnismol,* 29-35 and notes, wherein Yggdrasil is described at length.

3. *Ymir*: the giant out of whose body the gods made the world; cf. *Vafthruthnismol,* 21. In this stanza as quoted in Snorri's *Edda* the first line runs: "Of old was the age ere aught there was." *Yawning gap*: this phrase, "Ginnunga-gap," is sometimes used as a proper name.

4. *Bur's sons*: Othin, Vili, and Ve. Of Bur we know only that his wife was Bestla, daughter of Bolthorn; cf. *Hovamol,* 141. Vili and Ve are mentioned by name in the Eddic poems only in *Lokasenna,* 26. *Mithgarth* ("Middle Dwelling"): the world of men. *Leeks*: the leek was often used as the symbol of fine growth (cf. *Guthrunarkvitha* I, 17), and it was also supposed to have magic power (cf. *Sigrdrifumol,* 7).

5. Various editors have regarded this stanza as interpolated; Hoffory thinks it describes the northern summer night in which the sun does not set. Lines 3-5 are quoted by Snorri. In the manuscripts line 4 follows line 5. Regarding the sun and moon

6. Then sought the gods their assembly-seats,
The holy ones, and council held;
Names then gave they to noon and twilight,
Morning they named, and the waning moon,
Night and evening, the years to number.

7. At Ithavoll met the mighty gods,
Shrines and temples they timbered high;
Forges they set, and they smithied ore,
Tongs they wrought, and tools they fashioned.

8. In their dwellings at peace they played at tables,
Of gold no lack did the gods then know,—
Till thither came up giant-maids three,
Huge of might, out of Jotunheim.

---

as daughter and son of Mundilferi, cf. *Vafthruthnismol,* 23 and note, and *Grimnismol,* 37 and note.

6. Possibly an interpolation, but there seems no strong reason for assuming this. Lines 1-2 are identical with lines 1-2 of stanza 9, and line 2 may have been inserted here from that later stanza.

7. *Ithavoll* ("Field of Deeds"?): mentioned only here and in stanza 60 as the meeting-place of the gods; it appears in no other connection.

8. *Tables*: the exact nature of this game, and whether it more closely resembled chess or checkers, has been made the subject of a 400-page treatise, Willard Fiske's "Chess in Iceland." *Giant-maids*: perhaps the three great Norns, corresponding to the three fates; cf. stanza 20 and note. Possibly, however, something has been lost after this stanza, and the missing passage, replaced by the catalogue of the dwarfs (stanzas 9-16), may have explained the "giant-maids" otherwise than as Norns. In *Vafthruthnismol,* 49, the Norns (this time "three throngs" instead of simply "three") are spoken of as giant-maidens;

9\. Then sought the gods their assembly-seats,
The holy ones, and council held,
To find who should raise the race of dwarfs
Out of Brimir's blood and the legs of Blain.

10\. There was Motsognir the mightiest made
Of all the dwarfs, and Durin next;
Many a likeness of men they made,
The dwarfs in the earth, as Durin said.

11\. Nyi and Nithi, Northri and Suthri,
Austri and Vestri, Althjof, Dvalin,
Nar and Nain, Niping, Dain,
Bifur, Bofur, Bombur, Nori,
An and Onar, Ai, Mjothvitnir.

Fafnismol, 13, indicates the existence of many lesser Norns, belonging to various races. *Jotunheim*: the world of the giants.

9\. Here apparently begins the interpolated catalogue of the dwarfs, running through stanza 16; possibly, however, the interpolated section does not begin before stanza 11. Snorri quotes practically the entire section, the names appearing in a somewhat changed order. *Brimir* and *Blain*: nothing is known of these two giants, and it has been suggested that both are names for Ymir (cf. stanza 3). Brimir, however, appears in stanza 37 in connection with the home of the dwarfs. Some editors treat the words as common rather than proper nouns, Brimir meaning "the bloody moisture" and Blain being of uncertain significance.

10\. Very few of the dwarfs named in this and the following stanzas are mentioned elsewhere. It is not clear why Durin should have been singled out as authority for the list. The occasional repetitions suggest that not all the stanzas of the catalogue came from the same source. Most of the names presumably had some definite significance, as Northri, Suthri, Austri, and Vestri ("North," "South," "East," and "West"), Althjof

12. Vigg and Gandalf, Vindalf, Thrain,
Thekk and Thorin, Thror, Vit and Lit,
Nyr and Nyrath,— now have I told—
Regin and Rathsvith— the list aright.

13. Fili, Kili, Fundin, Nali,
Heptifili, Hannar, Sviur,
Frar, Hornbori, Fræg and Loni,
Aurvang, Jari, Eikinskjaldi.

14. The race of the dwarfs in Dvalin's throng
Down to Lofar the list must I tell;
The rocks they left, and through wet lands
They sought a home in the fields of sand.

15. There were Draupnir and Dolgthrasir,
Hor, Haugspori, Hlevang, Gloin,

("Mighty Thief"), Mjothvitnir ("Mead-Wolf"), Gandalf ("Magic Elf"), Vindalf ("Wind Elf"), Rathsvith ("Swift in Counsel"), Eikinskjaldi ("Oak Shield"), etc., but in many cases the interpretations are sheer guesswork.

12. The order of the lines in this and the succeeding four stanzas varies greatly in the manuscripts and editions, and the names likewise appear in many forms. *Regin*: probably not identical with Regin the son of Hreithmar, who plays an important part in the *Reginsmol* and *Fafnismol,* but cf. note on *Reginsmol,* introductory prose.

14. *Dvalin*: in Hovamol, 144, Dvalin seems to have given magic runes to the dwarfs, probably accounting for their skill in craftsmanship, while in *Fafnismol,* 13, he is mentioned as the father of some of the lesser Norns. The story that some of the dwarfs left the rocks and mountains to find a new home on the sands is mentioned, but unexplained, in Snorri's *Edda;* of *Lofar* we know only that he was descended from these wanderers.

Dori, Ori, Duf, Andvari,
Skirfir, Virfir, Skafith, Ai.

16. Alf and Yngvi, Eikinskjaldi,
Fjalar and Frosti, Fith and Ginnar;
So for all time shall the tale be known,
The list of all the forbears of Lofar.

17. Then from the throng did three come forth,
From the home of the gods, the mighty and gracious;
Two without fate on the land they found,
Ask and Embla, empty of might.

18. Soul they had not, sense they had not,
Heat nor motion, nor goodly hue;
Soul gave Othin, sense gave Hönir,
Heat gave Lothur and goodly hue.

---

15. *Andvari*: this dwarf appears prominently in the *Reginsmol,* which tells how the god Loki treacherously robbed him of his wealth; the curse which he laid on his treasure brought about the deaths of Sigurth, Gunnar, Atli, and many others.

17. Here the poem resumes its course after the interpolated section. Probably, however, something has been lost, for there is no apparent connection between the three giant-maids of stanza 8 and the three gods, Othin, Hönir and Lothur, who in stanza 17 go forth to create man and woman. The word "three" in stanzas 8 and 17 very likely confused some early reciter, or perhaps the compiler himself. *Ask* and *Embla*: ash and elm; Snorri gives them simply as the names of the first man and woman, but says that the gods made this pair out of trees.

18. *Hönir*: little is known of this god, save that he occasionally appears in the poems in company with Othin and Loki, and

19. An ash I know, Yggdrasil its name,
With water white is the great tree wet;
Thence come the dews that fall in the dales,
Green by Urth's well does it ever grow.

20. Thence come the maidens mighty in wisdom,
Three from the dwelling down 'neath the tree;
Urth is one named, Verthandi the next,—
On the wood they scored,— and Skuld the third.
Laws they made there, and life allotted
To the sons of men, and set their fates.

---

that he survives the destruction, assuming in the new age the gift of prophesy (cf. stanza 63). He was given by the gods as a hostage to the Wanes after their war, in exchange for Njorth (cf. stanza 21 and note). *Lothur*: apparently an older name for Loki, the treacherous but ingenious son of Laufey, whose divinity Snorri regards as somewhat doubtful. He was adopted by Othin, who subsequently had good reason to regret it. Loki probably represents the blending of two originally distinct figures, one of them an old fire-god, hence his gift of heat to the newly created pair.

19. *Yggdrasil*: cf. stanza 2 and note, and *Grimnismol,* 29-35 and notes. *Urth* ("The Past"): one of the three great Norns. The world-ash is kept green by being sprinkled with the marvelous healing water from her well.

20. *The maidens*: the three Norns; possibly this stanza should follow stanza 8. *Dwelling*: *Regius* has "sæ" (sea) instead of "sal" (hall, home), and many editors have followed this reading, although Snorri's prose paraphrase indicates "sal." *Urth, Verthandi* and *Skuld:* "Past," "Present" and "Future." *Wood,* etc.: the magic signs (runes) controlling the destinies of men were cut on pieces of wood. Lines 3-4 are probably interpolations from some other account of the Norns.

21. The war I remember, the first in the world,
When the gods with spears had smitten Gollveig,
And in the hall of Hor had burned her,—
Three times burned, and three times born,
Oft and again, yet ever she lives.

22. Heith they named her who sought their home,
The wide-seeing witch, in magic wise;
Minds she bewitched that were moved by her magic,
To evil women a joy she was.

---

21. This follows stanza 20 in *Regius;* in the *Hauksbok* version stanzas 25, 26, 27, 40 and 41 come between stanzas 20 and 21. Editors have attempted all sorts of rearrangements. *The war*: the first war was that between the gods and the Wanes. The cult of the Wanes (Vanir) seems to have originated among the seafaring folk of the Baltic and the southern shores of the North Sea, and to have spread thence into Norway in opposition to the worship of the older gods; hence the "war." Finally the two types of divinities were worshipped in common; hence the treaty which ended the war with the exchange of hostages. Chief among the Wanes were Njorth and his children, Freyr and Freyja, all of whom became conspicuous among the gods. Beyond this we know little of the Wanes, who seem originally to have been water-deities. *I remember*: the manuscripts have "she remembers," but the Volva is apparently still speaking of her own memories, as in stanza 2. *Gollveig* ("Gold-Might") : apparently the first of the Wanes to come among the gods, her ill-treatment being the immediate cause of the war. Müllenhoff maintains that Gollveig is another name for Freyja. Lines 5-6, one or both of them probably interpolated, seem to symbolize the refining of gold by fire. *Hor* ("The High One") : Othin.

22. *Heith* ("Shining One"?) : a name often applied to wise-women and prophetesses. The application of this stanza to Gollveig is far from clear, though the reference may be to the

23. On the host his spear did Othin hurl,
Then in the world did war first come;
The wall that girdled the gods was broken,
And the field by the warlike Wanes was trodden.

24. Then sought the gods their assembly-seats,
The holy ones, and council held,
Whether the gods should tribute give,
Or to all alike should worship belong.

25. Then sought the gods their assembly-seats,
The holy ones, and council held,
To find who with venom the air had filled,
Or had given Oth's bride to the giants' brood.

---

magic and destructive power of gold. It is also possible that the stanza is an interpolation. Bugge maintains that it applies to the Volva who is reciting the poem, and makes it the opening stanza, following it with stanzas 28 and 30, and then going on with stanzas 1 ff. The text of line 2 is obscure, and has been variously emended.

23. This stanza and stanza 24 have been transposed from the order in the manuscripts, for the former describes the battle and the victory of the Wanes, after which the gods took council, debating whether to pay tribute to the victors, or to admit them, as was finally done, to equal rights of worship.

25. Possibly, as Finn Magnusen long ago suggested, there is something lost after stanza 24, but it was not the custom of the Eddic poets to supply transitions which their hearers could generally be counted on to understand. The story referred to in stanzas 25-26 (both quoted by Snorri) is that of the rebuilding of Asgarth after its destruction by the Wanes. The gods employed a giant as builder, who demanded as his reward the sun and moon, and the goddess Freyja for his wife. The gods, terrified by the rapid progress of the work, forced Loki, who had advised the bargain, to delay the giant by a trick, so that the

26. In swelling rage then rose up Thor,—
Seldom he sits when he such things hears,—
And the oaths were broken, the words and bonds,
The mighty pledges between them made.

27. I know of the horn of Heimdall, hidden
Under the high-reaching holy tree;
On it there pours from Valfather's pledge
A mighty stream: would you know yet more?

---

work was not finished in the stipulated time (cf. *Grimnismol*, 44, note). The enraged giant then threatened the gods, whereupon Thor slew him. *Oth's bride*: Freyja; of Oth little is known beyond the fact that Snorri refers to him as a man who "went away on long journeys."

26. *Thor*: the thunder-god, son of Othin and Jorth (Earth); cf. particularly *Harbarthsljoth* and *Thrymskvitha, passim. Oaths,* etc.: the gods, by violating their oaths to the giant who rebuilt Asgarth, aroused the undying hatred of the giants' race, and thus the giants were among their enemies in the final battle.

27. Here the Volva turns from her memories of the past to a statement of some of Othin's own secrets in his eternal search for knowledge (stanzas 27-29). Bugge puts this stanza after stanza 29. *The horn of Heimdall*: the Gjallarhorn ("Shrieking Horn"), with which Heimdall, watchman of the gods, will summon them to the last battle. Till that time the horn is buried under Yggdrasil. *Valfather's pledge:* Othin's eye (the sun?), which he gave to the water-spirit Mimir (or Mim) in exchange for the latter's wisdom. It appears here and in stanza 29 as a drinking-vessel, from which Mimir drinks the magic mead, and from which he pours water on the ash Yggdrasil. Othin's sacrifice of his eye in order to gain knowledge of his final doom is one of the series of disasters leading up to the destruction of the gods. There were several differing versions of the story of Othin's relations with Mimir; another one, quite incompatible with this, appears in stanza 47. In the manuscripts *I know* and *I see* appear as "she knows" and "she sees" (cf. note on 21).

28. Alone I sat when the Old One sought me,
The terror of gods, and gazed in mine eyes:
"What hast thou to ask? why comest thou hither?
Othin, I know where thine eye is hidden."

29. I know where Othin's eye is hidden,
Deep in the wide-famed well of Mimir;
Mead from the pledge of Othin each morn
Does Mimir drink: would you know yet more?

30. Necklaces had I and rings from Heerfather,
Wise was my speech and my magic wisdom;
. . . .
Widely I saw over all the worlds.

---

28. The *Hauksbok* version omits all of stanzas 28-34, stanza 27 being there followed by stanzas 40 and 41. *Regius* indicates stanzas 28 and 29 as a single stanza. Bugge puts stanza 28 after stanza 22, as the second stanza of his reconstructed poem. The Volva here addresses Othin directly, intimating that, although he has not told her, she knows why he has come to her, and what he has already suffered in his search for knowledge regarding his doom. Her reiterated "would you know yet more?" seems to mean: "I have proved my wisdom by telling of the past and of your own secrets; is it your will that I tell likewise of the fate in store for you?" *The Old One:* Othin.

29. The first line, not in either manuscript, is a conjectural emendation based on Snorri's paraphrase. Bugge puts this stanza after stanza 20.

30. This is apparently the transitional stanza, in which the Volva, rewarded by Othin for her knowledge of the past (stanzas 1-29), is induced to proceed with her real prophecy (stanzas 31-66). Some editors turn the stanza into the third person, making it a narrative link. Bugge, on the other hand, puts it

31. On all sides saw I Valkyries assemble,
Ready to ride to the ranks of the gods;
Skuld bore the shield, and Skogul rode next,
Guth, Hild, Gondul, and Geirskogul.
Of Herjan's maidens the list have ye heard,
Valkyries ready to ride o'er the earth.

32. I saw for Baldr, the bleeding god,
The son of Othin, his destiny set:

---

after stanza 28 as the third stanza of the poem. No lacuna is indicated in the manuscripts, and editors have attempted various emendations. *Heerfather* ("Father of the Host"): Othin.

31. *Valkyries*: these "Choosers of the Slain" (cf. stanza 1, note) bring the bravest warriors killed in battle to Valhall, in order to re-enforce the gods for their final struggle. They are also called "Wish-Maidens," as the fulfillers of Othin's wishes. The conception of the supernatural warrior-maiden was presumably brought to Scandinavia in very early times from the South-Germanic races, and later it was interwoven with the likewise South-Germanic tradition of the swan-maiden. A third complication developed when the originally quite human women of the hero-legends were endowed with the qualities of both Valkyries and swan-maidens, as in the cases of Brynhild (cf. *Gripisspo,* introductory note), Svava (cf. *Helgakvitha Hjorvarthssonar,* prose after stanza 5 and note) and Sigrun (cf. *Helgakvitha Hundingsbana* I, 17 and note). The list of names here given may be an interpolation; a quite different list is given in *Grimnismol,* 36. *Ranks of the gods:* some editors regard the word thus translated as a specific place name. *Herjan* ("Leader of Hosts"): Othin. It is worth noting that the name *Hild* ("Warrior") is the basis of Bryn-hild ("Warrior in Mail-Coat").

32. *Baldr:* The death of Baldr, the son of Othin and Frigg, was the first of the great disasters to the gods. The story is fully told by Snorri. Frigg had demanded of all created things, saving only the mistletoe, which she thought too weak to be worth trou-

Famous and fair in the lofty fields,
Full grown in strength the mistletoe stood.

33. From the branch which seemed so slender and fair
Came a harmful shaft that Hoth should hurl;
But the brother of Baldr was born ere long,
And one night old fought Othin's son.

34. His hands he washed not, his hair he combed not,
Till he bore to the bale-blaze Baldr's foe.
But in Fensalir did Frigg weep sore
For Valhall's need: would you know yet more?

35. One did I see in the wet woods bound,
A lover of ill, and to Loki like;

---

bling about, an oath that they would not harm Baldr. Thus it came to be a sport for the gods to hurl weapons at Baldr, who, of course, was totally unharmed thereby. Loki, the trouble-maker, brought the mistletoe to Baldr's blind brother, Hoth, and guided his hand in hurling the twig. Baldr was slain, and grief came upon all the gods. Cf. *Baldrs Draumar*.

33. The lines in this and the following stanza have been combined in various ways by editors, lacunae having been freely conjectured, but the manuscript version seems clear enough. *The brother of Baldr:* Vali, whom Othin begot expressly to avenge Baldr's death. The day after his birth he fought and slew Hoth.

34. *Frigg:* Othin's wife. Some scholars have regarded her as a solar myth, calling her the sun-goddess, and pointing out that her home in *Fensalir* ("the sea-halls") symbolizes the daily setting of the sun beneath the ocean horizon.

35. The translation here follows the *Regius* version. The *Hauksbok* has the same final two lines, but in place of the first

By his side does Sigyn   sit, nor is glad
To see her mate: would you know yet more?

36. From the east there pours   through poisoned vales
With swords and daggers   the river Slith.
. . . .
. . . .

37. Northward a hall   in Nithavellir
Of gold there rose   for Sindri's race;
And in Okolnir   another stood,
Where the giant Brimir   his beer-hall had.

---

pair has, "I know that Vali   his brother gnawed, / With his bowels then   was Loki bound." Many editors have followed this version of the whole stanza or have included these two lines, often marking them as doubtful, with the four from *Regius.* After the murder of Baldr, the gods took Loki and bound him to a rock with the bowels of his son Narfi, who had just been torn to pieces by Loki's other son, Vali. A serpent was fastened above Loki's head, and the venom fell upon his face. Loki's wife, *Sigyn,* sat by him with a basin to catch the venom, but whenever the basin was full, and she went away to empty it, then the venom fell on Loki again, till the earth shook with his struggles. "And there he lies bound till the end." Cf. *Lokasenna,* concluding prose.

36. Stanzas 36-39 describe the homes of the enemies of the gods: the giants (36), the dwarfs (37), and the dead in the land of the goddess Hel (38-39). The *Hauksbok* version omits stanzas 36 and 37. *Regius* unites 36 with 37, but most editors have assumed a lacuna. *Slith* ("the Fearful"): a river in the giants' home. The "swords and daggers" may represent the icy cold.

37. *Nithavellir* ("the Dark Fields"): a home of the dwarfs. Perhaps the word should be "Nithafjoll" ("the Dark Crags"). *Sindri*: the great worker in gold among the dwarfs. *Okolnir*

38. A hall I saw, far from the sun,
On Nastrond it stands, and the doors face north;
Venom drops through the smoke-vent down,
For around the walls do serpents wind.

39. I saw there wading through rivers wild
Treacherous men and murderers too,
And workers of ill with the wives of men;
There Nithhogg sucked the blood of the slain,
And the wolf tore men; would you know yet more?

("the Not Cold"): possibly a volcano. *Brimir:* the giant (possibly Ymir) out of whose blood, according to stanza 9, the dwarfs were made; the name here appears to mean simply the leader of the dwarfs.

38. Stanzas 38 and 39 follow stanza 43 in the *Hauksbok* version. Snorri quotes stanzas 38, 39, 40 and 41, though not consecutively. *Nastrond* ("Corpse-Strand"): the land of the dead, ruled by the goddess Hel. Here the wicked undergo tortures. *Smoke-vent:* the phrase gives a picture of the Icelandic house, with its opening in the roof serving instead of a chimney.

39. The stanza is almost certainly in corrupt form. The third line is presumably an interpolation, and is lacking in most of the late paper manuscripts. Some editors, however, have called lines 1-3 the remains of a full stanza, with the fourth line lacking, and lines 4-5 the remains of another. The stanza depicts the torments of the two worst classes of criminals known to Old Norse morality—oath-breakers and murderers. *Nithhogg* ("the Dread Biter"): the dragon that lies beneath the ash Yggdrasil and gnaws at its roots, thus symbolizing the destructive elements in the universe; cf. *Grimnismol,* 32, 35. *The wolf:* presumably the wolf Fenrir, one of the children of Loki and the giantess Angrbotha (the others being Mithgarthsorm and the goddess Hel), who was chained by the gods with the marvelous chain Gleipnir, fashioned by a dwarf "out of six things: the

40. The giantess old in Ironwood sat,
In the east, and bore the brood of Fenrir;
Among these one in monster's guise
Was soon to steal the sun from the sky.

41. There feeds he full on the flesh of the dead,
And the home of the gods he reddens with gore;
Dark grows the sun, and in summer soon
Come mighty storms: would you know yet more?

42. On a hill there sat, and smote on his harp,
Eggther the joyous, the giants' warder;
Above him the cock in the bird-wood crowed,
Fair and red did Fjalar stand.

---

noise of a cat's step, the beards of women, the roots of mountains, the nerves of bears, the breath of fishes, and the spittle of birds." The chaining of Fenrir cost the god Tyr his right hand; cf. stanza 44.

40. The *Hauksbok* version inserts after stanza 39 the refrain-stanza (44), and puts stanzas 40 and 41 between 27 and 21. With this stanza begins the account of the final struggle itself. *The giantess:* her name is nowhere stated, and the only other reference to Ironwood is in *Grimnismol,* 39, in this same connection. The children of this giantess and the wolf Fenrir are the wolves Skoll and Hati, the first of whom steals the sun, the second the moon. Some scholars naturally see here an eclipse-myth.

41. In the third line many editors omit the comma after "sun," and put one after "soon," making the two lines run: "Dark grows the sun in summer soon, / Mighty storms —" etc. Either phenomenon in summer would be sufficiently striking.

42. In the *Hauksbok* version stanzas 42 and 43 stand between stanzas 44 and 38. *Eggther:* this giant, who seems to be the watchman of the giants, as Heimdall is that of the gods and Surt of the dwellers in the fire-world, is not mentioned elsewhere in

43. Then to the gods crowed Gollinkambi,
He wakes the heroes in Othin's hall;
And beneath the earth does another crow,
The rust-red bird at the bars of Hel.

44. Now Garm howls loud before Gnipahellir,
The fetters will burst, and the wolf run free;
Much do I know, and more can see
Of the fate of the gods, the mighty in fight.

45. Brothers shall fight and fell each other,
And sisters' sons shall kinship stain;

---

the poems. *Fjalar,* the cock whose crowing wakes the giants for the final struggle.

43. *Gollinkambi* ("Gold-Comb"): the cock who wakes the gods and heroes, as Fjalar does the giants. *The rust-red bird:* the name of this bird, who wakes the people of Hel's domain, is nowhere stated.

44. This is a refrain-stanza. In *Regius* it appears in full only at this point, but is repeated in abbreviated form before stanzas 50 and 59. In the *Hauksbok* version the full stanza comes first between stanzas 35 and 42, then, in abbreviated form, it occurs four times: before stanzas 45, 50, 55, and 59. In the *Hauksbok* line 3 runs: "Farther I see and more can say." *Garm:* the dog who guards the gates of Hel's kingdom; cf. *Baldrs Draumar,* 2 ff, and *Grimnismol,* 44. *Gniparhellir* ("the Cliff-Cave"): the entrance to the world of the dead. *The wolf:* Fenrir; cf. stanza 39 and note.

45. From this point on through stanza 57 the poem is quoted by Snorri, stanza 49 alone being omitted. There has been much discussion as to the status of stanza 45. Lines 4 and 5 look like an interpolation. After line 5 the *Hauksbok* has a line running: "The world resounds, the witch is flying." Editors have arranged these seven lines in various ways, with lacunae freely indicated. *Sisters' sons:* in all Germanic countries the relations between uncle and nephew were felt to be particularly close.

Hard is it on earth, with mighty whoredom;
Axe-time, sword-time, shields are sundered,
Wind-time, wolf-time, ere the world falls;
Nor ever shall men each other spare.

46. Fast move the sons of Mim, and fate
Is heard in the note of the Gjallarhorn;
Loud blows Heimdall, the horn is aloft,
In fear quake all who on Hel-roads are.

47. Yggdrasil shakes, and shiver on high
The ancient limbs, and the giant is loose;
To the head of Mim does Othin give heed,
But the kinsman of Surt shall slay him soon.

---

46. *Regius* combines the first three lines of this stanza with lines 3, 2, and 1 of stanza 47 as a single stanza. Line 4, not found in *Regius,* is introduced from the *Hauksbok* version, where it follows line 2 of stanza 47. *The sons of Mim:* the spirits of the water. On Mim (or Mimir) cf. stanza 27 and note. *Gjallarhorn:* the "Shrieking Horn" with which Heimdall, the watchman of the gods, calls them to the last battle.

47. In *Regius* lines 3, 2, and 1, in that order, follow stanza 46 without separation. Line 4 is not found in *Regius,* but is introduced from the *Hauksbok* version. *Yggdrasil:* cf. stanza 19 and note, and *Grimnismol,* 29-35. *The giant:* Fenrir. *The head of Mim:* various myths were current about Mimir. This stanza refers to the story that he was sent by the gods with Hönir as a hostage to the Wanes after their war (cf. stanza 21 and note), and that the Wanes cut off his head and returned it to the gods. Othin embalmed the head, and by magic gave it the power of speech, thus making Mimir's noted wisdom always available. Of course this story does not fit with that underlying the references to Mimir in stanzas 27 and 29. *The kinsman of Surt:* the wolf

48. How fare the gods? how fare the elves?
All Jotunheim groans, the gods are at council;
Loud roar the dwarfs by the doors of stone,
The masters of the rocks: would you know yet more?

49. Now Garm howls loud before Gnipahellir,
The fetters will burst, and the wolf run free;
Much do I know, and more can see
Of the fate of the gods, the mighty in fight.

50. From the east comes Hrym with shield held high;
In giant-wrath does the serpent writhe;
O'er the waves he twists, and the tawny eagle
Gnaws corpses screaming; Naglfar is loose.

Fenrir, who slays Othin in the final struggle; cf. stanza 53. Surt is the giant who rules the fire-world, Muspellsheim; cf. stanza 52.

48. This stanza in *Regius* follows stanza 51; in the *Hauksbok* it stands, as here, after 47. *Jotunheim:* the land of the giants.

49. Identical with stanza 44. In the manuscripts it is here abbreviated.

50. *Hrym:* the leader of the giants, who comes as the helmsman of the ship Naglfar (line 4). *The serpent:* Mithgarthsorm, one of the children of Loki and Angrbotha (cf. stanza 39, note). The serpent was cast into the sea, where he completely encircles the land; cf. especially *Hymiskvitha, passim. The eagle:* the giant Hræsvelg, who sits at the edge of heaven in the form of an eagle, and makes the winds with his wings; cf. *Vafthruthnismol,* 37, and *Skirnismol,* 27. *Naglfar:* the ship which was made out of dead men's nails to carry the giants to battle.

51. O'er the sea from the north there sails a ship
With the people of Hel, at the helm stands Loki;
After the wolf do wild men follow,
And with them the brother of Byleist goes.

52. Surt fares from the south with the scourge of branches,
The sun of the battle-gods shone from his sword;
The crags are sundered, the giant-women sink,
The dead throng Hel-way, and heaven is cloven.

53. Now comes to Hlin yet another hurt,
When Othin fares to fight with the wolf,
And Beli's fair slayer seeks out Surt,
For there must fall the joy of Frigg.

---

51. *North:* a guess; the manuscripts have "east," but there seems to be a confusion with stanza 50, line 1. *People of Hel:* the manuscripts have "people of Muspell," but these came over the bridge Bifrost (the rainbow), which broke beneath them, whereas the people of Hel came in a ship steered by Loki. *The wolf:* Fenrir. *The brother of Byleist:* Loki. Of Byleist (or Byleipt) no more is known.

52. *Surt:* the ruler of the fire-world. *The scourge of branches:* fire. This is one of the relatively rare instances in the Eddic poems of the type of poetic diction which characterizes the skaldic verse.

53. *Hlin:* apparently another name for Frigg, Othin's wife. After losing her son Baldr, she is fated now to see Othin slain by the wolf Fenrir. *Beli's slayer:* the god Freyr, who killed the giant Beli with his fist; cf. *Skirnismol,* 16 and note. On Freyr, who belonged to the race of the Wanes, and was the brother of Freyja, see especially *Skirnismol, passim. The joy of Frigg:* Othin.

54. Then comes Sigfather's mighty son,
Vithar, to fight with the foaming wolf;
In the giant's son does he thrust his sword
Full to the heart: his father is avenged.

55. Hither there comes the son of Hlothyn,
The bright snake gapes to heaven above;
. . . .
Against the serpent goes Othin's son.

56. In anger smites the warder of earth,—
Forth from their homes must all men flee;—
Nine paces fares the son of Fjorgyn,
And, slain by the serpent, fearless he sinks.

---

54. As quoted by Snorri the first line of this stanza runs: "Fares Othin's son to fight with the wolf." *Sigfather* ("Father of Victory"): Othin. His son, Vithar, is the silent god, famed chiefly for his great shield, and his strength, which is little less than Thor's. He survives the destruction. *The giant's son:* Fenrir.

55. This and the following stanza are clearly in bad shape. In *Regius* only lines 1 and 4 are found, combined with stanza 56 as a single stanza. Line 1 does not appear in the *Hauksbok* version, the stanza there beginning with line 2. Snorri, in quoting these two stanzas, omits 55, 2-4, and 56, 3, making a single stanza out of 55, 1, and 56, 4, 2, 1, in that order. Moreover, the *Hauksbok* manuscript at this point is practically illegible. The lacuna (line 3) is, of course, purely conjectural, and all sorts of arrangements of the lines have been attempted by editors. *Hlothyn:* another name for Jorth ("Earth"), Thor's mother; his father was Othin. *The snake:* Mithgarthsorm; cf. stanza 50 and note. *Othin's son:* Thor. The fourth line in *Regius* reads "against the wolf," but if this line refers to Thor at all, and not to Vithar, the *Hauksbok* reading, "serpent," is correct.

56. *The warder of earth:* Thor. *The son of Fjorgyn:* again

57. The sun turns black, earth sinks in the sea,
The hot stars down from heaven are whirled;
Fierce grows the steam and the life-feeding flame,
Till fire leaps high about heaven itself.

58. Now Garm howls loud before Gnipahellir,
The fetters will burst, and the wolf run free;
Much do I know, and more can see
Of the fate of the gods, the mighty in fight.

59. Now do I see the earth anew
Rise all green from the waves again;
The cataracts fall, and the eagle flies,
And fish he catches beneath the cliffs.

60. The gods in Ithavoll meet together,
Of the terrible girdler of earth they talk,

Thor, who, after slaying the serpent, is overcome by his venomous breath, and dies. Fjorgyn appears in both a masculine and a feminine form. In the masculine it is a name for Othin; in the feminine, as here and in *Harbarthsljoth,* 56, it apparently refers to Jorth.

57. With this stanza ends the account of the destruction.

58. Again the refrain-stanza (cf. stanza 44 and note), abbreviated in both manuscripts, as in the case of stanza 49. It is probably misplaced here.

59. Here begins the description of the new world which is to rise out of the wreck of the old one. It is on this passage that a few critics have sought to base their argument that the poem is later than the introduction of Christianity (*circa* 1000), but this theory has never seemed convincing (cf. introductory note).

60. The third line of this stanza is not found in *Regius. Ithavoll:* cf. stanza 7 and note. *The girdler of earth:* Mith-

And the mighty past they call to mind,
And the ancient runes of the Ruler of Gods.

61. In wondrous beauty once again
Shall the golden tables stand mid the grass,
Which the gods had owned in the days of old,
. . . .

62. Then fields unsowed bear ripened fruit,
All ills grow better, and Baldr comes back;
Baldr and Hoth dwell in Hropt's battle-hall,
And the mighty gods: would you know yet more?

63. Then Hönir wins the prophetic wand,
. . . .
And the sons of the brothers of Tveggi abide
In Vindheim now: would you know yet more?

---

garthsorm, who, lying in the sea, surrounded the land. *The Ruler of Gods:* Othin. The runes were both magic signs, generally carved on wood, and sung or spoken charms.

61. The *Hauksbok* version of the first two lines runs:
"The gods shall find there, wondrous fair,
The golden tables amid the grass."
No lacuna (line 4) is indicated in the manuscripts. *Golden tables:* cf. stanza 8 and note.

62. *Baldr:* cf. stanza 32 and note. Baldr and his brother, Hoth, who unwittingly slew him at Loki's instigation, return together, their union being a symbol of the new age of peace. *Hropt:* another name for Othin. His "battle-hall" is Valhall.

63. No lacuna (line 2) indicated in the manuscripts. *Hönir:* cf. stanza 18 and note. In this new age he has the gift of foretelling the future. *Tveggi* ("The Twofold"): another name for

64. More fair than the sun, a hall I see,
Roofed with gold, on Gimle it stands;
There shall the righteous rulers dwell,
And happiness ever there shall they have.

65. There comes on high, all power to hold,
A mighty lord, all lands he rules.
. . . .
. . . .

66. From below the dragon dark comes forth,
Nithhogg flying from Nithafjoll;
The bodies of men on his wings he bears,
The serpent bright: but now must I sink.

Othin. His brothers are Vili and Ve (cf. *Lokasenna,* 26, and note). Little is known of them, and nothing, beyond this reference, of their sons. *Vindheim* ("Home of the Wind"): heaven.

64. This stanza is quoted by Snorri. *Gimle:* Snorri makes this the name of the hall itself, while here it appears to refer to a mountain on which the hall stands. It is the home of the happy, as opposed to another hall, not here mentioned, for the dead. Snorri's description of this second hall is based on *Voluspo,* 38, which he quotes, and perhaps that stanza properly belongs after 64.

65. This stanza is not found in *Regius,* and is probably spurious. No lacuna is indicated in the *Hauksbok* version, but late paper manuscripts add two lines, running:

"Rule he orders, and rights he fixes,
Laws he ordains that ever shall live."

The name of this new ruler is nowhere given, and of course the suggestion of Christianity is unavoidable. It is not certain, however, that even this stanza refers to Christianity, and if it does, it may have been interpolated long after the rest of the poem was composed.

66. This stanza, which fits so badly with the preceding ones,

may well have been interpolated. It has been suggested that the dragon, making a last attempt to rise, is destroyed, this event marking the end of evil in the world. But in both manuscripts the final half-line does not refer to the dragon, but, as the gender shows, to the Volva herself, who sinks into the earth; a sort of conclusion to the entire prophecy. Presumably the stanza (barring the last half-line, which was probably intended as the conclusion of the poem) belongs somewhere in the description of the great struggle. *Nithhogg:* the dragon at the roots of Yggdrasil; cf. stanza 39 and note. *Nithafjoll* ("the Dark Crags"); nowhere else mentioned. *Must I:* the manuscripts have "must she."

HOVAMOL

The Ballad of the High One

Introductory Note

This poem follows the *Voluspo* in the *Codex Regius,* but is preserved in no other manuscript. The first stanza is quoted by Snorri, and two lines of stanza 84 appear in one of the sagas.

In its present shape it involves the critic of the text in more puzzles than any other of the Eddic poems. Without going in detail into the various theories, what happened seems to have been somewhat as follows. There existed from very early times a collection of proverbs and wise counsels, which were attributed to Othin just as the Biblical proverbs were to Solomon. This collection, which presumably was always elastic in extent, was known as "The High One's Words," and forms the basis of the present poem. To it, however, were added other poems and fragments dealing with wisdom which seemed by their nature to imply that the speaker was Othin. Thus a catalogue of runes, or charms, was tacked on, and also a set of proverbs, differing essentially in form from those comprising the main collection. Here and there bits of verse more nearly narrative crept in; and of course the loose structure of the poem made it easy for any reciter to insert new stanzas almost at will. This curious miscellany is what we now have as the *Hovamol.*

Five separate elements are pretty clearly recognizable: (1) the *Hovamol* proper (stanzas 1-80), a collection of proverbs and counsels for the conduct of life; (2) the *Loddfafnismol* (stanzas 111-138), a collection somewhat similar to the first, but specifically addressed to a certain Loddfafnir; (3) the *Ljothatal* (stanzas 147-165), a collection of charms; (4) the love-story of Othin and Billing's daughter (stanzas 96-102), with an introductory dissertation on the faithlessness of women in general (stanzas 81-95), which probably crept into the poem first, and then pulled the story, as an apt illustration, after it; (5) the story of how Othin got the mead of poetry—the draught which gave him the gift of tongues—from the maiden Gunnloth (stanzas 103-110). There is also a brief passage (stanzas 139-146) telling how Othin won the runes, this passage being a natural introduction to the *Ljothatal,* and doubtless brought into the poem for that reason.

Hovamol

It is idle to discuss the authorship or date of such a series of accretions as this. Parts of it are doubtless among the oldest relics of ancient Germanic poetry; parts of it may have originated at a relatively late period. Probably, however, most of its component elements go pretty far back, although we have no way of telling how or when they first became associated.

It seems all but meaningless to talk about "interpolations" in a poem which has developed almost solely through the process of piecing together originally unrelated odds and ends. The notes, therefore, make only such suggestions as are needed to keep the main divisions of the poem distinct.

Few gnomic collections in the world's literary history present sounder wisdom more tersely expressed than the *Hovamol.* Like the Book of Proverbs it occasionally rises to lofty heights of poetry. If it presents the worldly wisdom of a violent race, it also shows noble ideals of loyalty, truth, and unfaltering courage.

1\. Within the gates ere a man shall go,
(Full warily let him watch,)
Full long let him look about him;
For little he knows where a foe may lurk,
And sit in the seats within.

2\. Hail to the giver! a guest has come;
Where shall the stranger sit?
Swift shall he be who with swords shall try
The proof of his might to make.

1\. This stanza is quoted by Snorri, the second line being omitted in most of the *Prose Edda* manuscripts.

2\. Probably the first and second lines had originally nothing to do with the third and fourth, the last two not referring to host or guest, but to the general danger of backing one's views with the sword.

3. Fire he needs who with frozen knees
Has come from the cold without;
Food and clothes must the farer have,
The man from the mountains come.

4. Water and towels and welcoming speech
Should he find who comes to the feast;
If renown he would get, and again be greeted,
Wisely and well must he act.

5. Wits must he have who wanders wide,
But all is easy at home;
At the witless man the wise shall wink
When among such men he sits.

6. A man shall not boast of his keenness of mind,
But keep it close in his breast;
To the silent and wise does ill come seldom
When he goes as guest to a house;
(For a faster friend one never finds
Than wisdom tried and true.)

7. The knowing guest who goes to the feast,
In silent attention sits;
With his ears he hears, with his eyes he watches,
Thus wary are wise men all.

---

6. Lines 5 and 6 appear to have been added to the stanza.

8\. Happy the one who wins for himself
Favor and praises fair;
Less safe by far is the wisdom found
That is hid in another's heart.

9\. Happy the man who has while he lives
Wisdom and praise as well,
For evil counsel a man full oft
Has from another's heart.

10\. A better burden may no man bear
For wanderings wide than wisdom;
It is better than wealth on unknown ways,
And in grief a refuge it gives.

11\. A better burden may no man bear
For wanderings wide than wisdom;
Worse food for the journey he brings not afield
Than an over-drinking of ale.

12\. Less good there lies than most believe
In ale for mortal men;
For the more he drinks the less does man
Of his mind the mastery hold.

12\. Some editors have combined this stanza in various ways with the last two lines of stanza 11, as in the manuscript the first two lines of the latter are abbreviated, and, if they belong there at all, are presumably identical with the first two lines of stanza 10.

13. Over beer the bird of forgetfulness broods,
And steals the minds of men;
With the heron's feathers fettered I lay
And in Gunnloth's house was held.

14. Drunk I was, I was dead-drunk,
When with Fjalar wise I was;
'Tis the best of drinking if back one brings
His wisdom with him home.

15. The son of a king shall be silent and wise,
And bold in battle as well;
Bravely and gladly a man shall go,
Till the day of his death is come.

16. The sluggard believes he shall live forever,
If the fight he faces not;
But age shall not grant him the gift of peace,
Though spears may spare his life.

17. The fool is agape when he comes to the feast,
He stammers or else is still;
But soon if he gets a drink is it seen
What the mind of the man is like.

---

13. *The heron:* the bird of forgetfulness, referred to in line 1. *Gunnloth:* the daughter of the giant Suttung, from whom Othin won the mead of poetry. For this episode see stanzas 104-110.

14. *Fjalar:* apparently another name for Suttung. This stanza, and probably 13, seem to have been inserted as illustrative.

18. He alone is aware who has wandered wide,
And far abroad has fared,
How great a mind is guided by him
That wealth of wisdom has.

19. Shun not the mead, but drink in measure;
Speak to the point or be still;
For rudeness none shall rightly blame thee
If soon thy bed thou seekest.

20. The greedy man, if his mind be vague,
Will eat till sick he is;
The vulgar man, when among the wise,
To scorn by his belly is brought.

21. The herds know well when home they shall fare,
And then from the grass they go;
But the foolish man his belly's measure
Shall never know aright.

22. A paltry man and poor of mind
At all things ever mocks;
For never he knows, what he ought to know,
That he is not free from faults.

23. The witless man is awake all night,
Thinking of many things;
Care-worn he is when the morning comes,
And his woe is just as it was.

24. The foolish man for friends all those
Who laugh at him will hold;

When among the wise he marks it not
  Though hatred of him they speak.

25. The foolish man for friends all those
  Who laugh at him will hold;
But the truth when he comes to the council he learns,
  That few in his favor will speak.

26. An ignorant man thinks that all he knows,
  When he sits by himself in a corner;
But never what answer to make he knows,
  When others with questions come.

27. A witless man, when he meets with men,
  Had best in silence abide;
For no one shall find that nothing he knows,
  If his mouth is not open too much.
(But a man knows not, if nothing he knows,
  When his mouth has been open too much.)

28. Wise shall he seem who well can question,
  And also answer well;
Nought is concealed that men may say
  Among the sons of men.

29. Often he speaks who never is still
  With words that win no faith;

---

25. The first two lines are abbreviated in the manuscript, but are doubtless identical with the first two lines of stanza 24.

27. The last two lines were probably added as a commentary on lines 3 and 4.

The babbling tongue, if a bridle it find not,
Oft for itself sings ill.

30. In mockery no one a man shall hold,
Although he fare to the feast;
Wise seems one oft, if nought he is asked,
And safely he sits dry-skinned.

31. Wise a guest holds it to take to his heels,
When mock of another he makes;
But little he knows who laughs at the feast,
Though he mocks in the midst of his foes.

32. Friendly of mind are many men,
Till feasting they mock at their friends;
To mankind a bane must it ever be
When guests together strive.

33. Oft should one make an early meal,
Nor fasting come to the feast;
Else he sits and chews as if he would choke,
And little is able to ask.

34. Crooked and far is the road to a foe,
Though his house on the highway be;
But wide and straight is the way to a friend,
Though far away he fare.

35. Forth shall one go, nor stay as a guest
In a single spot forever;

Love becomes loathing if long one sits
By the hearth in another's home.

36. Better a house, though a hut it be,
A man is master at home;
A pair of goats and a patched-up roof
Are better far than begging.

37. Better a house, though a hut it be,
A man is master at home;
His heart is bleeding who needs must beg
When food he fain would have.

38. Away from his arms in the open field
A man should fare not a foot;
For never he knows when the need for a spear
Shall arise on the distant road.

39. If wealth a man has won for himself,
Let him never suffer in need;
Oft he saves for a foe what he plans for a friend,
For much goes worse than we wish.

40. None so free with gifts or food have I found
That gladly he took not a gift,

---

36. The manuscript has "little" in place of "a hut" in line 1, but this involves an error in the initial-rhymes, and the emendation has been generally accepted.

37. Lines 1 and 2 are abbreviated in the manuscript, but are doubtless identical with the first two lines of stanza 36.

39. In the manuscript this stanza follows stanza 40.

Nor one who so widely scattered his wealth
That of recompense hatred he had.

41. Friends shall gladden each other with arms and garments,
As each for himself can see;
Gift-givers' friendships are longest found,
If fair their fates may be.

42. To his friend a man a friend shall prove,
And gifts with gifts requite;
But men shall mocking with mockery answer,
And fraud with falsehood meet.

43. To his friend a man a friend shall prove,
To him and the friend of his friend;
But never a man shall friendship make
With one of his foeman's friends.

44. If a friend thou hast whom thou fully wilt trust,
And good from him wouldst get,
Thy thoughts with his mingle, and gifts shalt thou make,
And fare to find him oft.

---

40. The key-word in line 3 is missing in the manuscript, but editors have agreed in inserting a word meaning "generous."

41. In line 3 the manuscript adds "givers again" to "gift-givers."

45. If another thou hast whom thou hardly wilt trust,
Yet good from him wouldst get,
Thou shalt speak him fair, but falsely think,
And fraud with falsehood requite.

46. So is it with him whom thou hardly wilt trust,
And whose mind thou mayst not know;
Laugh with him mayst thou, but speak not thy mind,
Like gifts to his shalt thou give.

47. Young was I once, and wandered alone,
And nought of the road I knew;
Rich did I feel when a comrade I found,
For man is man's delight.

48. The lives of the brave and noble are best,
Sorrows they seldom feed;
But the coward fear of all things feels,
And not gladly the niggard gives.

49. My garments once in a field I gave
To a pair of carven poles;
Heroes they seemed when clothes they had,
But the naked man is nought.

50. On the hillside drear the fir-tree dies,
All bootless its needles and bark;
It is like a man whom no one loves,—
Why should his life be long?

51. Hotter than fire between false friends
 Does friendship five days burn;
When the sixth day comes the fire cools,
 And ended is all the love.

52. No great thing needs a man to give,
 Oft little will purchase praise;
With half a loaf and a half-filled cup
 A friend full fast I made.

53. A little sand has a little sea,
 And small are the minds of men;
Though all men are not equal in wisdom,
 Yet half-wise only are all.

54. A measure of wisdom each man shall have,
 But never too much let him know;
The fairest lives do those men live
 Whose wisdom wide has grown.

55. A measure of wisdom each man shall have,
 But never too much let him know;
For the wise man's heart is seldom happy,
 If wisdom too great he has won.

56. A measure of wisdom each man shall have,
 But never too much let him know;

55-56. The first pairs of lines are abbreviated in the manuscript.

Let no man the fate before him see,
For so is he freest from sorrow.

57. A brand from a brand is kindled and burned,
And fire from fire begotten;
And man by his speech is known to men,
And the stupid by their stillness.

58. He must early go forth who fain the blood
Or the goods of another would get;
The wolf that lies idle shall win little meat,
Or the sleeping man success.

59. He must early go forth whose workers are few,
Himself his work to seek;
Much remains undone for the morning-sleeper,
For the swift is wealth half won.

60. Of seasoned shingles and strips of bark
For the thatch let one know his need,
And how much of wood he must have for a month,
Or in half a year he will use.

61. Washed and fed to the council fare,
But care not too much for thy clothes;
Let none be ashamed of his shoes and hose,
Less still of the steed he rides,
(Though poor be the horse he has.)

61. The fifth line is probably a spurious addition.

62. When the eagle comes to the ancient sea,
He snaps and hangs his head;
So is a man in the midst of a throng,
Who few to speak for him finds.

63. To question and answer must all be ready
Who wish to be known as wise;
Tell one thy thoughts, but beware of two,—
All know what is known to three.

64. The man who is prudent a measured use
Of the might he has will make;
He finds when among the brave he fares
That the boldest he may not be.

65. . . . .
. . . .
Oft for the words that to others one speaks
He will get but an evil gift.

66. Too early to many a meeting I came,
And some too late have I sought;
The beer was all drunk, or not yet brewed;
Little the loathed man finds.

---

62. This stanza follows stanza 63 in the manuscript, but there are marks therein indicating the transposition.

65. The manuscript indicates no lacuna (lines 1 and 2). Many editors have filled out the stanza with two lines from late paper manuscripts, the passage running:

"A man must be watchful and wary as well,
And fearful of trusting a friend."

67. To their homes men would bid me hither and yon,
If at meal-time I needed no meat,
Or would hang two hams in my true friend's house,
Where only one I had eaten.

68. Fire for men is the fairest gift,
And power to see the sun;
Health as well, if a man may have it,
And a life not stained with sin.

69. All wretched is no man, though never so sick;
Some from their sons have joy,
Some win it from kinsmen, and some from their wealth,
And some from worthy works.

70. It is better to live than to lie a corpse,
The live man catches the cow;
I saw flames rise for the rich man's pyre,
And before his door he lay dead.

71. The lame rides a horse, the handless is herdsman,
The deaf in battle is bold;
The blind man is better than one that is burned,
No good can come of a corpse.

---

70. The manuscript has "and a worthy life" in place of "than to lie a corpse" in line 1, but Rask suggested the emendation as early as 1818, and most editors have followed him.

72. A son is better, though late he be born,
And his father to death have fared;
Memory-stones seldom stand by the road
Save when kinsman honors his kin.

73. Two make a battle, the tongue slays the head;
In each furry coat a fist I look for.

74. He welcomes the night whose fare is enough,
(Short are the yards of a ship,)
Uneasy are autumn nights;
Full oft does the weather change in a week,
And more in a month's time.

75. A man knows not, if nothing he knows,
That gold oft apes begets;
One man is wealthy and one is poor,
Yet scorn for him none should know.

76. Among Fitjung's sons saw I well-stocked folds,—
Now bear they the beggar's staff;

73-74. These seven lines are obviously a jumble. The two lines of stanza 73 not only appear out of place, but the verse-form is unlike that of the surrounding stanzas. In 74, the second line is clearly interpolated, and line 1 has little enough connection with lines 3, 4 and 5. It looks as though some compiler (or copyist) had inserted here various odds and ends for which he could find no better place.

75. The word "gold" in line 2 is more or less conjectural, the manuscript being obscure. The reading in line 4 is also doubtful.

Wealth is as swift as a winking eye,
Of friends the falsest it is.

77. Cattle die, and kinsmen die,
And so one dies one's self;
But a noble name will never die,
If good renown one gets.

78. Cattle die, and kinsmen die,
And so one dies one's self;
One thing I know that never dies,
The fame of a dead man's deeds.

79. Certain is that which is sought from runes,
That the gods so great have made,
And the Master-Poet painted;
. . . .
. . . . . . of the race of gods:
Silence is safest and best.

80. An unwise man, if a maiden's love
Or wealth he chances to win,

---

76. In the manuscript this stanza follows 78, the order being: 77, 78, 76, 80, 79, 81. *Fitjung* ("the Nourisher"): Earth.

79. This stanza is certainly in bad shape, and probably out of place here. Its reference to runes as magic signs suggests that it properly belongs in some list of charms like the *Ljothatal* (stanzas 147-165). The stanza-form is so irregular as to show either that something has been lost or that there have been interpolations. The manuscript indicates no lacuna; Gering fills out the assumed gap as follows:

"Certain is that which is sought from runes,
The runes—," etc.

His pride will wax, but his wisdom never,
Straight forward he fares in conceit.

* * *

81. Give praise to the day at evening, to a woman on her pyre,
To a weapon which is tried, to a maid at wedlock,
To ice when it is crossed, to ale that is drunk.

82. When the gale blows hew wood, in fair winds seek the water;
Sport with maidens at dusk, for day's eyes are many;
From the ship seek swiftness, from the shield protection,
Cuts from the sword, from the maiden kisses.

83. By the fire drink ale, over ice go on skates;
Buy a steed that is lean, and a sword when tarnished,

---

81. With this stanza the verse-form, as indicated in the translation, abruptly changes to Malahattr. What has happened seems to have been something like this. Stanza 80 introduces the idea of man's love for woman. Consequently some reciter or compiler (or possibly even a copyist) took occasion to insert at this point certain stanzas concerning the ways of women. Thus stanza 80 would account for the introduction of stanzas 81 and 82, which, in turn, apparently drew stanza 83 in with them. Stanza 84 suggests the fickleness of women, and is immediately followed—again with a change of verse-form—by a list of things equally untrustworthy (stanzas 85-90). Then, after a few more stanzas on love in the regular measure of the *Hovamol* (stanzas 91-95), is introduced, by way of illustration, Othin's story of his

The horse at home fatten, the hound in thy dwelling.

* * *

84. A man shall trust not the oath of a maid,
Nor the word a woman speaks;
For their hearts on a whirling wheel were fashioned,
And fickle their breasts were formed.

* * *

85. In a breaking bow or a burning flame,
A ravening wolf or a croaking raven,
In a grunting boar, a tree with roots broken,
In billowy seas or a bubbling kettle,

86. In a flying arrow or falling waters,
In ice new formed or the serpent's folds,
In a bride's bed-speech or a broken sword,
In the sport of bears or in sons of kings,

87. In a calf that is sick or a stubborn thrall,
A flattering witch or a foe new slain.

---

adventure with Billing's daughter (stanzas 96-102). Some such process of growth, whatever its specific stages may have been, must be assumed to account for the curious chaos of the whole passage from stanza 81 to stanza 102.

84. Lines 3 and 4 are quoted in the *Fostbrœthrasaga*.

85. Stanzas 85-88 and 90 are in Fornyrthislag, and clearly come from a different source from the rest of the *Hovamol*.

87. The stanza is doubtless incomplete. Some editors add from a late paper manuscript two lines running:

"In a light, clear sky or a laughing throng,
In the howl of a dog or a harlot's grief."

88. In a brother's slayer, if thou meet him abroad,
In a half-burned house, in a horse full swift—
One leg is hurt and the horse is useless—
None had ever such faith as to trust in them all.

* * *

89. Hope not too surely for early harvest,
Nor trust too soon in thy son;
The field needs good weather, the son needs wisdom,
And oft is either denied.

* * *

90. The love of women fickle of will
Is like starting o'er ice with a steed unshod,
A two-year-old restive and little tamed,
Or steering a rudderless ship in a storm,
Or, lame, hunting reindeer on slippery rocks.

* * *

91. Clear now will I speak, for I know them both,
Men false to women are found;
When fairest we speak, then falsest we think,
Against wisdom we work with deceit.

92. Soft words shall he speak and wealth shall he offer
Who longs for a maiden's love,
And the beauty praise of the maiden bright;
He wins whose wooing is best.

---

88. This stanza follows stanza 89 in the manuscript. Many editors have changed the order, for while stanza 89 is pretty clearly an interpolation wherever it stands, it seriously interferes with the sense if it breaks in between 87 and 88.

93. Fault for loving let no man find
Ever with any other;
Oft the wise are fettered, where fools go free,
By beauty that breeds desire.

94. Fault with another let no man find
For what touches many a man;
Wise men oft into witless fools
Are made by mighty love.

95. The head alone knows what dwells near the heart,
A man knows his mind alone;
No sickness is worse to one who is wise
Than to lack the longed-for joy.

96. This found I myself, when I sat in the reeds,
And long my love awaited;
As my life the maiden wise I loved,
Yet her I never had.

97. Billing's daughter I found on her bed,
In slumber bright as the sun;
Empty appeared an earl's estate
Without that form so fair.

---

96. Here begins the passage (stanzas 96-102) illustrating the falseness of woman by the story of Othin's unsuccessful love-affair with Billing's daughter. Of this person we know nothing beyond what is here told, but the story needs little comment.

98. "Othin, again at evening come,
If a woman thou wouldst win;
Evil it were if others than we
Should know of such a sin."

99. Away I hastened, hoping for joy,
And careless of counsel wise;
Well I believed that soon I should win
Measureless joy with the maid.

100. So came I next when night it was,
The warriors all were awake;
With burning lights and waving brands
I learned my luckless way.

101. At morning then, when once more I came,
And all were sleeping still,
A dog I found in the fair one's place,
Bound there upon her bed.

102. Many fair maids, if a man but tries them,
False to a lover are found;
That did I learn when I longed to gain
With wiles the maiden wise;

---

102. Rask adds at the beginning of this stanza two lines from a late paper manuscript, running:

"Few are so good that false they are never
To cheat the mind of a man."

He makes these two lines plus lines 1 and 2 a full stanza, and lines 3, 4, 5, and 6 a second stanza.

Foul scorn was my meed from the crafty maid,
And nought from the woman I won.

* * *

103. Though glad at home, and merry with guests,
A man shall be wary and wise;
The sage and shrewd, wide wisdom seeking,
Must see that his speech be fair;
A fool is he named who nought can say,
For such is the way of the witless.

104. I found the old giant, now back have I fared,
Small gain from silence I got;
Full many a word, my will to get,
I spoke in Suttung's hall.

105. The mouth of Rati made room for my passage,
And space in the stone he gnawed;

---

103. With this stanza the subject changes abruptly, and apparently the virtues of fair speech, mentioned in the last three lines, account for the introduction, from what source cannot be known, of the story of Othin and the mead of song (stanzas 104-110).

104. The giant *Suttung* ("the old giant") possessed the magic mead, a draught of which conferred the gift of poetry. Othin, desiring to obtain it, changed himself into a snake, bored his way through a mountain into Suttung's home, made love to the giant's daughter, Gunnloth, and by her connivance drank up all the mead. Then he flew away in the form of an eagle, leaving Gunnloth to her fate. While with Suttung he assumed the name of Bolverk ("the Evil-Doer").

105. *Rati* ("the Traveller"): the gimlet with which Othin bored through the mountain to reach Suttung's home.

Above and below the giants' paths lay,
So rashly I risked my head.

106. Gunnloth gave on a golden stool
A drink of the marvelous mead;
A harsh reward did I let her have
For her heroic heart,
And her spirit troubled sore.

107. The well-earned beauty well I enjoyed,
Little the wise man lacks;
So Othrörir now has up been brought
To the midst of the men of earth.

108. Hardly, methinks, would I home have come,
And left the giants' land,
Had not Gunnloth helped me, the maiden good,
Whose arms about me had been.

109. The day that followed, the frost-giants came,
Some word of Hor to win,
(And into the hall of Hor;)

---

106. Probably either the fourth or the fifth line is a spurious addition.

107. *Othrörir:* here the name of the magic mead itself, whereas in stanza 141 it is the name of the vessel containing it. Othin had no intention of bestowing any of the precious mead upon men, but as he was flying over the earth, hotly pursued by Suttung, he spilled some of it out of his mouth, and in this way mankind also won the gift of poetry.

109. *Hor:* Othin ("the High One"). The frost-giants, Suttung's kinsmen, appear not to have suspected Othin of being

Of Bolverk they asked, were he back midst the gods,
Or had Suttung slain him there?

110. On his ring swore Othin the oath, methinks;
Who now his troth shall trust?
Suttung's betrayal he sought with drink,
And Gunnloth to grief he left.

* * *

111. It is time to chant from the chanter's stool;
By the wells of Urth I was,
I saw and was silent, I saw and thought,
And heard the speech of Hor.
(Of runes heard I words, nor were counsels wanting,
At the hall of Hor,
In the hall of Hor;
Such was the speech I heard.)

---

identical with Bolverk, possibly because the oath referred to in stanza 110 was an oath made by Othin to Suttung that there was no such person as Bolverk among the gods. The giants, of course, fail to get from Othin the information they seek concerning Bolverk, but Othin is keenly conscious of having violated the most sacred of oaths, that sworn on his ring.

111. With this stanza begins the Loddfafnismol (stanzas 111-138). Loddfafnir is apparently a wandering singer, who, from his "chanter's stool," recites the verses which he claims to have received from Othin. *Wells of Urth:* cf. *Voluspo,* 19 and note. Urth ("the Past") is one of the three Norns. This stanza is apparently in corrupt form, and editors have tried many experiments with it, both in rejecting lines as spurious and in rearranging the words and punctuation. It looks rather as though the first four lines formed a complete stanza, and the last four had

112. I rede thee, Loddfafnir! and hear thou my rede,—
Profit thou hast if thou hearest,
Great thy gain if thou learnest:
Rise not at night, save if news thou seekest,
Or fain to the outhouse wouldst fare.

113. I rede thee, Loddfafnir! and hear thou my rede,—
Profit thou hast if thou hearest,
Great thy gain if thou learnest:
Beware of sleep on a witch's bosom,
Nor let her limbs ensnare thee.

114. Such is her might that thou hast no mind
For the council or meeting of men;
Meat thou hatest, joy thou hast not,
And sadly to slumber thou farest.

115. I rede thee, Loddfafnir! and hear thou my rede,—
Profit thou hast if thou hearest,
Great thy gain if thou learnest:

---

crept in later. The phrase translated "the speech of Hor" is "Hova mol," later used as the title for the entire poem.

112. Lines 1-3 are the formula, repeated (abbreviated in the manuscript) in most of the stanzas, with which Othin prefaces his counsels to Loddfafnir, and throughout this section, except in stanzas 111 and 138, Loddfafnir represents himself as simply quoting Othin's words. The material is closely analogous to that contained in the first eighty stanzas of the poem. In some cases (e. g., stanzas 117, 119, 121, 126 and 130) the formula precedes a full four-line stanza instead of two (or three) lines.

Seek never to win the wife of another,
Or long for her secret love.

116. I rede thee, Loddfafnir! and hear thou my rede,—
Profit thou hast if thou hearest,
Great thy gain if thou learnest:
If o'er mountains or gulfs thou fain wouldst go,
Look well to thy food for the way.

117. I rede thee, Loddfafnir! and hear thou my rede,—
Profit thou hast if thou hearest,
Great thy gain if thou learnest:
An evil man thou must not let
Bring aught of ill to thee;
For an evil man will never make
Reward for a worthy thought.

118. I saw a man who was wounded sore
By an evil woman's word;
A lying tongue his death-blow launched,
And no word of truth there was.

119. I rede thee, Loddfafnir! and hear thou my rede,—
Profit thou hast if thou hearest,
Great thy gain if thou learnest:
If a friend thou hast whom thou fully wilt trust,
Then fare to find him oft;
For brambles grow and waving grass
On the rarely trodden road.

120. I rede thee, Loddfafnir! and hear thou my rede,—
Profit thou hast if thou hearest,
Great thy gain if thou learnest:
A good man find to hold in friendship,
And give heed to his healing charms.

121. I rede thee, Loddfafnir! and hear thou my rede,—
Profit thou hast if thou hearest,
Great thy gain if thou learnest:
Be never the first to break with thy friend
The bond that holds you both;
Care eats the heart if thou canst not speak
To another all thy thought.

122. I rede thee, Loddfafnir! and hear thou my rede,—
Profit thou hast if thou hearest,
Great thy gain if thou learnest:
Exchange of words with a witless ape
Thou must not ever make.

123. For never thou mayst from an evil man
A good requital get;
But a good man oft the greatest love
Through words of praise will win thee.

124. Mingled is love when a man can speak
To another all his thought;

Nought is so bad as false to be,
No friend speaks only fair.

125. I rede thee, Loddfafnir! and hear thou my rede,—
Profit thou hast if thou hearest,
Great thy gain if thou learnest:
With a worse man speak not three words in dispute,
Ill fares the better oft
When the worse man wields a sword.

126. I rede thee, Loddfafnir! and hear thou my rede,—
Profit thou hast if thou hearest,
Great thy gain if thou learnest:
A shoemaker be, or a maker of shafts,
For only thy single self;
If the shoe is ill made, or the shaft prove false,
Then evil of thee men think.

127. I rede thee, Loddfafnir! and hear thou my rede,—
Profit thou hast if thou hearest,
Great thy gain if thou learnest:
If evil thou knowest, as evil proclaim it,
And make no friendship with foes.

128. I rede thee, Loddfafnir! and hear thou my rede,—
Profit thou hast if thou hearest,

Great thy gain if thou learnest:
In evil never joy shalt thou know,
But glad the good shall make thee.

129. I rede thee, Loddfafnir! and hear thou my rede,—
Profit thou hast if thou hearest,
Great thy gain if thou learnest:
Look not up when the battle is on,—
(Like madmen the sons of men become,—)
Lest men bewitch thy wits.

130. I rede thee, Loddfafnir! and hear thou my rede,—
Profit thou hast if thou hearest,
Great thy gain if thou learnest:
If thou fain wouldst win a woman's love,
And gladness get from her,
Fair be thy promise and well fulfilled;
None loathes what good he gets.

131. I rede thee, Loddfafnir! and hear thou my rede,—
Profit thou hast if thou hearest,
Great thy gain if thou learnest:
I bid thee be wary, but be not fearful;
(Beware most with ale or another's wife,
And third beware lest a thief outwit thee.)

---

129. Line 5 is apparently interpolated.

131. Lines 5-6 probably were inserted from a different poem.

132. I rede thee, Loddfafnir! and hear thou my rede,—
Profit thou hast if thou hearest,
Great thy gain if thou learnest:
Scorn or mocking ne'er shalt thou make
Of a guest or a journey-goer.

133. Oft scarcely he knows who sits in the house
What kind is the man who comes;
None so good is found that faults he has not,
Nor so wicked that nought he is worth.

134. I rede thee, Loddfafnir! and hear thou my rede,—
Profit thou hast if thou hearest,
Great thy gain if thou learnest:
Scorn not ever the gray-haired singer,
Oft do the old speak good;
(Oft from shrivelled skin come skillful counsels,
Though it hang with the hides,
And flap with the pelts,
And is blown with the bellies.)

---

133. Many editors reject the last two lines of this stanza as spurious, putting the first two lines at the end of the preceding stanza. Others, attaching lines 3 and 4 to stanza 132, insert as the first two lines of stanza 133 two lines from a late paper manuscript, running:

"Evil and good do men's sons ever
"Mingled bear in their breasts."

134. Presumably the last four lines have been added to this stanza, for the parallelism in the last three makes it probable that they belong together. The wrinkled skin of the old man is

135. I rede thee, Loddfafnir! and hear thou my rede,—
Profit thou hast if thou hearest,
Great thy gain if thou learnest:
Curse not thy guest, nor show him thy gate,
Deal well with a man in want.

136. Strong is the beam that raised must be
To give an entrance to all;
Give it a ring, or grim will be
The wish it would work on thee.

137. I rede thee, Loddfafnir! and hear thou my rede,—
Profit thou hast if thou hearest,
Great thy gain if thou learnest:
When ale thou drinkest, seek might of earth,
(For earth cures drink, and fire cures ills,
The oak cures tightness, the ear cures magic,
Rye cures rupture, the moon cures rage,
Grass cures the scab, and runes the sword-cut;)
The field absorbs the flood.

---

compared with the dried skins and bellies of animals kept for various purposes hanging in an Icelandic house.

136. This stanza suggests the dangers of too much hospitality. The beam (bolt) which is ever being raised to admit guests becomes weak thereby. It needs a ring to help it in keeping the door closed, and without the ability at times to ward off guests a man becomes the victim of his own generosity.

137. The list of "household remedies" in this stanza is doubtless interpolated. Their nature needs no comment here.

138. Now are Hor's words spoken in the hall,
Kind for the kindred of men,
Cursed for the kindred of giants:
Hail to the speaker, and to him who learns!
Profit be his who has them!
Hail to them who hearken!

* * *

139. I ween that I hung on the windy tree,
Hung there for nights full nine;
With the spear I was wounded, and offered I was
To Othin, myself to myself,
On the tree that none may ever know
What root beneath it runs.

---

138. In the manuscript this stanza comes at the end of the entire poem, following stanza 165. Most recent editors have followed Müllenhoff in shifting it to this position, as it appears to conclude the passage introduced by the somewhat similar stanza 111.

139. With this stanza begins the most confusing part of the *Hovamol:* the group of eight stanzas leading up to the *Ljothatal,* or list of charms. Certain paper manuscripts have before this stanza a title: "Othin's Tale of the Runes." Apparently stanzas 139, 140 and 142 are fragments of an account of how Othin obtained the runes; 141 is erroneously inserted from some version of the magic mead story (cf. stanzas 104-110); and stanzas 143, 144, 145, and 146 are from miscellaneous sources, all, however, dealing with the general subject of runes. With stanza 147 a clearly continuous passage begins once more. *The windy tree:* the ash Yggdrasil (literally "the Horse of Othin," so called because of this story), on which Othin, in order to win the magic runes, hanged himself as an offering to himself, and wounded himself with his own spear. Lines 5 and 6 have presumably been borrowed from *Svipdagsmol,* 30.

140. None made me happy with loaf or horn,
And there below I looked;
I took up the runes, shrieking I took them,
And forthwith back I fell.

141. Nine mighty songs I got from the son
Of Bolthorn, Bestla's father;
And a drink I got of the goodly mead
Poured out from Othrörir.

142. Then began I to thrive, and wisdom to get,
I grew and well I was;
Each word led me on to another word,
Each deed to another deed.

143. Runes shalt thou find, and fateful signs,
That the king of singers colored,
And the mighty gods have made;

---

141. This stanza, interrupting as it does the account of Othin's winning the runes, appears to be an interpolation. The meaning of the stanza is most obscure. Bolthorn was Othin's grandfather, and Bestla his mother. We do not know the name of the uncle here mentioned, but it has been suggested that this son of Bolthorn was Mimir (cf. *Voluspo,* 27 and note, and 47 and note). In any case, the nine magic songs which he learned from his uncle seem to have enabled him to win the magic mead (cf. stanzas 104-110). Concerning *Othrörir,* here used as the name of the vessel containing the mead, cf. stanza 107 and note.

143. This and the following stanza belong together, and in many editions appear as a single stanza. They presumably come from some lost poem on the authorship of the runes. Lines 2 and 3 follow line 4 in the manuscript; the transposition was suggested by Bugge. *The king of singers:* Othin. The magic signs (runes) were commonly carved in wood, then colored red.

Full strong the signs, full mighty the signs
That the ruler of gods doth write.

144. Othin for the gods, Dain for the elves,
And Dvalin for the dwarfs,
Alsvith for giants and all mankind,
And some myself I wrote.

145. Knowest how one shall write, knowest how one shall rede?
Knowest how one shall tint, knowest how one makes trial?
Knowest how one shall ask, knowest how one shall offer?
Knowest how one shall send, knowest how one shall sacrifice?

---

144. *Dain* and *Dvalin:* dwarfs; cf. *Voluspo,* 14, and note. Dain, however, may here be one of the elves rather than the dwarf of that name. The two names also appear together in *Grimnismol,* 33, where they are applied to two of the four harts that nibble at the topmost twigs of Yggdrasil. *Alsvith* ("the All-Wise") appears nowhere else as a giant's name. *Myself:* Othin. We have no further information concerning the list of those who wrote the runes for the various races, and these four lines seem like a confusion of names in the rather hazy mind of some reciter.

145. This Malahattr stanza appears to be a regular religious formula, concerned less with the runes which one "writes" and "tints" (cf. stanza 79) than with the prayers which one "asks" and the sacrifices which one "offers" and "sends." Its origin is wholly uncertain, but it is clearly an interpolation here. In the manuscript the phrase "knowest?" is abbreviated after the first line.

146. Better no prayer   than too big an offering,
  By thy getting measure thy gift;
Better is none   than too big a sacrifice,

. . . .

So Thund of old wrote   ere man's race began,
Where he rose on high   when home he came.

* * *

147. The songs I know   that king's wives know not,
  Nor men that are sons of men;
The first is called help,   and help it can bring thee
  In sorrow and pain and sickness.

148. A second I know,   that men shall need
  Who leechcraft long to use;

. . . .

. . . .

---

146. This stanza as translated here follows the manuscript reading, except in assuming a gap between lines 3 and 5. In Vigfusson and Powell's *Corpus Poeticum Boreale* the first three lines have somehow been expanded into eight. The last two lines are almost certainly misplaced; Bugge suggests that they belong at the end of stanza 144. *Thund:* another name for Othin. *When home he came:* presumably after obtaining the runes as described in stanzas 139 and 140.

147. With this stanza begins the *Ljothatal,* or list of charms. The magic songs themselves are not given, but in each case the peculiar application of the charm is explained. The passage, which is certainly approximately complete as far as it goes, runs to the end of the poem. In the manuscript and in most editions line 4 falls into two half-lines, running:

"In sickness and pain   and every sorrow."

149. A third I know, if great is my need
Of fetters to hold my foe;
Blunt do I make mine enemy's blade,
Nor bites his sword or staff.

150. A fourth I know, if men shall fasten
Bonds on my bended legs;
So great is the charm that forth I may go,
The fetters spring from my feet,
Broken the bonds from my hands.

151. A fifth I know, if I see from afar
An arrow fly 'gainst the folk;
It flies not so swift that I stop it not,
If ever my eyes behold it.

152. A sixth I know, if harm one seeks
With a sapling's roots to send me;
The hero himself who wreaks his hate
Shall taste the ill ere I.

153. A seventh I know, if I see in flames
The hall o'er my comrades' heads;
It burns not so wide that I will not quench it,
I know that song to sing.

---

148. *Second,* etc., appear in the manuscript as Roman numerals. The manuscript indicates no gap after line 2.

152. The sending of a root with runes written thereon was an excellent way of causing death. So died the Icelandic hero Grettir the Strong.

154. An eighth I know, that is to all
Of greatest good to learn;
When hatred grows among heroes' sons,
I soon can set it right.

155. A ninth I know, if need there comes
To shelter my ship on the flood;
The wind I calm upon the waves,
And the sea I put to sleep.

156. A tenth I know, what time I see
House-riders flying on high;
So can I work that wildly they go,
Showing their true shapes,
Hence to their own homes.

157. An eleventh I know, if needs I must lead
To the fight my long-loved friends;
I sing in the shields, and in strength they go
Whole to the field of fight,
Whole from the field of fight,
And whole they come thence home.

158. A twelfth I know, if high on a tree
I see a hanged man swing;

---

156. *House-riders:* witches, who ride by night on the roofs of houses, generally in the form of wild beasts. Possibly one of the last two lines is spurious.

157. The last line looks like an unwarranted addition, and line 4 may likewise be spurious.

158. Lines 4-5 are probably expanded from a single line.

So do I write and color the runes
That forth he fares,
And to me talks.

159. A thirteenth I know, if a thane full young
With water I sprinkle well;
He shall not fall, though he fares mid the host,
Nor sink beneath the swords.

160. A fourteenth I know, if fain I would name
To men the mighty gods;
All know I well of the gods and elves,—
Few be the fools know this.

161. A fifteenth I know, that before the doors
Of Delling sang Thjothrörir the dwarf;
Might he sang for the gods, and glory for elves,
And wisdom for Hroptatyr wise.

162. A sixteenth I know, if I seek delight
To win from a maiden wise;
The mind I turn of the white-armed maid,
And thus change all her thoughts.

---

159. The sprinkling of a child with water was an established custom long before Christianity brought its conception of baptism.

161. This stanza, according to Müllenhoff, was the original conclusion of the poem, the phrase "a fifteenth" being inserted only after stanzas 162-165 had crept in. *Delling:* a seldom mentioned god who married Not (Night). Their son was Dag (Day). *Thjothrörir:* not mentioned elsewhere. *Hroptatyr:* Othin.

163. A seventeenth I know, so that seldom shall go
A maiden young from me;
. . . .
. . . .

164. Long these songs thou shalt, Loddfafnir,
Seek in vain to sing;
Yet good it were if thou mightest get them,
Well, if thou wouldst them learn,
Help, if thou hadst them.

165. An eighteenth I know, that ne'er will I tell
To maiden or wife of man,—
The best is what none but one's self doth know,
So comes the end of the songs,—
Save only to her in whose arms I lie,
Or who else my sister is.

---

163. Some editors have combined these two lines with stanza 164. Others have assumed that the gap follows the first half-line, making "so that—from me" the end of the stanza.

164. This stanza is almost certainly an interpolation, and seems to have been introduced after the list of charms and the *Loddfafnismol* (stanzas 111-138) were combined in a single poem, for there is no other apparent excuse for the reference to Loddfafnir at this point. The words "if thou mightest get them" are a conjectural emendation.

165. This stanza is almost totally obscure. The third and fourth lines look like interpolations.

VAFTHRUTHNISMOL

The Ballad of Vafthruthnir

Introductory Note

The *Vafthruthnismol* follows the *Hovamol* in the *Codex Regius.* From stanza 20 on it is also included in the *Arnamagnæan Codex,* the first part evidently having appeared on a leaf now lost. Snorri quotes eight stanzas of it in the *Prose Edda,* and in his prose text closely paraphrases many others.

The poem is wholly in dialogue form except for a single narrative stanza (stanza 5). After a brief introductory discussion between Othin and his wife, Frigg, concerning the reputed wisdom of the giant Vafthruthnir, Othin, always in quest of wisdom, seeks out the giant, calling himself Gagnrath. The giant immediately insists that they shall demonstrate which is the wiser of the two, and propounds four questions (stanzas 11, 13, 15, and 17), each of which Othin answers. It is then the god's turn to ask, and he begins with a series of twelve numbered questions regarding the origins and past history of life. These Vafthruthnir answers, and Othin asks five more questions, this time referring to what is to follow the destruction of the gods, the last one asking the name of his own slayer. Again Vafthruthnir answers, and Othin finally propounds the unanswerable question: "What spake Othin himself in the ears of his son, ere in the bale-fire he burned?" Vafthruthnir, recognizing his questioner as Othin himself, admits his inferiority in wisdom, and so the contest ends.

The whole poem is essentially encyclopædic in character, and thus was particularly useful to Snorri in his preparation of the *Prose Edda.* The encyclopædic poem with a slight narrative outline seems to have been exceedingly popular; the *Grimnismol* and the much later *Alvissmol* represent different phases of the same type. The *Vafthruthnismol* and *Grimnismol* together, indeed, constitute a fairly complete dictionary of Norse mythology. There has been much discussion as to the probable date of the *Vafthruthnismol,* but it appears to belong to about the same period as the *Voluspo:* in other words, the middle of the tenth century. While there may be a few interpolated passages in the poem as we now have it, it is clearly a united whole, and evidently in relatively good condition.

Vafthruthnismol

Othin spake:

1. "Counsel me, Frigg, for I long to fare,
And Vafthruthnir fain would find;
In wisdom old with the giant wise
Myself would I seek to match."

Frigg spake:

2. "Heerfather here at home would I keep,
Where the gods together dwell;
Amid all the giants an equal in might
To Vafthruthnir know I none."

Othin spake:

3. "Much have I fared, much have I found,
Much have I got from the gods;
And fain would I know how Vafthruthnir now
Lives in his lofty hall."

Frigg spake:

4. "Safe mayst thou go, safe come again,
And safe be the way thou wendest!
Father of men, let thy mind be keen
When speech with the giant thou seekest."

5. The wisdom then of the giant wise

---

1. The phrases "Othin spake," "Frigg spake," etc., appear in abbreviated form in both manuscripts. *Frigg:* Othin's wife; cf. *Voluspo,* 34 and note. *Vafthruthnir* ("the Mighty in Riddles"): nothing is known of this giant beyond what is told in this poem.

2. *Heerfather* ("Father of the Host"): Othin.

5. This single narrative stanza is presumably a later interpo-

Forth did he fare to try;
He found the hall of the father of Im,
And in forthwith went Ygg.

Othin spake:

6. "Vafthruthnir, hail! to thy hall am I come,
For thyself I fain would see;
And first would I ask if wise thou art,
Or, giant, all wisdom hast won."

Vafthruthnir spake:

7. "Who is the man that speaks to me,
Here in my lofty hall?
Forth from our dwelling thou never shalt fare,
Unless wiser than I thou art."

Othin spake:

8. "Gagnrath they call me, and thirsty I come
From a journey hard to thy hall;
Welcome I look for, for long have I fared,
And gentle greeting, giant."

Vafthruthnir spake:

9. "Why standest thou there on the floor whilst thou speakest?
A seat shalt thou have in my hall;

---

lation. *Im:* the name appears to be corrupt, but we know nothing of any son of Vafthruthnir. *Ygg* ("the Terrible"): Othin.

8. *Gagnrath* ("the Gain-Counsellor"): Othin on his travels always assumes a name other than his own.

Then soon shall we know whose knowledge is more,
The guest's or the sage's gray."

Othin spake:

10. "If a poor man reaches the home of the rich,
Let him wisely speak or be still;
For to him who speaks with the hard of heart
Will chattering ever work ill."

Vafthruthnir spake:

11. "Speak forth now, Gagnrath, if there from the floor
Thou wouldst thy wisdom make known:
What name has the steed that each morn anew
The day for mankind doth draw?"

Othin spake:

12. "Skinfaxi is he, the steed who for men
The glittering day doth draw;
The best of horses to heroes he seems,
And brightly his mane doth burn."

Vafthruthnir spake:

13. "Speak forth now, Gagnrath, if there from the floor

---

10. This stanza sounds very much like many of those in the first part of the *Hovamol,* and may have been introduced here from some such source.

12. *Skinfaxi:* "Shining-Mane."

Thou wouldst thy wisdom make known:
What name has the steed that from East anew
Brings night for the noble gods?"

Othin spake:

14. "Hrimfaxi name they the steed that anew
Brings night for the noble gods;
Each morning foam from his bit there falls,
And thence come the dews in the dales."

Vafthruthnir spake:

15. "Speak forth now, Gagnrath, if there from the floor
Thou wouldst thy wisdom make known:
What name has the river that 'twixt the realms
Of the gods and the giants goes?"

Othin spake:

16. "Ifing is the river that 'twixt the realms
Of the gods and the giants goes;
For all time ever open it flows,
No ice on the river there is."

Vafthruthnir spake:

17. "Speak forth now, Gagnrath, if there from the floor

---

13. Here, and in general throughout the poem, the two-line introductory formulæ are abbreviated in the manuscripts.

14. *Hrimfaxi:* "Frosty-Mane."

16. *Ifing:* there is no other reference to this river, which never freezes, so that the giants cannot cross it.

Thou wouldst thy wisdom make known:
What name has the field where in fight shall meet
Surt and the gracious gods?"

Othin spake:

18. "Vigrith is the field where in fight shall meet
Surt and the gracious gods;
A hundred miles each way does it measure,
And so are its boundaries set."

Vafthruthnir spake:

19. "Wise art thou, guest! To my bench shalt thou go,
In our seats let us speak together;
Here in the hall our heads, O guest,
Shall we wager our wisdom upon."

Othin spake:

20. "First answer me well, if thy wisdom avails,
And thou knowest it, Vafthruthnir, now:
In earliest time whence came the earth,
Or the sky, thou giant sage?"

---

17. *Surt:* the ruler of the fire-world (Muspellsheim), who comes to attack the gods in the last battle; cf. *Voluspo,* 52.

18. *Vigrith:* "the Field of Battle." Snorri quotes this stanza. *A hundred miles:* a general phrase for a vast distance.

19. With this stanza Vafthruthnir, sufficiently impressed with his guest's wisdom to invite him to share his own seat, resigns the questioning to Othin.

20. The fragmentary version of this poem in the *Arnamagnæan Codex* begins in the middle of the first line of this stanza.

Vafthruthnir spake:

21. "Out of Ymir's flesh was fashioned the earth,
And the mountains were made of his bones;
The sky from the frost-cold giant's skull,
And the ocean out of his blood."

Othin spake:

22. "Next answer me well, if thy wisdom avails,
And thou knowest it, Vafthruthnir, now:
Whence came the moon, o'er the world of men
That fares, and the flaming sun?"

Vafthruthnir spake:

23. "Mundilferi is he who begat the moon,
And fathered the flaming sun;
The round of heaven each day they run,
To tell the time for men."

Othin spake:

24. "Third answer me well, if wise thou art called,
If thou knowest it, Vafthruthnir, now:
Whence came the day, o'er mankind that fares,
Or night with the narrowing moon?"

---

21. *Ymir:* the giant out of whose body the gods made the world; cf. *Voluspo,* 3 and note.

22. In this and in Othin's following questions, both manuscripts replace the words "next," "third," "fourth," etc., by Roman numerals.

23. *Mundilferi* ("the Turner"?): known only as the father of Mani (the Moon) and Sol (the Sun). Note that, curiously

Vafthruthnir spake:

25. "The father of day   is Delling called,
And the night was begotten by Nor;
Full moon and old   by the gods were fashioned,
To tell the time for men."

Othin spake:

26. "Fourth answer me well,   if wise thou art called,
If thou knowest it, Vafthruthnir, now:
Whence did winter come,   or the summer warm,
First with the gracious gods?"

Vafthruthnir spake:

27. "Vindsval he was   who was winter's father,
And Svosuth summer begat;"
. . . .
. . . .

---

enough, Mani is the boy and Sol the girl. According to Snorri, Sol drove the horses of the sun, and Mani those of the moon, for the gods, indignant that they should have been given such imposing names, took them from their father to perform these tasks. Cf. *Grimnismol,* 37.

25. *Delling* ("the Dayspring"? Probably another form of the name, Dogling, meaning "Son of the Dew" is more correct): the husband of Not (Night); their son was Dag (Day); cf. *Hovamol,* 161. *Nor:* Snorri calls the father of Night Norvi or Narfi, and puts him among the giants. Lines 3-4: cf. *Voluspo,* 6.

27. Neither the *Regius* nor the *Arnamagnæan Codex* indicates a lacuna. Most editors have filled out the stanza with two lines from late paper manuscripts: "And both of these   shall ever be, / Till the gods to destruction go." Bugge ingeniously paraphrases Snorri's prose: "Vindsval's father   was Vosuth called, / And rough is all his race." *Vindsval:* "the Wind-Cold," also called Vindljoni, "the Wind-Man." *Svosuth:* "the Gentle."

Othin spake:

28. "Fifth answer me well, if wise thou art called,
If thou knowest it, Vafthruthnir, now:
What giant first was fashioned of old,
And the eldest of Ymir's kin?"

Vafthruthnir spake:

29. "Winters unmeasured ere earth was made
Was the birth of Bergelmir;
Thruthgelmir's son was the giant strong,
And Aurgelmir's grandson of old."

Othin spake:

30. "Sixth answer me well, if wise thou art called,
If thou knowest it, Vafthruthnir, now:
Whence did Aurgelmir come with the giants' kin,
Long since, thou giant sage?"

Vafthruthnir spake:

31. "Down from Elivagar did venom drop,
And waxed till a giant it was;

---

28. *Ymir's kin:* the giants.

29. *Bergelmir:* when the gods slew Ymir in order to make the world out of his body, so much blood flowed from him that all the frost-giants were drowned except Bergelmir and his wife, who escaped in a boat; cf. stanza 35. Of *Thruthgelmir* ("the Mightily Burning") we know nothing, but Aurgelmir was the frost-giants' name for Ymir himself. Thus Ymir was the first of the giants, and so Othin's question is answered.

31. Snorri quotes this stanza, and the last two lines are taken from his version, as both of the manuscripts omit them. *Elivagar* ("Stormy Waves"): Mogk suggests that this river may have been the Milky Way. At any rate, the venom carried in its waters

And thence arose our giants' race,
And thus so fierce are we found."

Othin spake:

32. "Seventh answer me well, if wise thou art called,
If thou knowest it, Vafthruthnir, now:
How begat he children, the giant grim,
Who never a giantess knew?"

Vafthruthnir spake:

33. "They say 'neath the arms of the giant of ice
Grew man-child and maid together;
And foot with foot did the wise one fashion
A son that six heads bore."

Othin spake:

34. "Eighth answer me well, if wise thou art called,
If thou knowest it, Vafthruthnir, now:
What farthest back dost thou bear in mind?
For wide is thy wisdom, giant!"

---

froze into ice-banks over Ginnunga-gap (the "yawning gap" referred to in *Voluspo,* 3), and then dripped down to make the giant Ymir.

33. Snorri gives, without materially elaborating on it, the same account of how Ymir's son and daughter were born under his left arm, and how his feet together created a son. That this offspring should have had six heads is nothing out of the ordinary, for various giants had more than the normal number, and Hymir's mother is credited with a little matter of nine hundred heads; cf. *Hymiskvitha,* 8. Of the career of Ymir's six-headed son we know nothing; he may have been the Thruthgelmir of stanza 29.

Vafthruthnir spake:

35. "Winters unmeasured ere earth was made
Was the birth of Bergelmir;
This first knew I well, when the giant wise
In a boat of old was borne."

Othin spake:

36. "Ninth answer me well, if wise thou art called,
If thou knowest it, Vafthruthnir, now:
Whence comes the wind that fares o'er the waves,
Yet never itself is seen?"

Vafthruthnir spake:

37. "In an eagle's guise at the end of heaven
Hræsvelg sits, they say;
And from his wings does the wind come forth
To move o'er the world of men."

Othin spake:

38. "Tenth answer me now, if thou knowest all
The fate that is fixed for the gods:

---

35. Snorri quotes this stanza. *Bergelmir:* on him and his boat cf. stanza 29 and note.

37. Snorri quotes this stanza. *Hræsvelg* ("the Corpse-Eater"): on this giant in eagle's form cf. *Voluspo,* 50, and *Skirnismol,* 27.

38. With this stanza the question-formula changes, and Othin's questions from this point on concern more or less directly the great final struggle. Line 4 is presumably spurious. *Njorth:* on Njorth and the Wanes, who gave him as a hostage to the gods at the end of their war, cf. *Voluspo,* 21 and note.

Whence came up Njorth to the kin of the gods,—
(Rich in temples and shrines he rules,—)
Though of gods he was never begot?"

Vafthruthnir spake:

39. "In the home of the Wanes did the wise ones create him,
And gave him as pledge to the gods;
At the fall of the world shall he fare once more
Home to the Wanes so wise."

Othin spake:

40. "Eleventh answer me well, ...
. . . .
What men . . . . . . in . . . . home
Each day to fight go forth?"

Vafthruthnir spake:

41. "The heroes all in Othin's hall
Each day to fight go forth;

---

40. In both manuscripts, apparently through the carelessness of some older copyist, stanzas 40 and 41 are run together: "Eleventh answer me well, what men in the home mightily battle each day? They fell each other, and fare from the fight all healed full soon to sit." Luckily Snorri quotes stanza 41 in full, and the translation is from his version. Stanza 40 should probably run something like this: "Eleventh answer me well, if thou knowest all / The fate that is fixed for the gods: / What men are they who in Othin's home / Each day to fight go forth?"

41. *The heroes:* those brought to Valhall by the Valkyries. After the day's fighting they are healed of their wounds and all feast together.

They fell each other, and fare from the fight
All healed full soon to sit."

Othin spake:

42\. "Twelfth answer me now how all thou knowest
Of the fate that is fixed for the gods;
Of the runes of the gods and the giants' race
The truth indeed dost thou tell,
(And wide is thy wisdom, giant!)"

Vafthruthnir spake:

43\. "Of the runes of the gods and the giants' race
The truth indeed can I tell,
(For to every world have I won;)
To nine worlds came I, to Niflhel beneath,
The home where dead men dwell."

Othin spake:

44\. "Much have I fared, much have I found,
Much have I got of the gods:
What shall live of mankind when at last there comes
The mighty winter to men?"

Vafthruthnir spake:

45\. "In Hoddmimir's wood shall hide themselves
Lif and Lifthrasir then;

43\. *Nine worlds:* cf. *Voluspo,* 2. *Niflhel:* "Dark-Hell."

44\. *The mighty winter:* Before the final destruction three winters follow one another with no intervening summers.

45\. Snorri quotes this stanza. *Hoddmimir's wood:* probably

The morning dews for meat shall they have,
Such food shall men then find."

Othin spake:

46. "Much have I fared, much have I found,
Much have I got of the gods:
Whence comes the sun to the smooth sky back,
When Fenrir has snatched it forth?"

Vafthruthnir spake:

47. "A daughter bright Alfrothul bears
Ere Fenrir snatches her forth;
Her mother's paths shall the maiden tread
When the gods to death have gone."

Othin spake:

48. "Much have I fared, much have I found,
Much have I got of the gods:
What maidens are they, so wise of mind,
That forth o'er the sea shall fare?"

---

this is the ash-tree Yggdrasil, which is sometimes referred to as "Mimir's Tree," because Mimir waters it from his well; cf. *Voluspo,* 27 and note, and *Svipdagsmol,* 30 and note. Hoddmimir is presumably another name for Mimir. *Lif* ("Life") and *Lifthrasir* ("Sturdy of Life"?): nothing further is known of this pair, from whom the new race of men is to spring.

46. *Fenrir:* there appears to be a confusion between the wolf Fenrir (cf. *Voluspo,* 39 and note) and his son, the wolf Skoll, who steals the sun (cf. *Voluspo,* 40 and note).

47. Snorri quotes this stanza. *Alfrothul* ("the Elf-Beam"): the sun.

Vafthruthnir spake:

49. "O'er Mogthrasir's hill shall the maidens pass,
And three are their throngs that come;
They all shall protect the dwellers on earth,
Though they come of the giants' kin."

Othin spake:

50. "Much have I fared, much have I found,
Much have I got of the gods:
Who then shall rule the realm of the gods,
When the fires of Surt have sunk?"

Vafthruthnir spake:

51. "In the gods' home Vithar and Vali shall dwell,
When the fires of Surt have sunk;
Mothi and Magni shall Mjollnir have
When Vingnir falls in fight."

Othin spake:

52. "Much have I fared, much have I found,
Much have I got of the gods:

---

49. *Mogthrasir* ("Desiring Sons"): not mentioned elsewhere in the Eddic poems, or by Snorri. *The maidens:* apparently Norns, like the "giant-maids" in *Voluspo,* 8. These Norns, however, are kindly to men.

50. *Surt:* cf. *Voluspo,* 52 and note.

51. *Vithar:* a son of Othin, who slays the wolf Fenrir; cf. *Voluspo,* 54 and note. *Vali:* the son whom Othin begot to avenge Baldr's death; cf. *Voluspo,* 33 and note. *Mothi* ("Wrath") and *Magni* ("Might"): the sons of the god Thor, who after his death inherit his famous hammer, *Mjollnir.* Concerning this hammer cf. especially *Thrymskvitha, passim. Vingnir* ("the

What shall bring the doom of death to Othin,
When the gods to destruction go?"

Vafthruthnir spake:

53. "The wolf shall fell the father of men,
And this shall Vithar avenge;
The terrible jaws shall he tear apart,
And so the wolf shall he slay."

Othin spake:

54. "Much have I fared, much have I found,
Much have I got from the gods:
What spake Othin himself in the ears of his son,
Ere in the bale-fire he burned?"

Vafthruthnir spake:

55. "No man can tell what in olden time
Thou spak'st in the ears of thy son;
With fated mouth the fall of the gods
And mine olden tales have I told;
With Othin in knowledge now have I striven,
And ever the wiser thou art."

Hurler"): Thor. Concerning his death cf. *Voluspo*, 56. This stanza is quoted by Snorri.

53. *The wolf:* Fenrir; cf. *Voluspo*, 53 and 54.

54. *His son:* Baldr. Bugge changes lines 3-4 to run: "What did Othin speak in the ear of Baldr, / When to the bale-fire they bore him?" For Baldr's death cf. *Voluspo*, 32 and note. The question is, of course, unanswerable save by Othin himself, and so the giant at last recognizes his guest.

55. *Fated:* in stanza 19 Vafthruthnir was rash enough to wager his head against his guest's on the outcome of the contest of wisdom, so he knows that his defeat means his death.

GRIMNISMOL

The Ballad of Grimnir

Introductory Note

The *Grimnismol* follows the *Vafthruthnismol* in the *Codex Regius* and is also found complete in the *Arnamagnæan Codex,* where also it follows the *Vafthruthnismol.* Snorri quotes over twenty of its stanzas.

Like the preceding poem, the *Grimnismol* is largely encyclopedic in nature, and consists chiefly of proper names, the last forty-seven stanzas containing no less than two hundred and twenty-five of these. It is not, however, in dialogue form. As Müllenhoff pointed out, there is underneath the catalogue of mythological names a consecutive and thoroughly dramatic story. Othin, concealed under the name of Grimnir, is through an error tortured by King Geirröth. Bound between two blazing fires, he begins to display his wisdom for the benefit of the king's little son, Agnar, who has been kind to him. Gradually he works up to the great final moment, when he declares his true name, or rather names, to the terrified Geirröth, and the latter falls on his sword and is killed.

For much of this story we do not have to depend on guesswork, for in both manuscripts the poem itself is preceded by a prose narrative of considerable length, and concluded by a brief prose statement of the manner of Geirröth's death. These prose notes, of which there are many in the Eddic manuscripts, are of considerable interest to the student of early literary forms. Presumably they were written by the compiler to whom we owe the Eddic collection, who felt that the poems needed such annotation in order to be clear. Linguistic evidence shows that they were written in the twelfth or thirteenth century, for they preserve none of the older word-forms which help us to date many of the poems two or three hundred years earlier.

Without discussing in detail the problems suggested by these prose passages, it is worth noting, first, that the Eddic poems contain relatively few stanzas of truly narrative verse; and second, that all of them are based on narratives which must have been more or less familiar to the hearers of the poems. In other words, the poems seldom aimed to tell stories, although most of them followed a narrative sequence of ideas. The stories themselves appear to have lived in oral prose tradition, just as in the case of the sagas; and the prose notes of the manuscripts, in so far as they contain material not simply drawn from the poems themselves, are relics of this tradition. The early Norse poets rarely conceived verse as a suitable means for direct story-telling, and in some of the poems even the simplest action is told in prose "links" between dialogue stanzas.

The applications of this fact, which has been too often overlooked, are almost limitless, for it suggests a still unwritten chapter in the history of ballad poetry and the so-called "popular" epic. It implies that narrative among early peoples may frequently have had a period of prose existence before it was made into verse, and thus puts, for example, a long series of transitional stages before such a poem as the *Iliad.* In any case, the prose notes accompanying the Eddic poems prove that in addition to the poems themselves there existed in the twelfth century a considerable amount of narrative tradition, presumably in prose form, on which these notes were based by the compiler.

Interpolations in such a poem as the *Grimnismol* could have been made easily enough, and many stanzas have undoubtedly crept in from other poems, but the beginning and end of the poem are clearly marked, and presumably it has come down to us with the same essential outline it had when it was composed, probably in the first half of the tenth century.

King Hrauthung had two sons: one was called Agnar, and the other Geirröth. Agnar was ten winters old, and Geirröth eight. Once they both rowed in a boat with their fishing-gear to catch little fish; and the wind drove them out into the sea. In the darkness of the night they were wrecked on the shore; and going up, they found a poor peasant, with whom they stayed through the winter. The housewife took care of Agnar, and the peasant cared for

---

Prose. The texts of the two manuscripts differ in many minor details. *Hrauthung:* this mythical king is not mentioned elsewhere. *Geirröth:* the manuscripts spell his name in various ways.

Geirröth, and taught him wisdom. In the spring the peasant gave him a boat; and when the couple led them to the shore, the peasant spoke secretly with Geirröth. They had a fair wind, and came to their father's landing-place. Geirröth was forward in the boat; he leaped up on land, but pushed out the boat and said, "Go thou now where evil may have thee!" The boat drifted out to sea. Geirröth, however, went up to the house, and was well received, but his father was dead. Then Geirröth was made king, and became a renowned man.

Othin and Frigg sat in Hlithskjolf and looked over all the worlds. Othin said: "Seest thou Agnar, thy fosterling, how he begets children with a giantess in the cave? But Geirröth, my fosterling, is a king, and now rules over his land." Frigg said: "He is so miserly that he tortures his guests if he thinks that too many of them come to him." Othin replied that this was the greatest of lies; and they made a wager about this matter. Frigg sent her maidservant, Fulla, to Geirröth. She bade the king beware lest a magician who was come thither to his land should bewitch him, and told this sign concerning him, that no dog was so fierce as to leap at him. Now it was a very great slander that King Geirröth was not hospitable; but nevertheless he had them take the man whom the dogs would not attack. He wore a dark-blue mantle and called himself Grimnir, but said no more about himself, though

---

Frigg: Othin's wife. She and Othin nearly always disagreed in some such way as the one outlined in this story. *Hlithskjolf* ("Gate-Shelf"): Othin's watch-tower in heaven, whence he can overlook all the nine worlds; cf. *Skirnismol,* introductory prose. *Grimnir:* "the Hooded One."

he was questioned. The king had him tortured to make him speak, and set him between two fires, and he sat there eight nights. King Geirröth had a son ten winters old, and called Agnar after his father's brother. Agnar went to Grimnir, and gave him a full horn to drink from, and said that the king did ill in letting him be tormented without cause. Grimnir drank from the horn; the fire had come so near that the mantle burned on Grimnir's back. He spake:

1. Hot art thou, fire! too fierce by far;
   Get ye now gone, ye flames!
The mantle is burnt, though I bear it aloft,
   And the fire scorches the fur.

2. 'Twixt the fires now eight nights have I sat,
   And no man brought meat to me,
Save Agnar alone, and alone shall rule
   Geirröth's son o'er the Goths.

3. Hail to thee, Agnar! for hailed thou art
   By the voice of Veratyr;

2. In the original lines 2 and 4 are both too long for the meter, and thus the true form of the stanza is doubtful. For line 4 both manuscripts have "the land of the Goths" instead of simply "the Goths." The word "Goths" apparently was applied indiscriminately to any South-Germanic people, including the Burgundians as well as the actual Goths, and thus here has no specific application; cf. *Gripisspo,* 35 and note.

For a single drink shalt thou never receive
A greater gift as reward.

4. The land is holy that lies hard by
The gods and the elves together;
And Thor shall ever in Thruthheim dwell,
Till the gods to destruction go.

5. Ydalir call they the place where Ull
A hall for himself hath set;
And Alfheim the gods to Freyr once gave
As a tooth-gift in ancient times.

6. A third home is there, with silver thatched
By the hands of the gracious gods:
Valaskjolf is it, in days of old
Set by a god for himself.

7. Sökkvabekk is the fourth, where cool waves flow,

---

3. *Veratyr* ("Lord of Men"): Othin. The "gift" which Agnar receives is Othin's mythological lore.

4. *Thruthheim* ("the Place of Might"): the place where Thor, the strongest of the gods, has his hall, Bilskirnir, described in stanza 24.

5. *Ydalir* ("Yew-Dales"): the home of Ull, the archer among the gods, a son of Thor's wife, Sif, by another marriage. The wood of the yew-tree was used for bows in the North just as it was long afterwards in England. *Alfheim:* the home of the elves. *Freyr:* cf. *Skirnismol,* introductory prose and note. *Tooth-gift:* the custom of making a present to a child when it cuts its first tooth is, according to Vigfusson, still in vogue in Iceland.

6. *Valaskjolf* ("the Shelf of the Slain"): Othin's home, in which is his watch-tower, Hlithskjolf. Gering identifies this with Valhall, and as that is mentioned in stanza 8, he believes stanza 6 to be an interpolation.

And amid their murmur it stands;
There daily do Othin and Saga drink
In gladness from cups of gold.

8. The fifth is Glathsheim, and gold-bright there
Stands Valhall stretching wide;
And there does Othin each day choose
The men who have fallen in fight.

9. Easy is it to know for him who to Othin
Comes and beholds the hall;
Its rafters are spears, with shields is it roofed,
On its benches are breastplates strewn.

10. Easy is it to know for him who to Othin
Comes and beholds the hall;
There hangs a wolf by the western door,
And o'er it an eagle hovers.

11. The sixth is Thrymheim, where Thjazi dwelt,
The giant of marvelous might;

---

7. *Sökkvabekk* ("the Sinking Stream"): of this spot and of Saga, who is said to live there, little is known. Saga may be an hypostasis of Frigg, but Snorri calls her a distinct goddess, and the name suggests some relation to history or story-telling.

8. *Glathsheim* ("the Place of Joy"): Othin's home, the greatest and most beautiful hall in the world. *Valhall* ("Hall of the Slain"): cf. *Voluspo,* 31 and note. Valhall is not only the hall whither the slain heroes are brought by the Valkyries, but also a favorite home of Othin.

10. The opening formula is abbreviated in both manuscripts. *A wolf:* probably the wolf and the eagle were carved figures above the door.

Now Skathi abides, the god's fair bride,
In the home that her father had.

12. The seventh is Breithablik; Baldr has there
For himself a dwelling set,
In the land I know that lies so fair,
And from evil fate is free.

13. Himinbjorg is the eighth, and Heimdall there
O'er men holds sway, it is said;
In his well-built house does the warder of heaven
The good mead gladly drink.

14. The ninth is Folkvang, where Freyja decrees

---

11. *Thrymheim* ("the Home of Clamor"): on this mountain the giant Thjazi built his home. The god, or rather Wane, Njorth (cf. *Voluspo,* 21, note) married Thjazi's daughter, Skathi. She wished to live in her father's hall among the mountains, while Njorth loved his home, Noatun, by the sea. They agreed to compromise by spending nine nights at Thrymheim and then three at Noatun, but neither could endure the surroundings of the other's home, so Skathi returned to Thrymheim, while Njorth stayed at Noatun. Snorri quotes stanzas 11-15.

12. *Breithablik* ("Wide-Shining"): the house in heaven, free from everything unclean, in which Baldr (cf. *Voluspo,* 32, note), the fairest and best of the gods, lived.

13. *Himinbjorg* ("Heaven's Cliffs"): the dwelling at the end of the bridge Bifrost (the rainbow), where Heimdall (cf. *Voluspo,* 27) keeps watch against the coming of the giants. In this stanza the two functions of Heimdall—as father of mankind (cf. *Voluspo,* 1 and note, and *Rigsthula,* introductory prose and note) and as warder of the gods—seem both to be mentioned, but the second line in the manuscripts is apparently in bad shape, and in the editions is more or less conjectural.

14. *Folkvang* ("Field of the Folk"): here is situated Freyja's

Who shall have seats in the hall;
The half of the dead each day does she choose,
And half does Othin have.

15. The tenth is Glitnir; its pillars are gold,
And its roof with silver is set;
There most of his days does Forseti dwell,
And sets all strife at end.

16. The eleventh is Noatun; there has Njorth
For himself a dwelling set;
The sinless ruler of men there sits
In his temple timbered high.

17. Filled with growing trees and high-standing grass
Is Vithi, Vithar's land;

---

hall, Sessrymnir ("Rich in Seats"). Freyja, the sister of Freyr, is the fairest of the goddesses, and the most kindly disposed to mankind, especially to lovers. *Half of the dead:* Mogk has made it clear that Freyja represents a confusion between two originally distinct divinities: the wife of Othin (Frigg) and the northern goddess of love. This passage appears to have in mind her attributes as Othin's wife. Snorri has this same confusion, but there is no reason why the Freyja who was Freyr's sister should share the slain with Othin.

15. *Glitnir* ("the Shining"): the home of Forseti, a god of whom we know nothing beyond what Snorri tells us: "Forseti is the son of Baldr and Nanna, daughter of Nep. All those who come to him with hard cases to settle go away satisfied; he is the best judge among gods and men."

16. *Noatun* ("Ships'-Haven"): the home of Njorth, who calms the waves; cf. stanza 11 and *Voluspo,* 21.

17. *Vithi:* this land is not mentioned elsewhere. *Vithar* avenged his father, Othin, by slaying the wolf Fenrir.

But there did the son from his steed leap down,
When his father he fain would avenge.

18. In Eldhrimnir Andhrimnir cooks
Sæhrimnir's seething flesh,—
The best of food, but few men know
On what fare the warriors feast.

19. Freki and Geri does Heerfather feed,
The far-famed fighter of old:
But on wine alone does the weapon-decked god,
Othin, forever live.

20. O'er Mithgarth Hugin and Munin both
Each day set forth to fly;
For Hugin I fear lest he come not home,
But for Munin my care is more.

---

18. Stanzas 18-20 appear also in Snorri's *Edda.* Very possibly they are an interpolation here. *Eldhrimnir* ("Sooty with Fire"): the great kettle in Valhall, wherein the gods' cook, *Andhrimnir* ("The Sooty-Faced") daily cooks the flesh of the boar *Sæhrimnir* ("The Blackened"). His flesh suffices for all the heroes there gathered, and each evening he becomes whole again, to be cooked the next morning.

19. *Freki* ("The Greedy") and *Geri* ("The Ravenous"): the two wolves who sit by Othin's side at the feast, and to whom he gives all the food set before him, since wine is food and drink alike for him. *Heerfather:* Othin.

20. *Mithgarth* ("The Middle Home"): the earth. *Hugin* ("Thought") and *Munin* ("Memory"): the two ravens who sit on Othin's shoulders, and fly forth daily to bring him news of the world.

21. Loud roars Thund, and Thjothvitnir's fish
Joyously fares in the flood;
Hard does it seem to the host of the slain
To wade the torrent wild.

22. There Valgrind stands, the sacred gate,
And behind are the holy doors;
Old is the gate, but few there are
Who can tell how it tightly is locked.

23. Five hundred doors and forty there are,
I ween, in Valhall's walls;
Eight hundred fighters through one door fare
When to war with the wolf they go.

24. Five hundred rooms and forty there are
I ween, in Bilskirnir built;

---

21. *Thund* ("The Swollen" or "The Roaring"): the river surrounding Valhall. *Thjothvitnir's fish:* presumably the sun, which was caught by the wolf Skoll (cf. *Voluspo,* 40), Thjothvitnir meaning "the mighty wolf." Such a phrase, characteristic of all Skaldic poetry, is rather rare in the *Edda.* The last two lines refer to the attack on Valhall by the people of Hel; cf. *Voluspo,* 51.

22. *Valgrind* ("The Death-Gate"): the outer gate of Valhall; cf. *Sigurtharkvitha en skamma,* 68 and note.

23. This and the following stanza stand in reversed order in *Regius.* Snorri quotes stanza 23 as a proof of the vast size of Valhall. The last two lines refer to the final battle with Fenrir and the other enemies.

24. This stanza is almost certainly an interpolation, brought in through a confusion of the first two lines with those of stanza 23. Its description of Thor's house, Bilskirnir (cf. stanza 4 and

Of all the homes whose roofs I beheld,
My son's the greatest meseemed.

25. Heithrun is the goat who stands by Heerfather's hall,
And the branches of Lærath she bites;
The pitcher she fills with the fair, clear mead,
Ne'er fails the foaming drink.

26. Eikthyrnir is the hart who stands by Heerfather's hall
And the branches of Lærath he bites;
From his horns a stream into Hvergelmir drops,
Thence all the rivers run.

---

note) has nothing to do with that of Valhall. Snorri quotes the stanza in his account of Thor.

25. The first line in the original is, as indicated in the translation, too long, and various attempts to amend it have been made. *Heithrun:* the she-goat who lives on the twigs of the tree *Lærath* (presumably the ash Yggdrasil), and daily gives mead which, like the boar's flesh, suffices for all the heroes in Valhall. In Snorri's *Edda* Gangleri foolishly asks whether the heroes drink water, whereto Har replies, "Do you imagine that Othin invites kings and earls and other noble men, and then gives them water to drink?"

26. *Eikthyrnir* ("The Oak-Thorned," i.e., with antlers, "thorns," like an oak): this animal presumably represents the clouds. The first line, like that of stanza 25, is too long in the original. *Lærath:* cf. stanza 25, note. *Hvergelmir:* according to Snorri, this spring, "the Cauldron-Roaring," was in the midst of Niflheim, the world of darkness and the dead, beneath the third root of the ash Yggdrasil. Snorri gives a list of the rivers flowing thence nearly identical with the one in the poem.

27. Sith and Vith, Sækin and Ækin,
Svol and Fimbulthul, Gunnthro and Fjorm,
Rin and Rinnandi,
Gipul and Gopul, Gomul and Geirvimul,
That flow through the fields of the gods;
Thyn and Vin, Thol and Hol,
Groth and Gunnthorin.

28. Vino is one, Vegsvin another,
And Thjothnuma a third;
Nyt and Not, Non and Hron,
Slith and Hrith, Sylg and Ylg,
Vith and Von, Vond and Strond,
Gjol and Leipt, that go among men,
And hence they fall to Hel.

---

27. The entire passage from stanza 27 through stanza 35 is confused. The whole thing may well be an interpolation. Bugge calls stanzas 27-30 an interpolation, and editors who have accepted the passage as a whole have rejected various lines. The spelling of the names of the rivers varies greatly in the manuscripts and editions. It is needless here to point out the many attempted emendations of this list. For a passage presenting similar problems, cf. *Voluspo,* 10-16. Snorri virtually quotes stanzas 27-28 in his prose, though not consecutively. The name *Rin,* in line 3, is identical with that for the River Rhine which appears frequently in the hero poems, but the similarity is doubtless purely accidental.

28. *Slith* may possibly be the same river as that mentioned in *Voluspo,* 36, as flowing through the giants' land. *Leipt:* in *Helgakvitha Hundingsbana* II, 29, this river is mentioned as one by which a solemn oath is sworn, and Gering points the parallel to the significance of the Styx among the Greeks. The other rivers here named are not mentioned elsewhere in the poems.

29. Kormt and Ormt and the Kerlaugs twain
Shall Thor each day wade through,
(When dooms to give he forth shall go
To the ash-tree Yggdrasil;)
For heaven's bridge burns all in flame,
And the sacred waters seethe.

30. Glath and Gyllir, Gler and Skeithbrimir,
Silfrintopp and Sinir,
Gisl and Falhofnir, Golltopp and Lettfeti,
On these steeds the gods shall go
When dooms to give each day they ride
To the ash-tree Yggdrasil.

---

29. This stanza looks as though it originally had had nothing to do with the two preceding it. Snorri quotes it in his description of the three roots of Yggdrasil, and the three springs beneath them. "The third root of the ash stands in heaven and beneath this root is a spring which is very holy, and is called Urth's well." (Cf. *Voluspo,* 19) "There the gods have their judgment-seat, and thither they ride each day over Bifrost, which is also called the Gods' Bridge." Thor has to go on foot in the last days of the destruction, when the bridge is burning. Another interpretation, however, is that when Thor leaves the heavens (i.e., when a thunder-storm is over) the rainbow-bridge becomes hot in the sun. Nothing more is known of the rivers named in this stanza. Lines 3-4 are almost certainly interpolated from stanza 30.

30. This stanza, again possibly an interpolation, is closely paraphrased by Snorri following the passage quoted in the previous note. *Glath* ("Joyous") : identified in the *Skaldskaparmal* with Skinfaxi, the horse of day; cf. *Vafthruthnismol,* 12. *Gyllir:* "Golden." *Gler:* "Shining." *Skeithbrimir:* "Swift-Going." *Silfrintopp:* "Silver-Topped." *Sinir:* "Sinewy." *Gisl:* the meaning is doubtful; Gering suggests "Gleaming." *Falhofnir:*

31. Three roots there are that three ways run
'Neath the ash-tree Yggdrasil;
'Neath the first lives Hel, 'neath the second the frost-giants,
'Neath the last are the lands of men.

32. Ratatosk is the squirrel who there shall run
On the ash-tree Yggdrasil;
From above the words of the eagle he bears,
And tells them to Nithhogg beneath.

33. Four harts there are, that the highest twigs

"Hollow-Hoofed." *Golltopp* ("Gold-Topped"): this horse belonged to Heimdall (cf. *Voluspo,* 1 and 46). It is noteworthy that gold was one of the attributes of Heimdall's belongings, and, because his teeth were of gold, he was also called Gullintanni ("Gold-Toothed"). *Lettfeti:* "Light-Feet." Othin's eight-footed horse, Sleipnir, is not mentioned in this list.

31. The first of these roots is the one referred to in stanza 26; the second in stanza 29 (cf. notes). Of the third root there is nothing noteworthy recorded. After this stanza it is more than possible that one has been lost, paraphrased in the prose of Snorri's *Edda* thus: "An eagle sits in the branches of the ash-tree, and he is very wise; and between his eyes sits the hawk who is called Vethrfolnir."

32. *Ratatosk* ("The Swift-Tusked"): concerning this squirrel, the *Prose Edda* has to add only that he runs up and down the tree conveying the abusive language of the eagle (see note on stanza 31) and the dragon *Nithhogg* (cf. *Voluspo,* 39 and note) to each other. The hypothesis that Ratatosk "represents the undying hatred between the sustaining and the destroying elements—the gods and the giants," seems a trifle far-fetched.

33. Stanzas 33-34 may well be interpolated, and are certainly in bad shape in the Mss. Bugge points out that they are probably of later origin than those surrounding them. Snorri

Nibble with necks bent back;
Dain and Dvalin, ...
Duneyr and Dyrathror.

34. More serpents there are beneath the ash
Than an unwise ape would think;
Goin and Moin, Grafvitnir's sons,
Grabak and Grafvolluth,
Ofnir and Svafnir shall ever, methinks,
Gnaw at the twigs of the tree.

35. Yggdrasil's ash great evil suffers,
Far more than men do know;

---

closely paraphrases stanza 33, but without elaboration, and nothing further is known of the *four harts*. It may be guessed, however, that they are a late multiplication of the single hart mentioned in stanza 26, just as the list of dragons in stanza 34 seems to have been expanded out of Nithhogg, the only authentic dragon under the root of the ash. *Highest twigs:* a guess; the Mss. words are baffling. Something has apparently been lost from lines 3-4, but there is no clue as to its nature.

34. Cf. note on previous stanza. Nothing further is known of any of the serpents here listed, and the meanings of many of the names are conjectural. Snorri quotes this stanza. Editors have altered it in various ways in an attempt to regularize the meter. *Goin* and *Moin:* meaning obscure. *Grafvitnir:* "The Gnawing Wolf." *Grabak:* "Gray-Back." *Grafvolluth:* "The Field-Gnawer." *Ofnir* and *Svafnir* ("The Bewilderer" and "The Sleep-Bringer"): it is noteworthy that in stanza 54 Othin gives himself these two names.

35. Snorri quotes this stanza, which concludes the passage, beginning with stanza 25, describing Yggdrasil. If we assume that stanzas 27-34 are later interpolations—possibly excepting 32—this section of the poem reads clearly enough.

The hart bites its top, its trunk is rotting,
And Nithhogg gnaws beneath.

36. Hrist and Mist bring the horn at my will,
Skeggjold and Skogul;
Hild and Thruth, Hlok and Herfjotur,
Gol and Geironul,
Randgrith and Rathgrith and Reginleif
Beer to the warriors bring.

37. Arvak and Alsvith up shall drag
Weary the weight of the sun;
But an iron cool have the kindly gods
Of yore set under their yokes.

---

36. Snorri quotes this list of the Valkyries, concerning whom cf. *Voluspo,* 31 and note, where a different list of names is given. *Hrist:* "Shaker." *Mist:* "Mist." *Skeggjold:* "Ax-Time." *Skogul:* "Raging" (?). *Hild:* "Warrior." *Thruth:* "Might." *Hlok:* "Shrieking." *Herfjotur:* "Host-Fetter." *Gol:* "Screaming." *Geironul:* "Spear-Bearer." *Randgrith:* "Shield-Bearer." *Rathgrith:* Gering guesses "Plan-Destroyer." *Reginleif:* "Gods'-Kin." Manuscripts and editions vary greatly in the spelling of these names, and hence in their significance.

37. Müllenhoff suspects stanzas 37-41 to have been interpolated, and Edzardi thinks they may have come from the *Vafthruthnismol.* Snorri closely paraphrases stanzas 37-39, and quotes 40-41. *Arvak* ("Early Waker") and *Alsvith* ("All-Swift"): the horses of the sun, named also in *Sigrdrifumol,* 15. According to Snorri: "There was a man called Mundilfari, who had two children; they were so fair and lovely that he called his son Mani and his daughter Sol. The gods were angry at this presumption, and took the children and set them up in heaven; and they bade Sol drive the horses that drew the car of the sun

38. In front of the sun does Svalin stand,
The shield for the shining god;
Mountains and sea would be set in flames
If it fell from before the sun.

39. Skoll is the wolf that to Ironwood
Follows the glittering god,
And the son of Hrothvitnir, Hati, awaits
The burning bride of heaven.

40. Out of Ymir's flesh was fashioned the earth,
And the ocean out of his blood;
Of his bones the hills, of his hair the trees,
Of his skull the heavens high.

---

which the gods had made to light the world from the sparks which flew out of Muspellsheim. The horses were called Alsvith and Arvak, and under their yokes the gods set two bellows to cool them, and in some songs these are called 'the cold iron.'"

38. *Svalin* ("The Cooling"): the only other reference to this shield is in *Sigrdrifumol,* 15.

39. *Skoll* and *Hati:* the wolves that devour respectively the sun and moon. The latter is the son of Hrothvitnir ("The Mighty Wolf," i. e. Fenrir); cf. *Voluspo,* 40, and *Vafthruthnismol,* 46-47, in which Fenrir appears as the thief. *Ironwood:* a conjectural emendation of an obscure phrase; cf. *Voluspo,* 40.

40. This and the following stanza are quoted by Snorri. They seem to have come from a different source from the others of this poem; Edzardi suggests an older version of the *Vafthruthnismol.* This stanza is closely parallel to *Vafthruthnismol,* 21, which see, as also *Voluspo,* 3. Snorri, following this account, has a few details to add. The stones were made out of Ymir's teeth and such of his bones as were broken. Mithgarth was a mountain-wall made out of Ymir's eyebrows, and set around the earth because of the enmity of the giants.

41. Mithgarth the gods from his eyebrows made,
And set for the sons of men;
And out of his brain the baleful clouds
They made to move on high.

42. His the favor of Ull and of all the gods
Who first in the flames will reach;
For the house can be seen by the sons of the gods
If the kettle aside were cast.

43. In days of old did Ivaldi's sons
Skithblathnir fashion fair,
The best of ships for the bright god Freyr,
The noble son of Njorth.

---

42. With this stanza Othin gets back to his immediate situation, bound as he is between two fires. He calls down a blessing on the man who will reach into the fire and pull aside the great kettle which, in Icelandic houses, hung directly under the smoke-vent in the roof, and thus kept any one above from looking down into the interior. On *Ull,* the archer-god, cf. stanza 5 and note. He is specified here apparently for no better reason than that his name fits the initial-rhyme.

43. This and the following stanza are certainly interpolated, for they have nothing to do with the context, and stanza 45 continues the dramatic conclusion of the poem begun in stanza 42. This stanza is quoted by Snorri. *Ivaldi* ("The Mighty"): he is known only as the father of the craftsmen-dwarfs who made not only the ship Skithblathnir, but also Othin's spear Gungnir, and the golden hair for Thor's wife, Sif, after Loki had maliciously cut her own hair off. *Skithblathnir:* this ship ("Wooden-Bladed") always had a fair wind, whenever the sail was set; it could be folded up at will and put in the pocket. *Freyr:* concerning him and his father, see *Voluspo,* 21, note, and *Skirnismol,* introductory prose and note.

44. The best of trees must Yggdrasil be,
Skithblathnir best of boats;
Of all the gods is Othin the greatest,
And Sleipnir the best of steeds;
Bilrost of bridges, Bragi of skalds,
Hobrok of hawks, and Garm of hounds.

45. To the race of the gods my face have I raised,
And the wished-for aid have I waked;
For to all the gods has the message gone
That sit in Ægir's seats,
That drink within Ægir's doors.

---

44. Snorri quotes this stanza. Like stanza 43 an almost certain interpolation, it was probably drawn in by the reference to Skithblathnir in the stanza interpolated earlier. It is presumably in faulty condition. One Ms. has after the fifth line half of a sixth,—"Brimir of swords." *Yggdrasil:* cf. stanzas 25-35. *Skithblathnir:* cf. stanza 43, note. *Sleipnir:* Othin's eight-legged horse, one of Loki's numerous progeny, borne by him to the stallion Svathilfari. This stallion belonged to the giant who built a fortress for the gods, and came so near to finishing it, with Svathilfari's aid, as to make the gods fear he would win his promised reward—Freyja and the sun and moon. To delay the work, Loki turned himself into a mare, whereupon the stallion ran away, and the giant failed to complete his task within the stipulated time. *Bilrost:* probably another form of Bifrost (which Snorri has in his version of the stanza), on which cf. stanza 29. *Bragi:* the god of poetry. He is one of the later figures among the gods, and is mentioned only three times in the poems of the *Edda.* In Snorri's *Edda,* however, he is of great importance. His wife is Ithun, goddess of youth. Perhaps the Norwegian skald Bragi Boddason, the oldest recorded skaldic poet, had been traditionally apotheosized as early as the tenth century. *Hobrok:* nothing further is known of him. *Garm:* cf. *Voluspo,* 44.

45. With this stanza the narrative current of the poem is resumed. *Ægir:* the sea-god; cf. *Lokasenna,* introductory prose.

46. Grim is my name, Gangleri am I,
Herjan and Hjalmberi,
Thekk and Thrithi, Thuth and Uth,
Helblindi and Hor;

47. Sath and Svipal and Sanngetal,
Herteit and Hnikar,
Bileyg, Baleyg, Bolverk, Fjolnir,
Grim and Grimnir, Glapsvith, Fjolsvith.

48. Sithhott, Sithskegg, Sigfather, Hnikuth,

---

46. Concerning the condition of stanzas 46-50, quoted by Snorri, nothing definite can be said. Lines and entire stanzas of this "catalogue" sort undoubtedly came and went with great freedom all through the period of oral transmission. Many of the names are not mentioned elsewhere, and often their significance is sheer guesswork. As in nearly every episode Othin appeared in disguise, the number of his names was necessarily almost limitless. *Grim:* "The Hooded." *Gangleri:* "The Wanderer." *Herjan:* "The Ruler." *Hjalmberi:* "The Helmet-Bearer." *Thekk:* "The Much-Loved." *Thrithi:* "The Third" (in Snorri's *Edda* the stories are all told in the form of answers to questions, the speakers being Har, Jafnhar and Thrithi. Just what this tripartite form of Othin signifies has been the source of endless debate. Probably this line is late enough to betray the somewhat muddled influence of early Christianity.) *Thuth* and *Uth:* both names defy guesswork. *Helblindi:* "Hel-Blinder" (two manuscripts have *Herblindi*—"Host-Blinder"). *Hor:* "The High One."

47. *Sath:* "The Truthful." *Svipal:* "The Changing." *Sanngetal:* "The Truth-Teller." *Herteit:* "Glad of the Host." *Hnikar:* "The Overthrower." *Bileyg:* "The Shifty-Eyed." *Baleyg:* "The Flaming-Eyed." *Bolverk:* "Doer of Ill" (cf. *Hovamol,* 104 and note). *Fjolnir:* "The Many-Shaped." *Grimnir:* "The Hooded." *Glapsvith:* "Swift in Deceit." *Fjolsvith:* "Wide of Wisdom."

48. *Sithhott:* "With Broad Hat." *Sithskegg:* "Long-Bearded."

Allfather, Valfather, Atrith, Farmatyr:
A single name have I never had
Since first among men I fared.

49. Grimnir they call me in Geirröth's hall,
With Asmund Jalk am I;
Kjalar I was when I went in a sledge,
At the council Thror am I called,
As Vithur I fare to the fight;
Oski, Biflindi, Jafnhor and Omi,
Gondlir and Harbarth midst gods.

50. I deceived the giant Sokkmimir old
As Svithur and Svithrir of yore;
Of Mithvitnir's son the slayer I was
When the famed one found his doom.

Sigfather: "Father of Victory." *Hnikuth:* "Overthrower." *Valfather:* "Father of the Slain." *Atrith:* "The Rider." *Farmatyr:* "Helper of Cargoes" (i. e., god of sailors).

49. Nothing is known of Asmund, of Othin's appearance as Jalk, or of the occasion when he "went in a sledge" as Kjalar ("Ruler of Keels"?). *Thror* and *Vithur* are also of uncertain meaning. *Oski:* "God of Wishes." *Biflindi:* the manuscripts vary widely in the form of this name. *Jafnhor:* "Equally High" (cf. note on stanza 46). *Omi:* "The Shouter." *Gondlir:* "Wand-Bearer." *Harbarth:* "Graybeard" (cf. *Harbarthsljoth,* introduction).

50. Nothing further is known of the episode here mentioned. Sokkmimir is presumably Mithvitnir's son. Snorri quotes the names Svithur and Svithrir, but omits all the remainder of the stanza.

51. Drunk art thou, Geirröth, too much didst thou drink,

. . . .

Much hast thou lost, for help no more
From me or my heroes thou hast.

52. Small heed didst thou take to all that I told,
And false were the words of thy friends;
For now the sword of my friend I see,
That waits all wet with blood.

53. Thy sword-pierced body shall Ygg have soon,
For thy life is ended at last;
The maids are hostile; now Othin behold!
Now come to me if thou canst!

54. Now am I Othin, Ygg was I once,
Ere that did they call me Thund;
Vak and Skilfing, Vofuth and Hroptatyr,
Gaut and Jalk midst the gods;
Ofnir and Svafnir, and all, methinks,
Are names for none but me.

---

51. Again the poem returns to the direct action, Othin addressing the terrified Geirröth. The manuscripts show no lacuna. Some editors supply a second line from paper manuscripts: "Greatly by me art beguiled."

53. *Ygg:* Othin ("The Terrible"). *The maids:* the three Norns.

54. Possibly out of place, and probably more or less corrupt. *Thund:* "The Thunderer." *Vak:* "The Wakeful." *Skilfing:* "The Shaker." *Vofuth:* "The Wanderer." *Hroptatyr:* "Crier of the Gods." *Gaut:* "Father." *Ofnir* and *Svafnir:* cf. stanza 34.

King Geirröth sat and had his sword on his knee, half drawn from its sheath. But when he heard that Othin was come thither, then he rose up and sought to take Othin from the fire. The sword slipped from his hand, and fell with the hilt down. The king stumbled and fell forward, and the sword pierced him through, and slew him. Then Othin vanished, but Agnar long ruled there as king.

SKIRNISMOL

The Ballad of Skirnir

Introductory Note

The *Skirnismol* is found complete in the *Codex Regius,* and through stanza 27 in the *Arnamagnæan Codex*. Snorri quotes the concluding stanza. In *Regius* the poem is entitled "For Scirnis" ("Skirnir's Journey").

The *Skirnismol* differs sharply from the poems preceding it, in that it has a distinctly ballad quality. As a matter of fact, however, its verse is altogether dialogue, the narrative being supplied in the prose "links," concerning which cf. introductory note to the *Grimnismol.* The dramatic effectiveness and vivid characterization of the poem seem to connect it with the *Thrymskvitha,* and the two may possibly have been put into their present form by the same man. Bugge's guess that the *Skirnismol* was the work of the author of the *Lokasenna* is also possible, though it has less to support it.

Critics have generally agreed in dating the poem as we now have it as early as the first half of the tenth century; Finnur Jonsson puts it as early as 900, and claims it, as usual, for Norway. Doubtless it was current in Norway, in one form or another, before the first Icelandic settlements, but his argument that the thistle (stanza 31) is not an Icelandic plant has little weight, for such curse-formulas must have traveled freely from place to place. In view of the evidence pointing to a western origin for many or all of the Eddic poems, Jonsson's reiterated "Digtet er sikkert norsk og ikke islandsk" is somewhat exasperating. Wherever the *Skirnismol* was composed, it has been preserved in exceptionally good condition, and seems to be practically devoid of interpolations or lacunæ.

Freyr, the son of Njorth, had sat one day in Hlithskjolf, and looked over all the worlds. He looked into Jotunheim, and saw there a fair maiden, as she went from her father's house to her bower. Forthwith he felt a mighty love-sickness. Skirnir was the name of Freyr's servant; Njorth bade him ask speech of Freyr. He said:

1. "Go now, Skirnir! and seek to gain
Speech from my son;
And answer to win, for whom the wise one
Is mightily moved."

Skirnir spake:

2. "Ill words do I now await from thy son,
If I seek to get speech with him,
And answer to win, for whom the wise one
Is mightily moved."

Prose. Freyr: concerning his father, Njorth, and the race of the Wanes in general, cf. *Voluspo,* 21 and note. Snorri thus describes Njorth's family: "Njorth begat two children in Noatun; the son was named Freyr, and the daughter Freyja; they were fair of aspect and mighty. Freyr is the noblest of the gods; he rules over rain and sunshine, and therewith the fruitfulness of the earth; it is well to call upon him for plenty and welfare, for he rules over wealth for mankind. Freyja is the noblest of the goddesses. When she rides to the fight, she has one-half of the slain, and Othin has half. When she goes on a journey, she drives her two cats, and sits in a cart. Love-songs please her well, and it is good to call on her in love-matters." *Hlithskjolf:* Othin's watch-tower; cf. *Grimnismol,* introductory prose. *He said:* both manuscripts have "Then Skathi said:" (Skathi was Njorth's wife), but Bugge's emendation, based on Snorri's version, is doubtless correct.

1. *My son:* both manuscripts, and many editors, have "our son," which, of course, goes with the introduction of Skathi in the prose. As the stanza is clearly addressed to Skirnir, the change of pronouns seems justified. The same confusion occurs in stanza 2, where Skirnir in the manuscripts is made to speak of Freyr as

Skirnir spake:

3. "Speak prithee, Freyr, foremost of the gods,
For now I fain would know;
Why sittest thou here in the wide halls,
Days long, my prince, alone?"

Freyr spake:

4. "How shall I tell thee, thou hero young,
Of all my grief so great?
Though every day the elfbeam dawns,
It lights my longing never."

Skirnir spake:

5. "Thy longings, methinks, are not so large
That thou mayst not tell them to me;
Since in days of yore we were young together,
We two might each other trust."

Freyr spake:

6. "From Gymir's house I beheld go forth
A maiden dear to me;
Her arms glittered, and from their gleam
Shone all the sea and sky.

"your son" (plural). The plural pronoun in the original involves a metrical error, which is corrected by the emendation.

4. *Elfbeam:* the sun, so called because its rays were fatal to elves and dwarfs; cf. *Alvissmol,* 35.

6. *Gymir:* a mountain-giant, husband of Aurbotha, and father of Gerth, fairest among women. This is all Snorri tells of him in his paraphrase of the story.

7. Snorri's paraphrase of the poem is sufficiently close so that his addition of another sentence to Freyr's speech makes it prob-

7. "To me more dear than in days of old
Was ever maiden to man;
But no one of gods or elves will grant
That we both together should be."

Skirnir spake:

8. "Then give me the horse that goes through the dark
And magic flickering flames;
And the sword as well that fights of itself
Against the giants grim."

Freyr spake:

9. "The horse will I give thee that goes through the dark
And magic flickering flames,
And the sword as well that will fight of itself
If a worthy hero wields it."

---

able that a stanza has dropped out between 7 and 8. This has been tentatively reconstructed, thus: "Hither to me shalt thou bring the maid, / And home shalt thou lead her here, / If her father wills it or wills it not, / And good reward shalt thou get." Finn Magnusen detected the probable omission of a stanza here as early as 1821.

8. *The sword:* Freyr's gift of his sword to Skirnir eventually proves fatal, for at the last battle, when Freyr is attacked by Beli, whom he kills bare-handed, and later when the fire-demon, Surt, slays him in turn, he is weaponless; cf. *Voluspo,* 53 and note. *Against the giants grim:* the condition of this line makes it seem like an error in copying, and it is possible that it should be identical with the fourth line of the next stanza.

Skirnir spake to the horse:

10. "Dark is it without, and I deem it time
To fare through the wild fells,
(To fare through the giants' fastness;)
We shall both come back, or us both together
The terrible giant will take."

Skirnir rode into Jotunheim to Gymir's house. There were fierce dogs bound before the gate of the fence which was around Gerth's hall. He rode to where a herdsman sat on a hill, and said:

11. "Tell me, herdsman, sitting on the hill,
And watching all the ways,
How may I win a word with the maid
Past the hounds of Gymir here?"

The herdsman spake:

12. "Art thou doomed to die or already dead,
Thou horseman that ridest hither?
Barred from speech shalt thou ever be
With Gymir's daughter good."

Skirnir spake:

13. "Boldness is better than plaints can be
For him whose feet must fare;

---

10. Some editors reject line 3 as spurious.

12. Line 2 is in neither manuscript, and no gap is indicated. I have followed Grundtvig's conjectural emendation.

13. This stanza is almost exactly like many in the first part of

To a destined day has mine age been doomed,
And my life's span thereto laid."

Gerth spake:

14. "What noise is that which now so loud
I hear within our house?
The ground shakes, and the home of Gymir
Around me trembles too."

The Serving-Maid spake:

15. "One stands without who has leapt from his steed,
And lets his horse loose to graze;"
. . . .
. . . .

Gerth spake:

16. "Bid the man come in, and drink good mead
Here within our hall;
Though this I fear, that there without
My brother's slayer stands.

---

the *Hovamol,* and may well have been a separate proverb. After this stanza the scene shifts to the interior of the house.

15. No gap indicated in either manuscript. Bugge and Niedner have attempted emendations, while Hildebrand suggests that the last two lines of stanza 14 are spurious, 14, 1-2, and 15 thus forming a single stanza, which seems doubtful.

16. *Brother's slayer:* perhaps the brother is Beli, slain by Freyr; the only other references are in *Voluspo,* 53, and in Snorri's paraphrase of the *Skirnismol,* which merely says that Freyr's gift of his sword to Skirnir "was the reason why he was weaponless when he met Beli, and he killed him bare-handed." Skirnir himself seems never to have killed anybody.

17. "Art thou of the elves or the offspring of gods,
Or of the wise Wanes?
How camst thou alone through the leaping flame
Thus to behold our home?"

Skirnir spake:

18. "I am not of the elves, nor the offspring of gods,
Nor of the wise Wanes;
Though I came alone through the leaping flame
Thus to behold thy home.

19. "Eleven apples, all of gold,
Here will I give thee, Gerth,
To buy thy troth that Freyr shall be
Deemed to be dearest to you."

Gerth spake:

20. "I will not take at any man's wish
These eleven apples ever;
Nor shall Freyr and I one dwelling find
So long as we two live."

Skirnir spake:

21. "Then do I bring thee the ring that was burned

---

17. *Wise Wanes:* cf. *Voluspo,* 21 and note.

18. The *Arnamagnæan Codex* omits this stanza.

19. *Apples:* the apple was the symbol of fruitfulness, and also of eternal youth. According to Snorri, the goddess Ithun had charge of the apples which the gods ate whenever they felt themselves growing old.

Of old with Othin's son;
From it do eight of like weight fall
On every ninth night."

Gerth spake:

22. "The ring I wish not, though burned it was
Of old with Othin's son;
In Gymir's home is no lack of gold
In the wealth my father wields."

Skirnir spake:

23. "Seest thou, maiden, this keen, bright sword
That I hold here in my hand?
Thy head from thy neck shall I straightway hew,
If thou wilt not do my will."

Gerth spake:

24. "For no man's sake will I ever suffer
To be thus moved by might;
But gladly, methinks, will Gymir seek
To fight if he finds thee here."

Skirnir spake:

25. "Seest thou, maiden, this keen, bright sword
That I hold here in my hand?

---

21. *Ring:* the ring Draupnir ("Dropper") was made by the dwarfs for Othin, who laid it on Baldr's pyre when the latter's corpse was burned (cf. *Voluspo,* 32 and note, and *Baldrs Draumar*). Baldr, however, sent the ring back to Othin from hell. How Freyr obtained it is nowhere stated. Andvari's ring (Andvaranaut) had a similar power of creating gold; cf. *Reginsmol,* prose

Before its blade the old giant bends,—
Thy father is doomed to die.

26. "I strike thee, maid, with my magic staff,
To tame thee to work my will;
There shalt thou go where never again
The sons of men shall see thee.

27. "On the eagle's hill shalt thou ever sit,
And gaze on the gates of Hel;
More loathsome to thee than the light-hued snake
To men, shall thy meat become.

28. "Fearful to see, if thou comest forth,
Hrimnir will stand and stare,
(Men will marvel at thee;)

---

after stanza 4 and note. Lines 3 and 4 of this stanza, and the first two of stanza 22, are missing in the *Arnamagnæan Codex*.

25. The first two lines are abbreviated in both manuscripts.

26. With this stanza, bribes and threats having failed, Skirnir begins a curse which, by the power of his magic staff, is to fall on Gerth if she refuses Freyr.

27. *Eagle's hill:* the hill at the end of heaven, and consequently overlooking hell, where the giant Hræsvelg sits "in an eagle's guise," and makes the winds with his wings; cf. *Vafthruthnismol,* 37, also *Voluspo,* 50. The second line is faulty in both manuscripts; Hildebrand's emendation corrects the error, but omits an effective touch; the manuscript line may be rendered "And look and hanker for hell." The *Arnamagnæan Codex* breaks off with the fourth line of this stanza.

28. *Hrimnir:* a frost-giant, mentioned elsewhere only in *Hyndluljoth,* 33. Line 3 is probably spurious. *Watchman of the gods:* Heimdall; cf. *Voluspo,* 46.

More famed shalt thou grow than the watchman
of the gods!
Peer forth, then, from thy prison.

29. "Rage and longing, fetters and wrath,
Tears and torment are thine;
Where thou sittest down my doom is on thee
Of heavy heart
And double dole.

30. "In the giants' home shall vile things harm thee
Each day with evil deeds;
Grief shalt thou get instead of gladness,
And sorrow to suffer with tears.

31. "With three-headed giants thou shalt dwell ever,
Or never know a husband;
(Let longing grip thee, let wasting waste thee,—)

---

29. Three nouns of doubtful meaning, which I have rendered *rage, longing,* and *heart* respectively, make the precise force of this stanza obscure. Niedner and Sijmons mark the entire stanza as interpolated, and Jonsson rejects line 5.

30. In *Regius* and in nearly all the editions the first two lines of this stanza are followed by lines 3-5 of stanza 35. I have followed Niedner, Sijmons, and Gering. The two words here translated *vile things* are obscure; Gering renders the phrase simply "Kobolde."

31. The confusion noted as to the preceding stanza, and a metrical error in the third line, have led to various rearrangements and emendations; line 3 certainly looks like an interpolation. *Three-headed giants:* concerning giants with numerous heads, cf. *Vafthruthnismol,* 33, and *Hymiskvitha,* 8.

Be like to the thistle that in the loft
Was cast and there was crushed.

32. "I go to the wood, and to the wet forest,
To win a magic wand;
. . . .
I won a magic wand.

33. "Othin grows angry, angered is the best of the gods,
Freyr shall be thy foe,
Most evil maid, who the magic wrath
Of gods hast got for thyself.

34. "Give heed, frost-rulers, hear it, giants,
Sons of Suttung,
And gods, ye too,
How I forbid and how I ban
The meeting of men with the maid,
(The joy of men with the maid.)

---

32. No gap indicated in the manuscript; Niedner makes the line here given as 4 the first half of line 3, and fills out the stanza thus: "with which I will tame you, / Maid, to work my will." The whole stanza seems to be either interpolated or out of place; it would fit better after stanza 25.

33. Jonsson marks this stanza as interpolated. The word translated *most evil* is another case of guesswork.

34. Most editors reject line 3 as spurious, and some also reject line 6. Lines 2 and 3 may have been expanded out of a single line running approximately "Ye gods and Suttung's sons." *Suttung:* concerning this giant cf. *Hovamol*, 104 and note.

35. "Hrimgrimnir is he, the giant who shall have thee
In the depth by the doors of Hel;
To the frost-giants' halls each day shalt thou fare,
Crawling and craving in vain,
(Crawling and having no hope.)

36. "Base wretches there by the root of the tree
Will hold for thee horns of filth;
A fairer drink shalt thou never find,
Maid, to meet thy wish,
(Maid, to meet my wish.)

37. "I write thee a charm and three runes therewith,
Longing and madness and lust;
But what I have writ I may yet unwrite
If I find a need therefor."

---

35. Most editors combine lines 1-2 with stanza 36 (either with the first two lines thereof or the whole stanza), as lines 3-5 stand in the manuscript after line 2 of stanza 30. *Hrimgrimnir* ("The Frost-Shrouded"): a giant not elsewhere mentioned. Line 5, as a repetition of line 4, is probably a later addition.

36. For the combination of this stanza with the preceding one, cf. note on stanza 35. The scribe clearly did not consider that the stanza began with line 1, as the first word thereof in the manuscript does not begin with a capital letter and has no period before it. The first word of line 3, however, is so marked. Line 5 may well be spurious.

37. Again the scribe seems to have been uncertain as to the stanza divisions. This time the first line is preceded by a period, but begins with a small letter. Many editors have made line 2

Gerth spake:

38. "Find welcome rather, and with it take
The frost-cup filled with mead;
Though I did not believe that I should so love
Ever one of the Wanes."

Skirnir spake:

39. "My tidings all must I truly learn
Ere homeward hence I ride:
How soon thou wilt with the mighty son
Of Njorth a meeting make."

Gerth spake:

40. "Barri there is, which we both know well,
A forest fair and still;
And nine nights hence to the son of Njorth
Will Gerth there grant delight."

Then Skirnir rode home. Freyr stood without, and spoke to him, and asked for tidings:

41. "Tell me, Skirnir, ere thou take off the saddle,
Or farest forward a step:
What hast thou done in the giants' dwelling
To make glad thee or me?"

---

into two half-lines. *A charm:* literally, the rune Thurs (þ); the runic letters all had magic attributes; cf. *Sigrdrifumol,* 6-7 and notes.

40. *Barri:* "The Leafy."

Skirnir spake:

42. "Barri there is, which we both know well,
A forest fair and still;
And nine nights hence to the son of Njorth
Will Gerth there grant delight."

Freyr spake:

43. "Long is one night, longer are two;
How then shall I bear three?
Often to me has a month seemed less
Than now half a night of desire."

---

42. Abbreviated to initial letters in the manuscript.

43. The superscription is lacking in *Regius.* Snorri quotes this one stanza in his prose paraphrase, *Gylfaginning,* chapter 37. The two versions are substantially the same, except that Snorri makes the first line read, "Long is one night, long is the second."

HARBARTHSLJOTH

The Poem of Harbarth

Introductory Note

The *Harbarthsljoth* is found complete in the *Codex Regius,* where it follows the *Skirnismol,* and from the fourth line of stan a 19 to the end of the poem in the *Arnamagnæan Codex,* of which it occupies the first page and a half.

The poem differs sharply from those which precede it in the *Codex Regius,* both in metrical form and in spirit. It is, indeed, the most nearly formless of all the Eddic poems. The normal metre is the Malahattr (cf. Introduction, where an example is given). The name of this verse-form means "in the manner of conversation," and the *Harbarthsljoth's* verse fully justifies the term. The Atli poems exemplify the conventional use of Malahattr, but in the *Harbarthsljoth* the form is used with extraordinary freedom, and other metrical forms are frequently employed. A few of the speeches of which the poem is composed cannot be twisted into any known Old Norse metre, and appear to be simply prose.

How far this confusion is due to interpolations and faulty transmission of the original poem is uncertain. Finnur Jonsson has attempted a wholesale purification of the poem, but his arbitrary condemnation of words, lines, and entire stanzas as spurious is quite unjustified by any positive evidence. I have accepted Mogk's theory that the author was "a first-rate psychologist, but a poor poet," and have translated the poem as it stands in the manuscripts. I have preserved the metrical confusion of the original by keeping throughout so far as possible to the metres found in the poem; if the rhythm of the translation is often hard to catch, the difficulty is no less with the original Norse.

The poem is simply a contest of abuse, such as the early Norwegian and Icelander delighted in, the opposing figures being Thor and Othin, the latter appearing in the disguise of the ferryman Harbarth. Such billingsgate lent itself readily to changes, interpolations and omissions, and it is little wonder that the poem is chaotic. It consists mainly of boasting and of references, often luckily obscure, to disreputable events in the life of one or the other of the disputants. Some editors have sought to read a complex symbolism into it, particularly by representing it as a contest between the noble or warrior class (Othin) and the peasant (Thor). But it seems a pity to take such a vigorous piece of broad farce too seriously.

Verse-form, substance, and certain linguistic peculiarities, notably the suffixed articles, point to a relatively late date (eleventh century) for the poem in its present form. Probably it had its origin in the early days, but its colloquial nature and its vulgarity made it readily susceptible to changes.

Owing to the chaotic state of the text, and the fact that none of the editors or commentators have succeeded in improving it much, I have not in this case attempted to give all the important emendations and suggestions. The stanza-divisions are largely arbitrary.

Thor was on his way back from a journey in the East, and came to a sound; on the other side of the sound was a ferryman with a boat. Thor called out:

1. "Who is the fellow yonder, on the farther shore
of the sound?"

Prose. Harbarth ("Gray-Beard"): Othin. On the nature of the prose notes found in the manuscripts, cf. *Grimnismol,* introduction. *Thor:* the journeys of the thunder-god were almost as numerous as those of Othin; cf. *Thrymskvitha* and *Hymiskvitha.* Like the Robin Hood of the British ballads, Thor was often temporarily worsted, but always managed to come out ahead in the end. His "Journey in the East" is presumably the famous episode, related in full by Snorri, in the course of which he encountered the giant Skrymir, and in the house of Utgartha-Loki lifted the cat which turned out to be Mithgarthsorm. The *Hymiskvitha* relates a further incident of this journey.

Harbarthsljoth

The ferryman spake:

2. "What kind of a peasant is yon, that calls o'er the bay?"

Thor spake:

3. "Ferry me over the sound; I will feed thee therefor in the morning;
A basket I have on my back, and food therein, none better;
At leisure I ate, ere the house I left,
Of herrings and porridge, so plenty I had."

The ferryman spake:

4. "Of thy morning feats art thou proud, but the future thou knowest not wholly;
Doleful thine home-coming is: thy mother, methinks, is dead."

Thor spake:

5. "Now hast thou said what to each must seem
The mightiest grief, that my mother is dead."

---

2. The superscriptions to the speeches are badly confused in the manuscripts, but editors have agreed fairly well as to where they belong.

3. From the fact that in *Regius* line 3 begins with a capital letter, it is possible that lines 3-4 constitute the ferryman's reply, with something lost before stanza 4.

4. *Thy mother:* Jorth (Earth).

5. Some editors assume a lacuna after this stanza.

6. *Three good dwellings:* this has been generally assumed to mean three separate establishments, but it may refer simply to

The ferryman spake:

6. "Three good dwellings, methinks, thou hast not;
Barefoot thou standest, and wearest a beggar's dress;
Not even hose dost thou have."

Thor spake:

7. "Steer thou hither the boat; the landing here shall I show thee;
But whose the craft that thou keepest on the shore?"

The ferryman spake:

8. "Hildolf is he who bade me have it,
A hero wise; his home is at Rathsey's sound.
He bade me no robbers to steer, nor stealers of steeds,
But worthy men, and those whom well do I know.
Say now thy name, if over the sound thou wilt fare."

Thor spake:

9. "My name indeed shall I tell, though in danger I am,

---

the three parts of a single farm, the dwelling proper, the cattle-barn and the storehouse; i.e., Thor is not even a respectable peasant.

8. *Hildolf* ("slaughtering wolf"): not elsewhere mentioned in the *Edda. Rathsey* ("Isle of Counsel"): likewise not mentioned elsewhere.

9. *In danger:* Thor is "sekr," i.e., without the protection of any law, so long as he is in the territory of his enemies, the

And all my race; I am Othin's son,
Meili's brother, and Magni's father,
The strong one of the gods; with Thor now speech canst thou get.
And now would I know what name thou hast."

The ferryman spake:

10. "Harbarth am I, and seldom I hide my name."

Thor spake:

11. "Why shouldst thou hide thy name, if quarrel thou hast not?"

Harbarth spake:

12. "And though I had a quarrel, from such as thou art
Yet none the less my life would I guard,
Unless I be doomed to die."

---

giants. *Meili:* a practically unknown son of Othin, mentioned here only in the *Edda. Magni:* son of Thor and the giantess Jarnsaxa; after Thor's fight with Hrungnir (cf. stanza 14, note) Magni, though but three days old, was the only one of the gods strong enough to lift the dead giant's foot from Thor's neck. After rescuing his father, Magni said to him: "There would have been little trouble, father, had I but come sooner; I think I should have sent this giant to hell with my fist if I had met him first." Magni and his brother, Mothi, inherit Thor's hammer.

12. This stanza is hopelessly confused as to form, but none of the editorial rearrangements have materially altered the meaning. *Doomed to die:* the word "feigr" occurs constantly in the Old Norse poems and sagas; the idea of an inevitable but unknown fate seems to have been practically universal throughout the pre-Christian period. On the concealment of names from enemies, cf. *Fafnismol,* prose after stanza 1.

Thor spake:

13. "Great trouble, methinks, would it be to come to thee,
To wade the waters across, and wet my middle;
Weakling, well shall I pay thy mocking words,
If across the sound I come."

Harbarth spake:

14. "Here shall I stand and await thee here;
Thou hast found since Hrungnir died no fiercer man."

Thor spake:

15. "Fain art thou to tell how with Hrungnir I fought,
The haughty giant, whose head of stone was made;
And yet I felled him, and stretched him before me.
What, Harbarth, didst thou the while?"

---

13. This stanza, like the preceding one, is peculiarly chaotic in the manuscript, and has been variously emended.

14. *Hrungnir:* this giant rashly wagered his head that his horse, Gullfaxi, was swifter than Othin's Sleipnir. In the race, which Hrungnir lost, he managed to dash uninvited into the home of the gods, where he became very drunk. Thor ejected him, and accepted his challenge to a duel. Hrungnir, terrified, had a helper made for him in the form of a dummy giant nine miles high and three miles broad. Hrungnir himself had a three-horned heart of stone and a head of stone; his shield was of stone and his weapon was a grindstone. But Thjalfi, Thor's servant, told him the god would attack him out of the ground, wherefore Hrungnir laid down his shield and stood on it. The hammer Mjollnir shattered both the grindstone and Hrungnir's

Harbarth spake:

16. "Five full winters with Fjolvar was I,
And dwelt in the isle that is Algrön called;
There could we fight, and fell the slain,
Much could we seek, and maids could master."

Thor spake:

17. "How won ye success with your women?"

Harbarth spake:

18. "Lively women we had, if they wise for us were;
Wise were the women we had, if they kind for us were;
For ropes of sand they would seek to wind,
And the bottom to dig from the deepest dale.
Wiser than all in counsel I was,
And there I slept by the sisters seven,
And joy full great did I get from each.
What, Thor, didst thou the while?"

---

head, but part of the grindstone knocked Thor down, and the giant fell with his foot on Thor's neck (cf. note on stanza 9). Meanwhile Thjalfi dispatched the dummy giant without trouble.

16. *Fjolvar:* not elsewhere mentioned in the poems; perhaps the father of the "seven sisters" referred to in stanza 18. *Algrön* "The All-Green": not mentioned elsewhere in the *Edda.*

17. Thor is always eager for stories of this sort; cf. stanzas 31 and 33.

18. Lines 1-2 are obscure, but apparently Harbarth means that the women were wise to give in to him cheerfully, resistance to his power being as impossible as (lines 3-4) making ropes of sand or digging the bottoms out of the valleys. Nothing further is known of these unlucky "seven sisters."

Thor spake:

19. "Thjazi I felled, the giant fierce,
And I hurled the eyes of Alvaldi's son
To the heavens hot above;
Of my deeds the mightiest marks are these,
That all men since can see.
What, Harbarth, didst thou the while?"

Harbarth spake:

20. "Much love-craft I wrought with them who ride by night,
When I stole them by stealth from their husbands;
A giant hard was Hlebarth, methinks:
His wand he gave me as gift,
And I stole his wits away."

---

19. *Thjazi:* this giant, by a trick, secured possession of the goddess Ithun and her apples (cf. *Skirnismol,* 19, note), and carried her off into Jotunheim. Loki, through whose fault she had been betrayed, was sent after her by the gods. He went in Freyja's "hawk's-dress" (cf. *Thrymskvitha,* 3), turned Ithun into a nut, and flew back with her. Thjazi, in the shape of an eagle, gave chase. But the gods kindled a fire which burnt the eagle's wings, and then they killed him. Snorri's prose version does not attribute this feat particularly to Thor. Thjazi's daughter was Skathi, whom the gods permitted to marry Njorth as a recompense for her father's death. *Alvaldi:* of him we know only that he was the father of Thjazi, Ithi and Gang, who divided his wealth, each taking a mouthful of gold. The name is variously spelled. It is not known which stars were called "Thjazi's Eyes." In the middle of line 4 begins the fragmentary version of the poem found in the *Arnamagnæan Codex.*

20. *Riders by night:* witches, who were supposed to ride on wolves in the dark. Nothing further is known of this adventure.

Thor spake:

21. "Thou didst repay good gifts with evil mind."

Harbarth spake:

22. "The oak must have what it shaves from another;
In such things each for himself.
What, Thor, didst thou the while?"

Thor spake:

23. "Eastward I fared, of the giants I felled
Their ill-working women who went to the mountain;
And large were the giants' throng if all were alive;
No men would there be in Mithgarth more.
What, Harbarth, didst thou the while?"

Harbarth spake:

24. "In Valland I was, and wars I raised,
Princes I angered, and peace brought never;
The noble who fall in the fight hath Othin,
And Thor hath the race of the thralls."

---

22. *The oak, etc.:* this proverb is found elsewhere (e.g., *Grettissaga*) in approximately the same words. Its force is much like our "to the victor belong the spoils."

23. Thor killed no women of the giants' race on the "journey to the East" so fully described by Snorri, his great giant-killing adventure being the one narrated in the *Thrymskvitha.*

24. *Valland:* this mythical place ("Land of Slaughter") is elsewhere mentioned, but not further characterised; cf. prose introduction to *Völundarkvitha,* and *Helreith Brynhildar,* 2. On the bringing of slain heroes to Othin, cf. *Voluspo,* 31 and note,

Thor spake:

25. "Unequal gifts of men wouldst thou give to the gods,
If might too much thou shouldst have."

Harbarth spake:

26. "Thor has might enough, but never a heart;
For cowardly fear in a glove wast thou fain to crawl,
And there forgot thou wast Thor;
Afraid there thou wast, thy fear was such,
To fart or sneeze lest Fjalar should hear."

Thor spake:

27. "Thou womanish Harbarth, to hell would I smite thee straight,
Could mine arm reach over the sound."

---

and, for a somewhat different version, *Grimnismol,* 14. Nowhere else is it indicated that Thor has an asylum for dead peasants.

26. The reference here is to one of the most familiar episodes in Thor's eastward journey. He and his companions came to a house in the forest, and went in to spend the night. Being disturbed by an earthquake and a terrific noise, they all crawled into a smaller room opening from the main one. In the morning, however, they discovered that the earthquake had been occasioned by the giant Skrymir's lying down near them, and the noise by his snoring. The house in which they had taken refuge was his glove, the smaller room being the thumb. Skrymir was in fact Utgartha-Loki himself. That he is in this stanza called Fjalar (the name occurs also in *Hovamol,* 14) is probably due to a confusion of the names by which Utgartha-Loki went. Loki taunts Thor with this adventure in *Lokasenna,* 60 and 62, line 3 of this stanza being perhaps interpolated from *Lokasenna,* 60, 4.

Harbarth spake:

28. "Wherefore reach over the sound, since strife we have none?
What, Thor, didst thou do then?"

Thor spake:

29. "Eastward I was, and the river I guarded well,
Where the sons of Svarang sought me there;
Stones did they hurl; small joy did they have of winning;
Before me there to ask for peace did they fare.
What, Harbarth, didst thou the while?"

Harbarth spake:

30. "Eastward I was, and spake with a certain one,
I played with the linen-white maid, and met her by stealth;
I gladdened the gold-decked one, and she granted me joy."

Thor spake:

31. "Full fair was thy woman-finding."

---

29. *The river:* probably Ifing, which flows between the land of the gods and that of the giants; cf. *Vafthruthnismol,* 16. *Sons of Svarang:* presumably the giants; Svarang is not elsewhere mentioned in the poems, nor is there any other account of Thor's defense of the passage.

30. Othin's adventures of this sort were too numerous to make it possible to identify this particular person. *By stealth:* so the *Arnamagnæan Codex; Regius,* followed by several editors, has "long meeting with her."

Harbarth spake:

32. "Thy help did I need then, Thor, to hold the
white maid fast."

Thor spake:

33. "Gladly, had I been there, my help to thee had
been given."

Harbarth spake:

34. "I might have trusted thee then, didst thou not
betray thy troth."

Thor spake:

35. "No heel-biter am I, in truth, like an old leather
shoe in spring."

Harbarth spake:

36. "What, Thor, didst thou the while?"

Thor spake:

37. "In Hlesey the brides of the Berserkers slew I;
Most evil they were, and all they betrayed."

---

35. *Heel-biter:* this effective parallel to our "back-biter" is not found elsewhere in Old Norse.

37. *Hlesey:* "the Island of the Sea-God" (Hler = Ægir), identified with the Danish island Läsö, in the Kattegat. It appears again, much out of place, in *Oddrunargratr,* 28. *Berserkers:* originally men who could turn themselves into bears, hence the name, "bear-shirts"; cf. the werewolf or loupgarou. Later the name was applied to men who at times became seized with a madness for bloodshed; cf. *Hyndluljoth,* 23 and note. The women here mentioned are obviously of the earlier type.

Harbarth spake:

38. "Shame didst thou win, that women thou slewest,
Thor."

Thor spake:

39. "She-wolves they were like, and women but little;
My ship, which well I had trimmed, did they shake;
With clubs of iron they threatened, and Thjalfi they drove off.
What, Harbarth, didst thou the while?"

Harbarth spake:

40. "In the host I was that hither fared,
The banners to raise, and the spear to redden."

Thor spake:

41. "Wilt thou now say that hatred thou soughtest to bring us?"

Harbarth spake:

42. "A ring for thy hand shall make all right for thee,
As the judge decides who sets us two at peace."

---

39. *Thjalfi:* Thor's servant; cf. note on stanza 14.

40. To what expedition this refers is unknown, but apparently Othin speaks of himself as allied to the foes of the gods.

41. *Hatred:* so *Regius;* the other manuscript has, apparently, "sickness."

42. Just what Othin means, or why his words should so have enraged Thor, is not evident, though he may imply that Thor is open to bribery. Perhaps a passage has dropped out before stanza 43.

Thor spake:

43. "Where foundest thou so foul and scornful a speech?
More foul a speech I never before have heard."

Harbarth spake:

44. "I learned it from men, the men so old,
Who dwell in the hills of home."

Thor spake:

45. "A name full good to heaps of stones thou givest
When thou callest them hills of home."

Harbarth spake:

46. "Of such things speak I so."

Thor spake:

47. "Ill for thee comes thy keenness of tongue,
If the water I choose to wade;
Louder, I ween, than a wolf thou cryest,
If a blow of my hammer thou hast."

Harbarth spake:

48. "Sif has a lover at home, and him shouldst thou meet;
More fitting it were on him to put forth thy strength."

---

44. Othin refers to the dead, from whom he seeks information through his magic power.

48. *Sif:* Thor's wife, the lover being presumably Loki; cf. *Lokasenna*, 54.

Thor spake:

49. "Thy tongue still makes thee say what seems most ill to me,
Thou witless man! Thou liest, I ween."

Harbarth spake:

50. "Truth do I speak, but slow on thy way thou art;
Far hadst thou gone if now in the boat thou hadst fared."

Thor spake:

51. "Thou womanish Harbarth! here hast thou held me too long."

Harbarth spake:

52. "I thought not ever that Asathor would be hindered
By a ferryman thus from faring."

Thor spake:

53. "One counsel I bring thee now: row hither thy boat;
No more of scoffing; set Magni's father across."

Harbarth spake:

54. "From the sound go hence; the passage thou hast not."

---

52. *Asathor:* Thor goes by various names in the poems: e.g., Vingthor, Vingnir, Hlorrithi. Asathor means "Thor of the Gods."

53. *Magni:* Thor's son; cf. stanza 9 and note.

Thor spake:

55. "The way now show me, since thou takest me not
o'er the water."

Harbarth spake:

56. "To refuse it is little, to fare it is long;
A while to the stock, and a while to the stone;
Then the road to thy left, till Verland thou reachest;
And there shall Fjorgyn her son Thor find,
And the road of her children she shows him to
Othin's realm."

Thor spake:

57. "May I come so far in a day?"

Harbarth spake:

58. "With toil and trouble perchance,
While the sun still shines, or so I think."

Thor spake:

59. "Short now shall be our speech, for thou speakest
in mockery only;

---

56. *Line 2:* the phrases mean simply "a long way"; cf. "over stock and stone." *Verland:* the "Land of Men" to which Thor must come from the land of the giants. The *Arnamagnæan Codex* has "Valland" (cf. stanza 24 and note), but this is obviously an error. *Fjorgyn:* a feminine form of the same name, which belongs to Othin (cf. *Voluspo,* 56 and note); here it evidently means Jorth (Earth), Thor's mother. *The road:* the rainbow bridge, Bifrost; cf. *Grimnismol,* 29 and note.

58. *Line 2:* so *Regius;* the other manuscript has "ere sunrise."

The passage thou gavest me not   I shall pay thee
    if ever we meet."

Harbarth spake:

60. "Get hence where every evil thing shall have thee!"

---

60. The *Arnamagnæan Codex* clearly indicates Harbarth as the speaker of this line, but *Regius* has no superscription, and begins the line with a small letter not preceded by a period, thereby assigning it to Thor.

HYMISKVITHA

The Lay of Hymir

Introductory Note

The *Hymiskvitha* is found complete in both manuscripts; in *Regius* it follows the *Harbarthsljoth,* while in the *Arnamagnæan Codex* it comes after the *Grimnismol.* Snorri does not quote it, although he tells the main story involved.

The poem is a distinctly inferior piece of work, obviously based on various narrative fragments, awkwardly pieced together. Some critics, Jessen and Edzardi for instance, have maintained that the compiler had before him three distinct poems, which he simply put together; others, like Finnur Jonsson and Mogk, think that the author made a new poem of his own on the basis of earlier poems, now lost. It seems probable that he took a lot of odds and ends of material concerning Thor, whether in prose or in verse, and worked them together in a perfunctory way, without much caring how well they fitted. His chief aim was probably to impress the credulous imaginations of hearers greedy for wonders.

The poem is almost certainly one of the latest of those dealing with the gods, though Finnur Jonsson, in order to support his theory of a Norwegian origin, has to date it relatively early. If, as seems probable, it was produced in Iceland, the chances are that it was composed in the first half of the eleventh century. Jessen, rather recklessly, goes so far as to put it two hundred years later. In any case, it belongs to a period of literary decadence,—the great days of Eddic poetry would never have permitted the nine hundred headed person found in Hymir's home—and to one in which the usual forms of diction in mythological poetry had yielded somewhat to the verbal subtleties of skaldic verse.

While the skaldic poetry properly falls outside the limits of this book, it is necessary here to say a word about it. There is preserved, in the sagas and elsewhere, a very considerable body of lyric poetry, the authorship of each poem being nearly always definitely stated, whether correctly or otherwise. This type of poetry is marked by an extraordinary complexity of diction, with a peculiarly difficult vocabulary of its own. It was to explain some of the "kennings" which composed this special vocabulary that Snorri wrote one of the sections of the *Prose Edda.* As an illustration, in a single stanza of one poem in the *Egilssaga,* a sword is called "the halo of the helm," "the wound-hoe," "the blood-snake" (possibly; no one is sure what the compound word means) and "the ice of the girdle," while men appear in the same stanza as "Othin's ash-trees," and battle is spoken of as "the iron game." One of the eight lines has defied translation completely.

Skaldic diction made relatively few inroads into the earlier Eddic poems, but in the *Hymiskvitha* these circumlocutions are fairly numerous. This sets the poem somewhat apart from the rest of the mythological collection. Only the vigor of the two main stories—Thor's expedition after Hymir's kettle and the fishing trip in which he caught Mithgarthsorm—saves it from complete mediocrity.

---

1. Of old the gods made feast together,
And drink they sought ere sated they were;
Twigs they shook, and blood they tried:
Rich fare in Ægir's hall they found.

---

1. *Twigs:* Vigfusson comments at some length on "the rite practised in the heathen age of inquiring into the future by dipping bunches of chips or twigs into the blood (of sacrifices) and shaking them." But the two operations may have been separate, the twigs being simply "divining-rods" marked with runes. In either case, the gods were seeking information by magic as to where they could find plenty to drink. *Ægir:* a giant who is also the god of the sea; little is known of him outside of what is told here and in the introductory prose to the *Lokasenna,* though Snorri has a brief account of him, giving his home as Hlesey (Läsö, cf. *Harbarthsljoth,* 37). *Grimnismol,* 45, has a reference to this same feast.

2. The mountain-dweller sat merry as boyhood,
But soon like a blinded man he seemed;
The son of Ygg gazed in his eyes:
"For the gods a feast shalt thou forthwith get."

3. The word-wielder toil for the giant worked,
And so revenge on the gods he sought;
He bade Sif's mate the kettle bring:
"Therein for ye all much ale shall I brew."

4. The far-famed ones could find it not,
And the holy gods could get it nowhere;
Till in truthful wise did Tyr speak forth,
And helpful counsel to Hlorrithi gave.

5. "There dwells to the east of Elivagar
Hymir the wise at the end of heaven;
A kettle my father fierce doth own,
A mighty vessel a mile in depth."

---

2. *Mountain-dweller:* the giant (Ægir). *Line 2:* the principal word in the original has defied interpretation, and any translation of the line must be largely guesswork. *Ygg:* Othin; his son is Thor. Some editors assume a gap after this stanza.

3. *Word-wielder:* Thor. *The giant:* Ægir. *Sif:* Thor's wife; cf. *Harbarthsljoth,* 48. *The kettle:* Ægir's kettle is possibly the sea itself.

4. *Tyr:* the god of battle; his two great achievements were thrusting his hand into the mouth of the wolf Fenrir so that the gods might bind him, whereby he lost his hand (cf. *Voluspo,* 39, note), and his fight with the hound Garm in the last battle, in which they kill each other. *Hlorrithi:* Thor.

5. *Elivagar* ("Stormy Waves"): possibly the Milky Way;

Thor spake:

6. "May we win, dost thou think, this whirler of water?"

Tyr spake:

"Aye, friend, we can, if cunning we are."

7. Forward that day with speed they fared,
From Asgarth came they to Egil's home;
The goats with horns bedecked he guarded;
Then they sped to the hall where Hymir dwelt.

8. The youth found his grandam, that greatly he loathed,

---

cf. *Vafthruthnismol,* 31, note. *Hymir:* this giant figures only in this episode. It is not clear why Tyr, who is elsewhere spoken of as a son of Othin, should here call Hymir his father. Finnur Jonsson, in an attempt to get round this difficulty, deliberately changed the word "father" to "grandfather," but this does not help greatly.

6. Neither manuscript has any superscriptions, but most editors have supplied them as above. From this point through stanza 11 the editors have varied considerably in grouping the lines into stanzas. The manuscripts indicate the third lines of stanzas 7, 8, 9, and 10 as beginning stanzas, but this makes more complications than the present arrangement. It is possible that, as Sijmons suggests, two lines have been lost after stanza 6.

7. *Egil:* possibly, though by no means certainly, the father of Thor's servant, Thjalfi, for, according to Snorri, Thor's first stop on this journey was at the house of a peasant whose children, Thjalfi and Roskva, he took into his service; cf. stanza 38, note. The *Arnamagnæan Codex* has "Ægir" instead of "Egil," but, aside from the fact that Thor had just left Ægir's house, the sea-god can hardly have been spoken of as a goat-herd.

8. *The youth:* Tyr, whose extraordinary grandmother is Hymir's mother. We know nothing further of her, or of *the other,*

And full nine hundred heads she had;
But the other fair with gold came forth,
And the bright-browed one brought beer to her son.

9. "Kinsman of giants, beneath the kettle
Will I set ye both, ye heroes bold;
For many a time my dear-loved mate
To guests is wrathful and grim of mind."

10. Late to his home the misshapen Hymir,
The giant harsh, from his hunting came;
The icicles rattled as in he came,
For the fellow's chin-forest frozen was.

11. "Hail to thee, Hymir! good thoughts mayst thou have;
Here has thy son to thine hall now come;
(For him have we waited, his way was long;)
And with him fares the foeman of Hroth,
The friend of mankind, and Veur they call him.

---

who is Hymir's wife and Tyr's mother. It may be guessed, however, that she belonged rather to the race of the gods than to that of the giants.

11. Two or three editors give this stanza a superscription ("The concubine spake," "The daughter spake"). Line 3 is commonly regarded as spurious. *The foeman of Hroth:* of course this means Thor, but nothing is known of any enemy of his by this name. Several editors have sought to make a single word meaning "the famous enemy" out of the phrase. Concerning Thor as the friend of man, particularly of the peasant class, cf. introduction to *Harbarthsljoth*. *Veur:* another name, of uncertain meaning, for Thor.

12. "See where under the gable they sit!
Behind the beam do they hide themselves."
The beam at the glance of the giant broke,
And the mighty pillar in pieces fell.

13. Eight fell from the ledge, and one alone,
The hard-hammered kettle, of all was whole;
Forth came they then, and his foes he sought,
The giant old, and held with his eyes.

14. Much sorrow his heart foretold when he saw
The giantess' foeman come forth on the floor;
Then of the steers did they bring in three;
Their flesh to boil did the giant bid.

15. By a head was each the shorter hewed,
And the beasts to the fire straight they bore;
The husband of Sif, ere to sleep he went,
Alone two oxen of Hymir's ate.

16. To the comrade hoary of Hrungnir then
Did Hlorrithi's meal full mighty seem;
"Next time at eve we three must eat
The food we have s the hunting's spoil."

---

13. *Eight:* the giant's glance, besides breaking the beam, knocks down all the kettles with such violence that all but the one under which Thor and Tyr are hiding are broken.

14. Hymir's wrath does not permit him to ignore the duties of a host to his guests, always strongly insisted on.

15. Thor's appetite figures elsewhere; cf. *Thrymskvitha,* 24.

16. *The comrade of Hrungnir:* Hymir, presumably simply because both are giants; cf. *Harbarthsljoth,* 14 and note.

17\. . . . .
Fain to row on the sea was Veur, he said,
If the giant bold would give him bait.

Hymir spake:

18\. "Go to the herd, if thou hast it in mind,
Thou slayer of giants, thy bait to seek;
For there thou soon mayst find, methinks,
Bait from the oxen easy to get."

19\. Swift to the wood the hero went,
Till before him an ox all black he found;
From the beast the slayer of giants broke
The fortress high of his double horns.

Hymir spake:

20\. "Thy works, methinks, are worse by far,

17\. The manuscripts indicate no lacuna, and many editors unite stanza 17 with lines 1 and 2 of 18. Sijmons and Gering assume a gap after these two lines, but it seems more probable that the missing passage, if any, belonged before them, supplying the connection with the previous stanza.

18\. The manuscripts have no superscription. Many editors combine lines 3 and 4 with lines 1 and 2 of stanza 19. In Snorri's extended paraphrase of the story, Hymir declines to go fishing with Thor on the ground that the latter is too small a person to be worth bothering about. "You would freeze," he says, "if you stayed out in mid-ocean as long as I generally do." *Bait* (line 4): the word literally means "chaff," hence any small bits; Hymir means that Thor should collect dung for bait.

19\. Many editors combine lines 3 and 4 with stanza 20. *Fortress,* etc.: the ox's head; cf. introductory note concerning the diction of this poem. Several editors assume a lacuna after stanza 19, but this seems unnecessary.

Thou steerer of ships, than when still thou sittest."

. . . .
. . . .

21. The lord of the goats bade the ape-begotten
Farther to steer the steed of the rollers;
But the giant said that his will, forsooth,
Longer to row was little enough.

22. Two whales on his hook did the mighty Hymir
Soon pull up on a single cast;
In the stern the kinsman of Othin sat,
And Veur with cunning his cast prepared.

23. The warder of men, the worm's destroyer,
Fixed on his hook the head of the ox;
There gaped at the bait the foe of the gods,
The girdler of all the earth beneath.

---

20. The manuscripts have no superscription. *Steerer of ships:* probably merely a reference to Thor's intention to go fishing. The lacuna after stanza 20 is assumed by most editors.

21. *Lord of the goats:* Thor, because of his goat-drawn chariot. *Ape-begotten:* Hymir; the word "api," rare until relatively late times in its literal sense, is fairly common with the meaning of "fool." Giants were generally assumed to be stupid. *Steed of the rollers:* a ship, because boats were pulled up on shore by means of rollers.

23. *Warder of men:* Thor; cf. stanza 11. *Worm's destroyer:* likewise Thor, who in the last battle slays, and is slain by, Mithgarthsorm; cf. *Voluspo, 56. The foe of the gods:* Mithgarthsorm, who lies in the sea, and surrounds the whole earth.

24. The venomous serpent swiftly up
To the boat did Thor, the bold one, pull;
With his hammer the loathly hill of the hair
Of the brother of Fenrir he smote from above.

25. The monsters roared, and the rocks resounded,
And all the earth so old was shaken;
. . . .
Then sank the fish in the sea forthwith.

26. . . . .
Joyless as back they rowed was the giant;
Speechless did Hymir sit at the oars,
With the rudder he sought a second wind.

Hymir spake:

27. "The half of our toil wilt thou have with me,

---

24. *Hill of the hair:* head,—a thoroughly characteristic skaldic phrase. *Brother of Fenrir:* Mithgarthsorm was, like the wolf Fenrir and the goddess Hel, born to Loki and the giantess Angrbotha (cf. *Voluspo,* 39 and note), and I have translated this line accordingly; but the word used in the text has been guessed as meaning almost anything from "comrade" to "enemy."

25. No gap is indicated in the manuscripts, but that a line or more has been lost is highly probable. In Snorri's version, Thor pulls so hard on the line that he drives both his feet through the flooring of the boat, and stands on bottom. When he pulls the serpent up, Hymir cuts the line with his bait-knife, which explains the serpent's escape. Thor, in a rage, knocks Hymir overboard with his hammer, and then wades ashore. The lines of stanzas 25 and 26 have been variously grouped.

26. No gap is indicated in the manuscripts, but line 2 begins with a small letter. *A second wind:* another direction, i. e., he put about for the shore.

And now make fast our goat of the flood;
Or home wilt thou bear the whales to the house,
Across the gorge of the wooded glen?"

28. Hlorrithi stood and the stem he gripped,
And the sea-horse with water awash he lifted;
Oars and bailer and all he bore
With the surf-swine home to the giant's house.

29. His might the giant again would match,
For stubborn he was, with the strength of Thor;
None truly strong, though stoutly he rowed,
Would he call save one who could break the cup.

30. Hlorrithi then, when the cup he held,
Struck with the glass the pillars of stone;
As he sat the posts in pieces he shattered,
Yet the glass to Hymir whole they brought.

31. But the loved one fair of the giant found
A counsel true, and told her thought:

---

27. No superscription in the manuscripts. In its place Bugge supplies a line—"These words spake Hymir, the giant wise." The manuscripts reverse the order of lines 2 and 3, and in both of them line 4 stands after stanza 28. *Goat of the flood:* boat.

28. *Sea-horse:* boat. *Surf-swine:* the whales.

29. Snorri says nothing of this episode of Hymir's cup. The glass which cannot be broken appears in the folklore of various races.

31. *The loved one:* Hymir's wife and Tyr's mother; cf. stanza 8 and note. The idea that a giant's skull is harder than stone or anything else is characteristic of the later Norse folk-stories, and

"Smite the skull of Hymir, heavy with food,
For harder it is than ever was glass."

32. The goats' mighty ruler then rose on his knee,
And with all the strength of a god he struck;
Whole was the fellow's helmet-stem,
But shattered the wine-cup rounded was.

Hymir spake:

33. "Fair is the treasure that from me is gone,
Since now the cup on my knees lies shattered;"
So spake the giant: "No more can I say
In days to be, 'Thou art brewed, mine ale.'

34. "Enough shall it be if out ye can bring
Forth from our house the kettle here."
Tyr then twice to move it tried,
But before him the kettle twice stood fast.

35. The father of Mothi the rim seized firm,
And before it stood on the floor below;
Up on his head Sif's husband raised it,
And about his heels the handles clattered.

---

in one of the so-called "mythical sagas" we find a giant actually named Hard-Skull.

32. *Helmet-stem:* head.

33. The manuscripts have no superscription. Line 4 in the manuscripts is somewhat obscure, and Bugge, followed by some editors, suggests a reading which may be rendered (beginning with the second half of line 3): "No more can I speak / Ever again as I spoke of old."

35. *The father of Mothi* and *Sif's husband:* Thor.

36. Not long had they fared, ere backwards looked
The son of Othin, once more to see;
From their caves in the east beheld he coming
With Hymir the throng of the many-headed.

37. He stood and cast from his back the kettle,
And Mjollnir, the lover of murder, he wielded;
. . . .
So all the whales of the waste he slew.

38. Not long had they fared ere one there lay
Of Hlorrithi's goats half-dead on the ground;
In his leg the pole-horse there was lame;
The deed the evil Loki had done.

---

36. *The many-headed:* The giants, although rarely designated as a race in this way, sometimes had two or more heads; cf. stanza 8, *Skirnismol,* 31 and *Vafthruthnismol*, 33. Hymir's mother is, however, the only many-headed giant actually to appear in the action of the poems, and it is safe to assume that the tradition as a whole belongs to the period of Norse folk-tales of the *märchen* order.

37. No gap is indicated in the manuscripts. Some editors put the missing line as 2, some as 3, and some, leaving the present three lines together, add a fourth, and metrically incorrect, one from late paper manuscripts: "Who with Hymir followed after." *Whales of the waste:* giants.

38. According to Snorri, when Thor set out with Loki (not Tyr) for the giants' land, he stopped first at a peasant's house (cf. stanza 7 and note). There he proceeded to cook his own goats for supper. The peasant's son, Thjalfi, eager to get at the marrow, split one of the leg-bones with his knife. The next morning, when Thor was ready to proceed with his journey, he called the goats to life again, but one of them proved irretrievably lame. His wrath led the peasant to give him both his children as

39. But ye all have heard,— for of them who have
The tales of the gods, who better can tell?—
What prize he won from the wilderness-dweller,
Who both his children gave him to boot.

40. The mighty one came to the council of gods,
And the kettle he had that Hymir's was;
So gladly their ale the gods could drink
In Ægir's hall at the autumn-time.

---

servants (cf. stanza 39). Snorri does not indicate that Loki was in any way to blame.

39. This deliberate introduction of the story-teller is exceedingly rare in the older poetry.

40. The translation of the last two lines is mostly guess-work, as the word rendered "gods" is uncertain, and the one rendered "at the autumn-time" is quite obscure.

LOKASENNA

Loki's Wrangling

Introductory Note

The *Lokasenna* is found only in *Regius,* where it follows the *Hymiskvitha;* Snorri quotes four lines of it, grouped together as a single stanza.

The poem is one of the most vigorous of the entire collection, and seems to have been preserved in exceptionally good condition. The exchange or contest of insults was dear to the Norse heart, and the *Lokasenna* consists chiefly of Loki's taunts to the assembled gods and goddesses, and their largely ineffectual attempts to talk back to him. The author was evidently well versed in mythological lore, and the poem is full of references to incidents not elsewhere recorded. As to its date and origin there is the usual dispute, but the latter part of the tenth century and Iceland seem the best guesses.

The prose notes are long and of unusual interest. The introductory one links the poem closely to the *Hymiskvitha,* much as the *Reginsmol, Fafnismol* and *Sigrdrifumol* are linked together; the others fill in the narrative gaps in the dialogue—very like stage directions,—and provide a conclusion by relating Loki's punishment, which, presumably, is here connected with the wrong incident. It is likely that often when the poem was recited during the two centuries or so before it was committed to writing, the speaker inserted some such explanatory comments, and the compiler of the collection followed this example by adding such explanations as he thought necessary. The *Lokasenna* is certainly much older than the *Hymiskvitha,* the connection between them being purely one of subject-matter; and the twelfth-century compiler evidently knew a good deal less about mythology than the author whose work he was annotating.

Ægir, who was also called Gymir, had prepared ale for the gods, after he had got the mighty kettle, as now has been told. To this feast came Othin and Frigg, his wife. Thor came not, as he was on a journey in the East. Sif,

Thor's wife, was there, and Bragi with Ithun, his wife. Tyr, who had but one hand, was there; the wolf Fenrir had bitten off his other hand when they had bound him. There were Njorth and Skathi his wife, Freyr and Freyja, and Vithar, the son of Othin. Loki was there, and Freyr's

---

Prose. Ægir: the sea-god; Snorri gives Hler as another of his names, but he is not elsewhere called Gymir, which is the name of the giant, Gerth's father, in the *Skirnismol.* On Ægir cf. *Grimnismol,* 45, and *Hymiskvitha,* 1. *Frigg:* though Othin's wife is often mentioned, she plays only a minor part in the Eddic poems; cf. *Voluspo,* 34, *Vafthruthnismol,* 1, and *Grimnismol,* introductory prose. *Thor:* the compiler is apparently a trifle confused as to Thor's movements; the "journey in the East" here mentioned cannot be the one described in the *Hymiskvitha,* nor yet the one narrated by Snorri, as Loki was with Thor throughout that expedition. He probably means no more than that Thor was off killing giants. *Sif:* concerning Thor's wife the chief incident is that Loki cut off her hair, and, at the command of the wrathful Thor, was compelled to have the dwarfs fashion her a new supply of hair out of gold; cf. *Harbarthsljoth,* 48. *Bragi:* the god of poetry; cf. *Grimnismol,* 44 and note. *Ithun:* the goddess of youth; cf. note on *Skirnismol,* 19. Ithun is not mentioned by name in any other of the Eddic poems, but Snorri tells in detail how the giant Thjazi stole her and her apples, explaining the reference in *Harbarthsljoth,* 19 (q. v.). *Tyr:* the god of battle; cf. *Hymiskvitha,* 4, and (concerning his dealings with the wolf Fenrir) *Voluspo,* 39, note. *Njorth:* the chief of the Wanes, and father of *Freyr* and *Freyja;* cf. (concerning the whole family) *Skirnismol,* introductory prose and note, also *Voluspo,* 21 and note. *Skathi:* Njorth's wife was the daughter of the giant Thjazi; cf. *Harbarthsljoth,* 19, note, and *Grimnismol,* 11. *Vithar:* the silent god, the son of Othin who avenged his father by slaying the wolf Fenrir; cf. *Voluspo,* 54, *Vafthruthnismol,* 51, and *Grimnismol,* 17. *Loki:* the mischief-making fire-god; in addition to the many references to his career in the *Lokasenna,* cf. particularly *Voluspo,* 32 and 35, and notes. *Byggvir and Beyla:* not mentioned elsewhere in the poems; Freyr's conspicuous servant is Skirnir, hero of the *Skirnismol. Fimafeng* ("The Swift Handler")

servants Byggvir and Beyla. Many were there of the gods and elves.

Ægir had two serving-men, Fimafeng and Eldir. Glittering gold they had in place of firelight; the ale came in of itself; and great was the peace. The guests praised much the ability of Ægir's serving-men. Loki might not endure that, and he slew Fimafeng. Then the gods shook their shields and howled at Loki and drove him away to the forest, and thereafter set to drinking again. Loki turned back, and outside he met Eldir. Loki spoke to him:

1. "Speak now, Eldir, for not one step
   Farther shalt thou fare;
   What ale-talk here do they have within,
   The sons of the glorious gods?"

Eldir spake:

2. "Of their weapons they talk, and their might in war,
   The sons of the glorious gods;
   From the gods and elves who are gathered here
   No friend in words shalt thou find."

Loki spake:

3. "In shall I go into Ægir's hall,
   For the feast I fain would see;

and *Eldir* ("The Man of the Fire"): mentioned only in connection with this incident. *Glittering gold:* Ægir's use of gold to light his hall, which was often thought of as under the sea, was responsible for the phrase "flame of the flood," and sundry kindred phrases, meaning "gold."

Bale and hatred I bring to the gods,
And their mead with venom I mix."

Eldir spake:

4. "If in thou goest to Ægir's hall,
And fain the feast wouldst see,
And with slander and spite wouldst sprinkle the gods,
Think well lest they wipe it on thee."

Loki spake:

5. "Bethink thee, Eldir, if thou and I
Shall strive with spiteful speech;
Richer I grow in ready words
If thou speakest too much to me."

Then Loki went into the hall, but when they who were there saw who had entered, they were all silent.

Loki spake:

6. "Thirsty I come into this thine hall,
I, Lopt, from a journey long,
To ask of the gods that one should give
Fair mead for a drink to me.

7. "Why sit ye silent, swollen with pride,
Ye gods, and no answer give?

---

6. *Lopt:* like Lothur (cf. *Voluspo,* 18) another name for Loki; cf. *Hyndluljoth,* 43, and *Svipdagsmol,* 42.

7. In the manuscript this stanza begins with a small letter, and Heinzel unites it with stanza 6.

and a seat prepare me,
o fare."

seat will the gods prepare
their midst for thee;
s know well what men they wish
at their mighty feasts."

oki spake:

member, Othin, in olden days
That we both our blood have mixed;
Then didst thou promise no ale to pour,
Unless it were brought for us both."

Othin spake:

10. "Stand forth then, Vithar, and let the wolf's father
Find a seat at our feast;

---

8. ***Bragi:*** cf. note on introductory prose. Why Loki taunts him with cowardice (stanzas 11-13-15) is not clear, for poetry, of which Bragi was the patron, was generally associated in the Norse mind with peculiar valor, and most of the skaldic poets were likewise noted fighters.

9. There exists no account of any incident in which Othin and Loki thus swore blood-brotherhood, but they were so often allied in enterprises that the idea is wholly reasonable. The common process of "mingling blood" was carried out quite literally, and the promise of which Loki speaks is characteristic of those which, in the sagas, often accompanied the ceremony; cf. *Brot af Sigurtharkvithu,* 18 and note.

10. In stanzas 10-31 the manuscript has nothing to indicate the identity of the several speakers, but these are uniformly clear

Lest evil should Loki speak aloud
Here within Ægir's hall."

Then Vithar arose and poured drink for Loki; but before he drank he spoke to the gods:

11. "Hail to you, gods! ye goddesses, hail!
Hail to the holy throng!
Save for the god who yonder sits,
Bragi there on the bench."

Bragi spake:

12. "A horse and a sword from my hoard will I give,
And a ring gives Bragi to boot,
That hatred thou makst not among the gods;
So rouse not the great ones to wrath."

Loki spake:

13. "In horses and rings thou shalt never be rich,
Bragi, but both shalt thou lack;
Of the gods and elves here together met
Least brave in battle art thou,
(And shyest thou art of the shot.)"

Bragi spake:

14. "Now were I without as I am within,

---

enough through the context. *Vithar:* cf. note on introductory prose. *The wolf's father:* Loki; cf. *Voluspo,* 39 and note.

13. Sijmons makes one line of lines 4-5 by cutting out a part of each; Finnur Jonsson rejects 5 as spurious.

14. The text of line 4 is somewhat obscure, and has been

And here in Ægir's hall,
Thine head would I bear in mine hands away,
And pay thee the price of thy lies."

Loki spake:

15. "In thy seat art thou bold, not so are thy deeds,
Bragi, adorner of benches!
Go out and fight if angered thou feelest,
No hero such forethought has."

Ithun spake:

16. "Well, prithee, Bragi, his kinship weigh,
Since chosen as wish-son he was;
And speak not to Loki such words of spite
Here within Ægir's hall."

Loki spake:

17. "Be silent, Ithun! thou art, I say,

---

variously emended, one often adopted suggestion making the line read, "Little is that for thy lies."

15. *Adorner of benches:* this epithet presumably implies that Bragi is not only slothful, but also effeminate, for a very similar word, "pride of the benches," means a bride.

16. *Ithun:* Bragi's wife; cf. note on introductory prose. The goddesses who, finding that their husbands are getting the worst of it, take up the cudgels with Loki, all find themselves confronted with undeniable facts in their own careers; cf. stanzas 26 (Frigg), 52 (Skathi) and 54 (Sif). Gefjun and Freyja are silenced in similar fashion. *Wish-son:* adopted son; Loki was the son of the giant Farbauti and the giantess Laufey, and hence was not of the race of the gods, but had been virtually adopted by Othin, who subsequently had good reason to regret it.

Of women most lustful in love,
Since thou thy washed-bright arms didst wind
About thy brother's slayer."

Ithun spake:

18. "To Loki I speak not with spiteful words
Here within Ægir's hall;
And Bragi I calm, who is hot with beer,
For I wish not that fierce they should fight."

Gefjun spake:

19. "Why, ye gods twain, with bitter tongues
Raise hate among us here?
Loki is famed for his mockery foul,
And the dwellers in heaven he hates."

Loki spake:

20. "Be silent, Gefjun! for now shall I say
Who led thee to evil life;
The boy so fair gave a necklace bright,
And about him thy leg was laid."

---

17. We do not even know who Ithun's brother was, much less who slew him.

19. *Gefjun:* a goddess, not elsewhere mentioned in the poems, who, according to Snorri, was served by the women who died maidens. Beyond this nothing is known of her. Lines 3-4 in the manuscript are puzzling, and have been freely emended.

20. Nothing is known of the incident here mentioned. There is a good deal of confusion as to various of the gods and goddesses, and it has been suggested that Gefjun is really Frigg under another name, with a little of Freyja—whose attributes were frequently confused with Frigg's—thrown in. Certainly Othin's

Othin spake:

21\. "Mad art thou, Loki, and little of wit,
The wrath of Gefjun to rouse;
For the fate that is set for all she sees,
Even as I, methinks."

Loki spake:

22\. "Be silent, Othin! not justly thou settest
The fate of the fight among men;
Oft gavst thou to him who deserved not the gift,
To the baser, the battle's prize."

Othin spake:

23\. "Though I gave to him who deserved not the gift,
To the baser, the battle's prize;
Winters eight wast thou under the earth,
Milking the cows as a maid,
(Ay, and babes didst thou bear;
Unmanly thy soul must seem.)"

---

answer (stanza 21, lines 3-4) fits Frigg perfectly, for she shared his knowledge of the future, whereas it has no relation to anything known of Gefjun. As for the necklace (line 3), it may be the Brisings' necklace, which appears in the *Thrymskvitha* as Freyja's, but which, in some mythological writings, is assigned to Frigg.

21\. Snorri quotes line 1; cf. note on stanza 29.

23\. There is no other reference to Loki's having spent eight years underground, or to his cow-milking. On one occasion, however, he did bear offspring. A giant had undertaken to build the gods a fortress, his reward being Freyja and the sun and moon, provided the work was done by a given time. His sole helper was his horse, Svathilfari. The work being nearly done, and the gods fearing to lose Freyja and the sun and moon, Loki

Loki spake:

24. "They say that with spells in Samsey once
Like witches with charms didst thou work;
And in witch's guise among men didst thou go;
Unmanly thy soul must seem."

Frigg spake:

25. "Of the deeds ye two of old have done
Ye should make no speech among men;
Whate'er ye have done in days gone by,
Old tales should ne'er be told."

Loki spake:

26. "Be silent, Frigg! thou art Fjorgyn's wife,
But ever lustful in love;
For Vili and Ve, thou wife of Vithrir,
Both in thy bosom have lain."

---

turned himself into a mare, and so effectually distracted Svathilfari from his task that shortly afterwards Loki gave birth to Othin's eight-legged horse, Sleipnir. In such contests of abuse a man was not infrequently taunted with having borne children; cf. *Helgakvitha Hundingsbana* I, 39-45. One or two of the last three lines may be spurious.

24. *Samsey:* perhaps the Danish island of Samsö. Othin was the god of magic, but there is no other reference to his ever having disguised himself as a witch.

25. *Frigg:* Othin's wife; cf. note to introductory prose.

26. *Fjorgyn:* Othin; cf. *Voluspo,* 56 and note. *Vili and Ve:* Othin's brothers, who appear merely as, with Othin, the sons of Bur and Bestla; cf. *Voluspo,* 4. The *Ynglingasaga* says that, during one of Othin's protracted absences, his two brothers took Frigg as their mistress. *Vithrir:* another name for Othin.

Frigg spake:

27. "If a son like Baldr were by me now,
Here within Ægir's hall,
From the sons of the gods thou shouldst go not forth
Till thy fierceness in fight were tried."

Loki spake:

28. "Thou wilt then, Frigg, that further I tell
Of the ill that now I know;
Mine is the blame that Baldr no more
Thou seest ride home to the hall."

Freyja spake:

29. "Mad art thou, Loki, that known thou makest
The wrong and shame thou hast wrought;
The fate of all does Frigg know well,
Though herself she says it not."

Loki spake:

30. "Be silent, Freyja! for fully I know thee,
Sinless thou art not thyself;

---

27. On the death of Baldr, slain through Loki's cunning by the blind Hoth, cf. *Voluspo,* 32 and note.

29. *Freyja:* daughter of Njorth and sister of Freyr; cf. note on introductory prose. Snorri, in speaking of Frigg's knowledge of the future, makes a stanza out of *Lokasenna,* 21, 1; 47, 2; 29, 3-4, thus: "Mad art thou, Loki, and little of wit, / Why, Loki, leavst thou this not? / The fate of all does Frigg know well, / Though herself she says it not."

30. According to Snorri, Freyja was a model of fidelity to her husband, Oth.

Of the gods and elves who are gathered here,
Each one as thy lover has lain."

Freyja spake:

31. "False is thy tongue, and soon shalt thou find
That it sings thee an evil song;
The gods are wroth, and the goddesses all,
And in grief shalt thou homeward go."

Loki spake:

32. "Be silent, Freyja! thou foulest witch,
And steeped full sore in sin;
In the arms of thy brother the bright gods caught thee
When Freyja her wind set free."

Njorth spake:

33. "Small ill does it work though a woman may have
A lord or a lover or both;
But a wonder it is that this womanish god
Comes hither, though babes he has borne."

---

32. Before each of stanzas 32-42 the manuscript indicates the speaker, through the initial letter of the name written in the margin. *Thy brother:* Freyr; there is no other indication that such a relation existed between these two, but they themselves were the product of such a union; cf. stanza 36 and note.

33. *Njorth:* father of Freyr and Freyja, and given by the Wanes as a hostage, in exchange for Hönir, at the close of the first war; cf. *Voluspo,* 21 and note, also *Skirnismol,* introductory prose and note. *Babes:* cf. stanza 23 and note. Bugge suggests that this clause may have been a late insertion.

Loki spake:

34. "Be silent, Njorth; thou wast eastward sent,
To the gods as a hostage given;
And the daughters of Hymir their privy had
When use did they make of thy mouth."

Njorth spake:

35. "Great was my gain, though long was I gone,
To the gods as a hostage given;
The son did I have whom no man hates,
And foremost of gods is found."

Loki spake:

36. "Give heed now, Njorth, nor boast too high,
No longer I hold it hid;
With thy sister hadst thou so fair a son,
Thus hadst thou no worse a hope."

Tyr spake:

37. "Of the heroes brave is Freyr the best
Here in the home of the gods;

---

34. *Daughters of Hymir:* we have no clue to who these were, though Hymir is doubtless the frost-giant of the *Hymiskvitha* (q.v.). Loki's point is that Njorth is not a god, but the product of an inferior race (the Wanes).

35. *The son:* Freyr.

36. *Thy sister:* the *Ynglingasaga* supports this story of Njorth's having had two children by his sister before he came among the gods. Snorri, on the other hand, specifically says that Freyr and Freyja were born after Njorth came to the gods.

37. *Tyr:* the god of battle; cf. notes on *Hymiskvitha,* 4, and *Voluspo,* 39. *Freyr;* concerning his noble qualities cf. *Skirnismol,* introductory prose and note.

He harms not maids nor the wives of men,
And the bound from their fetters he frees."

Loki spake:

38. "Be silent, Tyr! for between two men
Friendship thou ne'er couldst fashion;
Fain would I tell how Fenrir once
Thy right hand rent from thee."

Tyr spake:

39. "My hand do I lack, but Hrothvitnir thou,
And the loss brings longing to both;
Ill fares the wolf who shall ever await
In fetters the fall of the gods."

Loki spake:

40. "Be silent, Tyr! for a son with me
Thy wife once chanced to win;
Not a penny, methinks, wast thou paid for the wrong,
Nor wast righted an inch, poor wretch."

Freyr spake:

41. "By the mouth of the river the wolf remains

---

38. Snorri mentions Tyr's incompetence as a peacemaker. *Fenrir:* the wolf, Loki's son; cf. *Voluspo,* 39.

39. *Hrothvitnir* ("The Mighty Wolf"): Fenrir, who awaits in chains the final battle and death at the hands of Vithar. The manuscript has a metrical error in line 3, which has led to various emendations, all with much the same meaning.

40. *Thy wife:* there is no other reference to Tyr's wife, nor do we know who was the son in question.

Till the gods to destruction go;
Thou too shalt soon, if thy tongue is not stilled,
Be fettered, thou forger of ill."

Loki spake:

42. "The daughter of Gymir with gold didst thou buy,
And sold thy sword to boot;
But when Muspell's sons through Myrkwood ride,
Thou shalt weaponless wait, poor wretch."

Byggvir spake:

43. "Had I birth so famous as Ingunar-Freyr,
And sat in so lofty a seat,

---

41. *The mouth of the river:* according to Snorri, the chained Fenrir "roars horribly, and the slaver runs from his mouth, and makes the river called Vam; he lies there till the doom of the gods." Freyr's threat is actually carried out; cf. concluding prose.

42. *The daughter of Gymir:* Gerth, heroine of the *Skirnismol,* which gives the details of Freyr's loss of his sword. *Muspell's sons:* the name Muspell is not used elsewhere in the poems; Snorri uses it frequently, but only in this same phrase, "Muspell's sons." They are the dwellers in the fire-world, Muspellsheim, led by Surt against the gods in the last battle; cf. *Voluspo,* 47 and 52 and notes. *Myrkwood:* here the dark forest bounding the fire-world; in the *Atlakvitha* (stanza 3) the name is used of another boundary forest.

43. *Byggvir:* one of Freyr's two servants; cf. introductory prose. *Ingunar-Freyr:* the name is not used elsewhere in the poems, or by Snorri; it may be the genitive of a woman's name, Ingun, the unknown sister of Njorth who was Freyr's mother (cf. stanza 36), or a corruption of the name Ingw, used for Freyr (Fro) in old German mythology.

I would crush to marrow this croaker of ill,
And beat all his body to bits."

Loki spake:

44. "What little creature goes crawling there,
Snuffling and snapping about?
At Freyr's ears ever wilt thou be found,
Or muttering hard at the mill."

Byggvir spake:

45. "Byggvir my name, and nimble am I,
As gods and men do grant;
And here am I proud that the children of Hropt
Together all drink ale."

Loki spake:

46. "Be silent, Byggvir! thou never couldst set
Their shares of the meat for men;
Hid in straw on the floor, they found thee not
When heroes were fain to fight."

Heimdall spake:

47. "Drunk art thou, Loki, and mad are thy deeds,
Why, Loki, leavst thou this not?

---

44. Beginning with this stanza, the names of the speakers are lacking in the manuscript. *The mill:* i.e., at slaves' tasks.

45. Nothing further is known of either Byggvir's swiftness or his cowardice. *Hropt:* Othin.

47. *Heimdall:* besides being the watchman of the gods (cf. *Voluspo,* 27), he appears also as the god of light (cf. *Thrymskvitha,* 14), and possibly also as a complex cultural deity in the

For drink beyond measure will lead all men
No thought of their tongues to take."

Loki spake:

48. "Be silent, Heimdall! in days long since
Was an evil fate for thee fixed;
With back held stiff must thou ever stand,
As warder of heaven to watch."

Skathi spake:

49. "Light art thou, Loki, but longer thou mayst not
In freedom flourish thy tail;
On the rocks the gods bind thee with bowels torn
Forth from thy frost-cold son."

Loki spake:

50. "Though on rocks the gods bind me with bowels torn
Forth from my frost-cold son,

Rigsthula. He was a son of Othin, born of nine sisters; cf. *Hyndluljoth,* 37-40. In the last battle he and Loki slay one another. Line 2 is quoted by Snorri; cf. stanza 29, note.

49. *Skathi:* the wife of Njorth, and daughter of the giant Thjazi, concerning whose death cf. *Harbarthsljoth,* 19, note. *Bowels,* etc.: according to the prose note at the end of the *Lokasenna,* the gods bound Loki with the bowels of his son Vali, and changed his other son, Narfi, into a wolf. Snorri turns the story about, Vali being the wolf, who tears his brother to pieces, the gods then using Narfi's intestines to bind Loki. Narfi—and presumably Vali—were the sons of Loki and his wife, Sigyn. They appear only in this episode, though Narfi (or Nari) is named by Snorri in his list of Loki's children. Cf. concluding prose, and note.

I was first and last at the deadly fight
There where Thjazi we caught."

Skathi spake:

51. "Wert thou first and last at the deadly fight
There where Thjazi was caught,
From my dwellings and fields shall ever come forth
A counsel cold for thee."

Loki spake:

52. "More lightly thou spakest with Laufey's son,
When thou badst me come to thy bed;
Such things must be known if now we two
Shall seek our sins to tell."

Then Sif came forward and poured mead for Loki in a crystal cup, and said:

53. "Hail to thee, Loki, and take thou here
The crystal cup of old mead;
For me at least, alone of the gods,
Blameless thou knowest to be."

---

52. *Laufey's son:* Loki; not much is known of his parents beyond their names. His father was the giant Farbauti, his mother Laufey, sometimes called Nal. There is an elaborate but far-fetched hypothesis explaining these three on the basis of a nature-myth. There is no other reference to such a relation between Skathi and Loki as he here suggests.

53. *Sif:* Thor's wife; cf. *Harbarthsljoth,* 48, where her infidelity is again mentioned. The manuscript omits the proper name

He took the horn, and drank therefrom:

54. "Alone thou wert if truly thou wouldst
All men so shyly shun;
But one do I know full well, methinks,
Who had thee from Hlorrithi's arms,—
(Loki the crafty in lies.)"

Beyla spake:

55. "The mountains shake, and surely I think
From his home comes Hlorrithi now;
He will silence the man who is slandering here
Together both gods and men."

Loki spake:

56. "Be silent, Beyla! thou art Byggvir's wife,
And deep art thou steeped in sin;
A greater shame to the gods came ne'er,
Befouled thou art with thy filth."

Then came Thor forth, and spake:

57. "Unmanly one, cease, or the mighty hammer,
Mjollnir, shall close thy mouth;

---

from the preceding prose, and a few editors have, obviously in error, attributed the speech to Beyla.

54. *Hlorrithi:* Thor. Line 5 is probably spurious.

55. *Beyla:* Freyr's servant, wife of Byggvir; cf. introductory prose and note.

57. *Mjollnir:* concerning Thor's famous hammer see particularly *Thrymskvitha,* 1 and note. *Shoulder-cliff:* head; concerning

Thy shoulder-cliff shall I cleave from thy neck,
And so shall thy life be lost."

Loki spake:

58. "Lo, in has come the son of Earth:
Why threaten so loudly, Thor?
Less fierce thou shalt go to fight with the wolf
When he swallows Sigfather up."

Thor spake:

59. "Unmanly one, cease, or the mighty hammer,
Mjollnir, shall close thy mouth;
I shall hurl thee up and out in the East,
Where men shall see thee no more."

Loki spake:

60. "That thou hast fared on the East-road forth
To men shouldst thou say no more;

---

the use of such diction in the *Edda,* cf. introductory note to *Hymiskvitha.* The manuscript indicates line 3 as the beginning of a stanza, but this is apparently a scribal error.

58. *Son of Earth:* Thor, son of Othin and Jorth (Earth). The manuscript omits the word "son," but all editors have agreed in supplying it. *The wolf:* Fenrir, Loki's son, who slays Othin (*Sigfather:* "Father of Victory") in the final battle. Thor, according to Snorri and to the *Voluspo,* 56, fights with Mithgarthsorm and not with Fenrir, who is killed by Vithar.

59. Lines 1-2 are abbreviated in the manuscript, as also in stanzas 61 and 63.

60. Loki's taunt that Thor hid in the thumb of Skrymir's glove is similar to that of Othin, *Harbarthsljoth,* 26, in the note to which the story is outlined. Line 4 is identical with line 3 of *Harbarthsljoth,* 26.

In the thumb of a glove didst thou hide, thou
great one,
And there forgot thou wast Thor."

Thor spake:

61. "Unmanly one, cease, or the mighty hammer,
Mjollnir, shall close thy mouth;
My right hand shall smite thee with Hrungnir's
slayer,
Till all thy bones are broken."

Loki spake:

62. "A long time still do I think to live,
Though thou threatenest thus with thy hammer;
Rough seemed the straps of Skrymir's wallet,
When thy meat thou mightest not get,
(And faint from hunger didst feel.)"

Thor spake:

63. "Unmanly one, cease, or the mighty hammer,
Mjollnir, shall close thy mouth;

---

61. *Hrungnir's slayer:* the hammer; the story of how Thor slew this stone-headed giant is indicated in *Harbarthsljoth,* 14-15, and outlined in the note to stanza 14 of that poem.

62. On the day following the adventure of the glove, Thor, Loki and Thor's servants proceed on their way in company with Skrymir, who puts all their food in his wallet. At evening Skrymir goes to sleep, and Thor tries to get at the food, but cannot loosen the straps of the wallet. In a rage he smites Skrymir three times on the head with his hammer, but the giant —who, it subsequently appears, deftly dodges the blows—is totally undisturbed. Line 5 may well be spurious.

The slayer of Hrungnir shall send thee to hell,
And down to the gate of death."

Loki spake:

64. "I have said to the gods and the sons of the gods
The things that whetted my thoughts;
But before thee alone do I now go forth,
For thou fightest well, I ween.

65. "Ale hast thou brewed, but, Ægir, now
Such feasts shalt thou make no more;
O'er all that thou hast which is here within
Shall play the flickering flames,
(And thy back shall be burnt with fire.)"

And after that Loki hid himself in Franang's waterfall in the guise of a salmon, and there the gods took him. He was bound with the bowels of his son Vali, but his son Narfi was changed to a wolf. Skathi took a poison-snake and fastened it up over Loki's face, and the poison dropped thereon. Sigyn, Loki's wife, sat there and held a shell under the poison, but when the shell was full she bore away the poison, and meanwhile the poison dropped on Loki. Then he struggled so hard that the whole earth shook therewith; and now that is called an earthquake.

---

65. *The flames:* the fire that consumes the world on the last day; cf. *Voluspo,* 57. Line 5 may be spurious.

Prose: Snorri tells the same story, with minor differences, but makes it the consequence of Loki's part in the slaying of Baldr, which undoubtedly represents the correct tradition. The compiler of the poems either was confused or thought the incident was useful as indicating what finally happened to Loki. Possibly he did not mean to imply that Loki's fate was brought upon him by his abuse of the gods, but simply tried to round out the story. *Franang:* "Gleaming Water." *Vali* and *Narfi:* cf. stanza 49 and note. *Sigyn:* cf. *Voluspo,* 35, the only other place where she is mentioned in the poems. Snorri omits the naive note about earthquakes, his narrative ending with the words, "And there he lies till the destruction of the gods."

THRYMSKVITHA

The Lay of Thrym

Introductory Note

The *Thrymskvitha* is found only in the *Codex Regius,* where it follows the *Lokasenna.* Snorri does not quote from it, nor, rather oddly, does the story occur in the *Prose Edda.*

Artistically the *Thrymskvitha* is one of the best, as it is, next to the *Voluspo,* the most famous, of the entire collection. It has, indeed, been called "the finest ballad in the world," and not without some reason. Its swift, vigorous action, the sharpness of its characterization and the humor of the central situation combine to make it one of the most vivid short narrative poems ever composed. Of course we know nothing specific of its author, but there can be no question that he was a poet of extraordinary ability. The poem assumed its present form, most critics agree, somewhere about 900, and thus it is one of the oldest in the collection. It has been suggested, on the basis of stylistic similarity, that its author may also have composed the *Skirnismol,* and possibly *Baldrs Draumar.* There is also some resemblance between the *Thrymskvitha* and the *Lokasenna* (note, in this connection, Bugge's suggestion that the *Skirnismol* and the *Lokasenna* may have been by the same man), and it is not impossible that all four poems have a single authorship.

The *Thrymskvitha* has been preserved in excellent condition, without any serious gaps or interpolations. In striking contrast to many of the poems, it contains no prose narrative links, the story being told in narrative verse—a rare phenomenon in the poems of the *Edda.*

1\. Wild was Vingthor when he awoke,
And when his mighty hammer he missed;

1\. *Vingthor* ("Thor the Hurler"): another name for Thor, equivalent to Vingnir (*Vafthruthnismol,* 51). Concerning Thor and his hammer, Mjollnir, cf. *Hymiskvitha, Lokasenna,* and *Harbarthsljoth, passim. Jorth:* Earth, Thor's mother, Othin being his father.

He shook his beard, his hair was bristling,
As the son of Jorth about him sought.

2. Hear now the speech that first he spake:
"Harken, Loki, and heed my words,
Nowhere on earth is it known to man,
Nor in heaven above: our hammer is stolen."

3. To the dwelling fair of Freyja went they,
Hear now the speech that first he spake:
"Wilt thou, Freyja, thy feather-dress lend me,
That so my hammer I may seek?"

Freyja spake:

4. "Thine should it be though of silver bright,
And I would give it though 'twere of gold."
Then Loki flew, and the feather-dress whirred,
Till he left behind him the home of the gods,
And reached at last the realm of the giants.

---

2. *Loki:* cf. *Lokasenna, passim.*

3. *Freyja:* Njorth's daughter, and sister of Freyr; cf. *Lokasenna,* introductory prose and note, also *Skirnismol,* introductory prose. Freyja's house was Sessrymnir ("Rich in Seats") built in Folkvang ("Field of the Folk"); cf. *Grimnismol,* 14. *Feather-dress:* this flying equipment of Freyja's is also used in the story of Thjazi, wherein Loki again borrows the "hawk's dress" of Freyja, this time to rescue Ithun; cf. *Harbarthsljoth,* 19 and note.

4. The manuscript and most editions have lines 1-2 in inverse order. Several editors assume a lacuna before line 1, making a stanza out of the two conjectural lines (Bugge actually supplies them) and lines 1-2 of stanza 4. Thus they either make a separate stanza out of lines 3-5 or unite them in a six-line stanza with 5. The manuscript punctuation and capitalization—not

5. Thrym sat on a mound,   the giants' master,
Leashes of gold   he laid for his dogs,
And stroked and smoothed   the manes of his steeds.

Thrym spake:

6. "How fare the gods,   how fare the elves?
Why comst thou alone   to the giants' land?"

Loki spake:

"Ill fare the gods,   ill fare the elves!
Hast thou hidden   Hlorrithi's hammer?"

Thrym spake:

7. "I have hidden   Hlorrithi's hammer,
Eight miles down   deep in the earth;
And back again   shall no man bring it
If Freyja I win not   to be my wife."

8. Then Loki flew,   and the feather-dress whirred,
Till he left behind him   the home of the giants,
And reached at last   the realm of the gods.
There in the courtyard   Thor he met:
Hear now the speech   that first he spake:

---

wholly trustworthy guides—indicate the stanza divisions as in this translation.

5. *Thrym:* a frost-giant. Gering declares that this story of the theft of Thor's hammer symbolizes the fact that thunderstorms rarely occur in winter.

6. *Line 1:* cf. *Voluspo,* 48, 1. The manuscript does not indicate Loki as the speaker of lines 3-4. *Hlorrithi:* Thor.

7. No superscription in the manuscript. Vigfusson made up

9. "Hast thou found tidings as well as trouble?
Thy news in the air shalt thou utter now;
Oft doth the sitter his story forget,
And lies he speaks who lays himself down."

Loki spake:

10. "Trouble I have, and tidings as well:
Thrym, king of the giants, keeps thy hammer,
And back again shall no man bring it
If Freyja he wins not to be his wife."

11. Freyja the fair then went they to find;
Hear now the speech that first he spake:
"Bind on, Freyja, the bridal veil,
For we two must haste to the giants' home."

12. Wrathful was Freyja, and fiercely she snorted,
And the dwelling great of the gods was shaken,
And burst was the mighty Brisings' necklace:
"Most lustful indeed should I look to all
If I journeyed with thee to the giants' home."

---

and inserted lines like "Then spake Loki the son of Laufey" whenever he thought they would be useful.

9. The manuscript marks line 2, instead of line 1, as the beginning of a stanza, which has caused editors some confusion in grouping the lines of stanzas 8 and 9.

10. No superscription in the manuscript.

12. Many editors have rejected either line 2 or line 3. Vigfusson inserts one of his own lines before line 4. *Brisings' necklace:* a marvelous necklace fashioned by the dwarfs, here called Brisings (i.e., "Twiners"); cf. *Lokasenna,* 20 and note.

13. Then were the gods together met,
And the goddesses came and council held,
And the far-famed ones a plan would find,
How they might Hlorrithi's hammer win.

14. Then Heimdall spake, whitest of the gods,
Like the Wanes he knew the future well:
"Bind we on Thor the bridal veil,
Let him bear the mighty Brisings' necklace;

15. "Keys around him let there rattle,
And down to his knees hang woman's dress;
With gems full broad upon his breast,
And a pretty cap to crown his head."

16. Then Thor the mighty his answer made:
"Me would the gods unmanly call
If I let bind the bridal veil."

17. Then Loki spake, the son of Laufey:
"Be silent, Thor, and speak not thus;

---

13. Lines 1-3 are identical with *Baldrs Draumar*, 1, 1-3.

14. *Heimdall:* the phrase "whitest of the gods" suggests that Heimdall was the god of light as well as being the watchman. His wisdom was probably connected with his sleepless watching over all the worlds; cf. *Lokasenna*, 47 and note. On the Wanes cf. *Voluspo*, 21 and note. They are not elsewhere spoken of as peculiarly gifted with knowledge of future events.

16. Possibly a line has been lost from this stanza.

17. *Laufey:* Loki's mother, cf. *Lokasenna*, 52 and note.

Else will the giants in Asgarth dwell
If thy hammer is brought not home to thee."

18. Then bound they on Thor the bridal veil,
And next the mighty Brisings' necklace.

19. Keys around him let they rattle,
And down to his knees hung woman's dress;
With gems full broad upon his breast,
And a pretty cap to crown his head.

20. Then Loki spake, the son of Laufey:
"As thy maid-servant thither I go with thee;
We two shall haste to the giants' home."

21. Then home the goats to the hall were driven,
They wrenched at the halters, swift were they to run;
The mountains burst, earth burned with fire,
And Othin's son sought Jotunheim.

22. Then loud spake Thrym, the giants' leader:
"Bestir ye, giants, put straw on the benches;

18-19. The manuscript abbreviates all six lines, giving only the initial letters of the words. The stanza division is thus arbitrary; some editors have made one stanza of the six lines, others have combined the last two lines of stanza 19 with stanza 20. It is possible that a couple of lines have been lost.

21. *Goats:* Thor's wagon was always drawn by goats; cf. *Hymiskvitha,* 38 and note. *Jotunheim:* the world of the giants.

22. *Njorth:* cf. *Voluspo,* 21, and *Grimnismol,* 11 and 16. *Noatun*

Now Freyja they bring to be my bride,
The daughter of Njorth out of Noatun.

23. "Gold-horned cattle go to my stables,
Jet-black oxen, the giant's joy;
Many my gems, and many my jewels,
Freyja alone did I lack, methinks."

24. Early it was to evening come,
And forth was borne the beer for the giants;
Thor alone ate an ox, and eight salmon,
All the dainties as well that were set for the women;
And drank Sif's mate three tuns of mead.

25. Then loud spake Thrym, the giants' leader:
"Who ever saw bride more keenly bite?
I ne'er saw bride with a broader bite,
Nor a maiden who drank more mead than this!"

26. Hard by there sat the serving-maid wise,
So well she answered the giant's words:
"From food has Freyja eight nights fasted,
So hot was her longing for Jotunheim."

("Ships'-Haven"): Njorth's home, where his wife, Skathi, found it impossible to stay; cf. *Grimnismol,* 11 and note.

24. Grundtvig thinks this is all that is left of two stanzas describing Thor's supper. Some editors reject line 4. In line 3 the manuscript has "he," the reference being, of course, to Thor, on whose appetite cf. *Hymiskvitha,* 15. *Sif:* Thor's wife; cf. *Lokasenna,* note to introductory prose and stanza 53.

27. Thrym looked 'neath the veil, for he longed to kiss,
But back he leaped the length of the hall:
"Why are so fearful the eyes of Freyja?
Fire, methinks, from her eyes burns forth."

28. Hard by there sat the serving-maid wise,
So well she answered the giant's words:
"No sleep has Freyja for eight nights found,
So hot was her longing for Jotunheim."

29. Soon came the giant's luckless sister,
Who feared not to ask the bridal fee:
"From thy hands the rings of red gold take,
If thou wouldst win my willing love,
(My willing love and welcome glad.)"

30. Then loud spake Thrym, the giants' leader:
"Bring in the hammer to hallow the bride;
On the maiden's knees let Mjollnir lie,
That us both the hand of Vor may bless."

---

27. For clearness I have inserted Thrym's name in place of the pronoun of the original. *Fire:* the noun is lacking in the manuscript; most editors have inserted it, however, following a late paper manuscript.

28. In the manuscript the whole stanza is abbreviated to initial letters, except for "sleep," "Freyja," and "found."

29. *Luckless:* so the manuscript, but many editors have altered the word "arma" to "aldna," meaning "old," to correspond with line 1 of stanza 32. Line 5 may well be spurious.

30. *Hallow:* just what this means is not clear, but there are

31. The heart in the breast   of Hlorrithi laughed
When the hard-souled one   his hammer beheld;
First Thrym, the king   of the giants, he killed,
Then all the folk   of the giants he felled.

32. The giant's sister   old he slew,
She who had begged   the bridal fee;
A stroke she got   in the shilling's stead,
And for many rings   the might of the hammer.

33. And so his hammer   got Othin's son.

---

references to other kinds of consecration, though not of a bride, with the "sign of the hammer." According to Vigfusson, "the hammer was the holy sign with the heathens, answering to the cross of the Christians." In Snorri's story of Thor's resuscitation of his cooked goat (cf. *Hymiskvitha*, 38, note) the god "hallows" the goat with his hammer. One of the oldest runic signs, supposed to have magic power, was named Thor's-hammer. *Vor:* the goddess of vows, particularly between men and women; Snorri lists a number of little-known goddesses similar to Vor, all of them apparently little more than names for Frigg.

33. Some editors reject this line, which, from a dramatic standpoint, is certainly a pity. In the manuscript it begins with a capital letter, like the opening of a new stanza.

ALVISSMOL

The Ballad of Alvis

Introductory Note

No better summary of the Alvissmol can be given than Gering's statement that "it is a versified chapter from the skaldic Poetics." The narrative skeleton, contained solely in stanzas 1-8 and in 35, is of the slightest; the dwarf Alvis, desirous of marrying Thor's daughter, is compelled by the god to answer a number of questions to test his knowledge. That all his answers are quite satisfactory makes no difference whatever to the outcome. The questions and answers differ radically from those of the *Vafthruthnismol.* Instead of being essentially mythological, they all concern synonyms. Thor asks what the earth, the sky, the moon, and so on, are called " in each of all the worlds," but there is no apparent significance in the fact that the gods call the earth one thing and the giants call it another; the answers are simply strings of poetic circumlocutions, or "kennings." Concerning the use of these "kennings" in skaldic poetry, cf. introductory note to the *Hymiskvitha.*

Mogk is presumably right in dating the poem as late as the twelfth century, assigning it to the period of "the Icelandic renaissance of skaldic poetry." It appears to have been the work of a man skilled in poetic construction,—Thor's questions, for instance, are neatly balanced in pairs,—and fully familiar with the intricacies of skaldic diction, but distinctly weak in his mythology. In other words, it is learned rather than spontaneous poetry. Finnur Jonsson's attempt to make it a tenth century Norwegian poem baffles logic. Vigfusson is pretty sure the poem shows marked traces of Celtic influence, which is by no means incompatible with Mogk's theory (cf. introductory note to the *Rigsthula*).

The poem is found only in *Regius,* where it follows the *Thrymskvitha.* Snorri quotes stanzas 20 and 30, the manuscripts of the *Prose Edda* giving the name of the poem as *Alvissmol, Alsvinnsmol* or *Olvismol.* It is apparently in excellent condition, without serious errors of transmission, although interpolations or omissions in such a poem might have been made so easily as to defy detection.

The translation of the many synonyms presents, of course,

unusual difficulties, particularly as many of the Norse words can be properly rendered in English only by more or less extended phrases. I have kept to the original meanings as closely as I could without utterly destroying the metrical structure.

Alvis spake:

1. "Now shall the bride my benches adorn,
And homeward haste forthwith;
Eager for wedlock to all shall I seem,
Nor at home shall they rob me of rest."

Thor spake:

2. "What, pray, art thou? Why so pale round the nose?
By the dead hast thou lain of late?
To a giant like dost thou look, methinks;
Thou wast not born for the bride."

Alvis spake:

3. "Alvis am I, and under the earth
My home 'neath the rocks I have;

---

1. *Alvis* ("All-Knowing"): a dwarf, not elsewhere mentioned. The manuscript nowhere indicates the speakers' names. The bride in question is Thor's daughter; Thruth ("Might") is the only daughter of his whose name is recorded, and she does not appear elsewhere in the poems. Her mother was Sif, Thor's wife, whereas the god's sons were born of a giantess. *Benches:* cf. *Lokasenna,* 15 and note.

2. The dwarfs, living beyond the reach of the sun, which was fatal to them (cf. stanzas 16 and 35), were necessarily pale. Line 3 is, of course, ironical.

3. *Wagon-guider:* Thor, who travels habitually on his goat-drawn wagon. Bugge changes "Vagna vers" to "Vapna verþs,"

With the wagon-guider a word do I seek;
Let the gods their bond not break."

Thor spake:

4. "Break it shall I, for over the bride
Her father has foremost right;
At home was I not when the promise thou hadst,
And I give her alone of the gods."

Alvis spake:

5. "What hero claims such right to hold
O'er the bride that shines so bright?
Not many will know thee, thou wandering man!
Who was bought with rings to bear thee?"

Thor spake:

6. "Vingthor, the wanderer wide, am I,
And I am Sithgrani's son;
Against my will shalt thou get the maid,
And win the marriage word."

---

rendering the line "I am come to seek the cost of the weapons." In either case, Alvis does not as yet recognize Thor.

4. Apparently the gods promised Thor's daughter in marriage to Alvis during her father's absence, perhaps as a reward for some craftsmanship of his (cf. Bugge's suggestion as to stanza 3). The text of line 4 is most uncertain.

5. *Hero:* ironically spoken; Alvis takes Thor for a tramp, the god's uncouth appearance often leading to such mistakes; cf. *Harbarthsljoth,* 6. Line 4 is a trifle uncertain; some editors alter the wording to read "What worthless woman bore thee?"

6. *Vingthor* ("Thor the Hurler"): cf. *Thrymskvitha,* 1. *Sithgrani* ("Long-Beard"): Othin.

Alvis spake:

7. "Thy good-will now shall I quickly get,
And win the marriage word;
I long to have, and I would not lack,
This snow-white maid for mine."

Thor spake:

8. "The love of the maid I may not keep thee
From winning, thou guest so wise,
If of every world thou canst tell me all
That now I wish to know.

9. "Answer me, Alvis! thou knowest all,
Dwarf, of the doom of men:
What call they the earth, that lies before all,
In each and every world?"

Alvis spake:

10. " 'Earth' to men, 'Field' to the gods it is,
'The Ways' is it called by the Wanes;

---

8. *Every world:* concerning the nine worlds, cf. *Voluspo,* 2 and note. Many editors follow this stanza with one spoken by Alvis, found in late paper manuscripts, as follows: "Ask then, Vingthor, since eager thou art / The lore of the dwarf to learn; / Oft have I fared in the nine worlds all, / And wide is my wisdom of each."

10. *Men,* etc.: nothing could more clearly indicate the author's mythological inaccuracy than his confusion of the inhabitants of the nine worlds. Men (dwellers in Mithgarth) appear in each of Alvis's thirteen answers; so do the gods (Asgarth) and the giants (Jotunheim). The elves (Alfheim) appear in eleven

'Ever Green' by the giants, 'The Grower' by elves,
'The Moist' by the holy ones high."

Thor spake:

11. "Answer me, Alvis! thou knowest all,
Dwarf, of the doom of men:
What call they the heaven, beheld of the high one,
In each and every world?"

Alvis spake:

12. "'Heaven' men call it, 'The Height' the gods,
The Wanes 'The Weaver of Winds';
Giants 'The Up-World,' elves 'The Fair-Roof,'
The dwarfs 'The Dripping Hall.'"

---

answers, the Wanes (Vanaheim) in nine, and the dwarfs (who occupied no special world, unless one identifies them with the dark elves of Svartalfaheim) in seven. The dwellers "in hell" appear in six stanzas; the phrase probably refers to the world of the dead, though Mogk thinks it may mean the dwarfs. In stanzas where the gods are already listed appear names elsewhere applied only to them,—"holy ones," "sons of the gods" and "high ones,"—as if these names meant beings of a separate race. "Men" appears twice in the same stanza, and so do the giants, if one assumes that they are "the sons of Suttung." Altogether it is useless to pay much attention to the mythology of Alvis's replies.

11. Lines 1, 2, and 4 of Thor's questions are regularly abbreviated in the manuscript. *Beheld,* etc.: the word in the manuscript is almost certainly an error, and all kinds of guesses have been made to rectify it. All that can be said is that it means "beheld of" or "known to" somebody.

Thor spake:

13. "Answer me, Alvis! thou knowest all,
Dwarf, of the doom of men:
What call they the moon, that men behold,
In each and every world?"

Alvis spake:

14. "'Moon' with men, 'Flame' the gods among,
'The Wheel' in the house of hell;
'The Goer' the giants, 'The Gleamer' the dwarfs,
The elves 'The Teller of Time.'"

Thor spake:

15. "Answer me, Alvis! thou knowest all,
Dwarf, of the doom of men:
What call they the sun, that all men see,
In each and every world?"

Alvis spake:

16. "Men call it 'Sun,' gods 'Orb of the Sun,'
'The Deceiver of Dvalin' the dwarfs;
The giants 'The Ever-Bright,' elves 'Fair Wheel,'
'All-Glowing' the sons of the gods."

---

14. *Flame:* a doubtful word; Vigfusson suggests that it properly means a "mock sun." *Wheel:* the manuscript adds the adjective "whirling," to the destruction of the metre; cf. *Hovamol,* 84, 3.

16. *Deceiver of Dvalin:* Dvalin was one of the foremost dwarfs; cf. *Voluspo,* 14, *Fafnismol,* 13, and *Hovamol,* 144. The

Thor spake:

17. "Answer me, Alvis! thou knowest all,
Dwarf, of the doom of men:
What call they the clouds, that keep the rains,
In each and every world?"

Alvis spake:

18. " 'Clouds' men name them, 'Rain-Hope' gods call them,
The Wanes call them 'Kites of the Wind';
'Water-Hope' giants, 'Weather-Might' elves,
'The Helmet of Secrets' in hell."

Thor spake:

19. "Answer me, Alvis! thou knowest all,
Dwarf, of the doom of men:
What call they the wind, that widest fares,
In each and every world?"

Alvis spake:

20. " 'Wind' do men call it, the gods 'The Waverer,'
'The Neigher' the holy ones high;

---

sun "deceives" him because, like the other dwarfs living underground, he cannot live in its light, and always fears lest sunrise may catch him unaware. The sun's rays have power to turn the dwarfs into stone, and the giantess Hrimgerth meets a similar fate (cf. *Helgakvitha Hjorvarthssonar,* 30). Alvis suffers in the same way; cf. stanza 35.

20. Snorri quotes this stanza in the *Skaldskaparmal. Waverer:* the word is uncertain, the *Prose Edda* manuscripts giving it in various forms. *Blustering Blast:* two *Prose Edda* manuscripts give a totally different word, meaning "The Pounder."

'The Wailer' the giants, 'Roaring Wender' the elves,
In hell 'The Blustering Blast.' "

Thor spake:

21. "Answer me, Alvis! thou knowest all,
Dwarf, of the doom of men:
What call they the calm, that quiet lies,
In each and every world?"

Alvis spake:

22. " 'Calm' men call it, 'The Quiet' the gods,
The Wanes 'The Hush of the Winds';
'The Sultry' the giants, elves 'Day's Stillness,'
The dwarfs 'The Shelter of Day.' "

Thor spake:

23. "Answer me, Alvis! thou knowest all,
Dwarf, of the doom of men:
What call they the sea, whereon men sail,
In each and every world?"

Alvis spake:

24. " 'Sea' men call it, gods 'The Smooth-Lying,'
'The Wave' is it called by the Wanes;

---

22. *Hush,* etc.: the manuscript, by inserting an additional letter, makes the word practically identical with that translated "Kite" in stanza 18. Most editors have agreed as to the emendation.

24. *Drink-Stuff:* Gering translates the word thus; I doubt it, but can suggest nothing better.

'Eel-Home' the giants, 'Drink-Stuff' the elves,
For the dwarfs its name is 'The Deep.' "

Thor spake:

25. "Answer me, Alvis! thou knowest all,
Dwarf, of the doom of men:
What call they the fire, that flames for men,
In each of all the worlds?"

Alvis spake:

26. " 'Fire' men call it, and 'Flame' the gods,
By the Wanes is it 'Wildfire' called;
'The Biter' by giants, 'The Burner' by dwarfs,
'The Swift' in the house of hell."

Thor spake:

27. "Answer me, Alvis! thou knowest all,
Dwarf, of the doom of men:
What call they the wood, that grows for mankind,
In each and every world?"

Alvis spake:

28. "Men call it 'The Wood,' gods 'The Mane of the Field,'

---

26. *Wildfire:* the word may mean any one of various things, including "Wave," which is not unlikely.

28. *In hell:* the word simply means "men," and it is only a guess, though a generally accepted one, that here it refers to the dead.

'Seaweed of Hills' in hell;
'Flame-Food' the giants, 'Fair-Limbed' the elves,
'The Wand' is it called by the Wanes."

Thor spake:

29. "Answer me, Alvis! thou knowest all,
Dwarf, of the doom of men:
What call they the night, the daughter of Nor,
In each and every world?"

Alvis spake:

30. " 'Night' men call it, 'Darkness' gods name it,
'The Hood' the holy ones high;
The giants 'The Lightless,' the elves 'Sleep's Joy,'
The dwarfs 'The Weaver of Dreams.' "

Thor spake:

31. "Answer me, Alvis! thou knowest all,
Dwarf, of the doom of men:
What call they the seed, that is sown by men,
In each and every world?"

---

29. *Nor:* presumably the giant whom Snorri calls Norvi or Narfi, father of Not (Night) and grandfather of Dag (Day). Cf. *Vafthruthnismol,* 25.

30. Snorri quotes this stanza in the *Skaldskaparmal.* The various *Prose Edda* manuscripts differ considerably in naming the gods, the giants, etc. *Lightless:* some manuscripts have "The Unsorrowing."

32. *Grain:* the two words translated "grain" and "corn" apparently both meant primarily barley, and thence grain in

Alvis spake:

32. "Men call it 'Grain,' and 'Corn' the gods,
'Growth' in the world of the Wanes;
'The Eaten' by giants, 'Drink-Stuff' by elves,
In hell 'The Slender Stem.' "

Thor spake:

33. "Answer me, Alvis! thou knowest all,
Dwarf, of the doom of men:
What call they the ale, that is quaffed of men,
In each and every world?"

Alvis spake:

34. " 'Ale' among men, 'Beer' the gods among,
In the world of the Wanes 'The Foaming';
'Bright Draught' with giants, 'Mead' with dwellers in hell,
'The Feast-Draught' with Suttung's sons."

Thor spake:

35. "In a single breast I never have seen
More wealth of wisdom old;

---

general, the first being the commoner term of the two. *Drink-Stuff:* the word is identical with the one used, and commented on, in stanza 24, and again I have followed Gering's interpretation for want of a better one. If his guess is correct, the reference here is evidently to grain as the material from which beer and other drinks are brewed.

34. *Suttung's sons:* these ought to be the giants, but the giants are specifically mentioned in line 3. The phrase "Suttung's sons" occurs in *Skirnismol,* 34, clearly meaning the giants. Concerning Suttung as the possessor of the mead of poetry, cf. *Hovamol,* 104.

But with treacherous wiles must I now betray
thee:
The day has caught thee, dwarf!
(Now the sun shines here in the hall.)"

---

35. Concerning the inability of the dwarfs to endure sunlight, which turns them into stone, cf. stanza 16 and note. Line 5 may be spurious.

BALDRS DRAUMAR

Baldr's Dreams

Introductory Note

Baldrs Draumar is found only in the *Arnamagnæan Codex,* where it follows the *Harbarthsljoth* fragment. It is preserved in various late paper manuscripts, with the title *Vegtamskvitha* (The Lay of Vegtam), which has been used by some editors.

The poem, which contains but fourteen stanzas, has apparently been preserved in excellent condition. Its subject-matter and style link it closely with the *Voluspo.* Four of the five lines of stanza 11 appear, almost without change, in the *Voluspo,* 32-33, and the entire poem is simply an elaboration of the episode outlined in those and the preceding stanzas. It has been suggested that *Baldrs Draumar* and the *Voluspo* may have been by the same author. There is also enough similarity in style between *Baldrs Draumar* and the *Thrymskvitha* (note especially the opening stanza) to give color to Vigfusson's guess that these two poems had a common authorship. In any case, *Baldrs Draumar* presumably assumed its present form not later than the first half of the tenth century.

Whether the Volva (wise-woman) of the poem is identical with the speaker in the *Voluspo* is purely a matter for conjecture. Nothing definitely opposes such a supposition. As in the longer poem she foretells the fall of the gods, so in this case she prophesies the first incident of that fall, the death of Baldr. Here she is called up from the dead by Othin, anxious to know the meaning of Baldr's evil dreams; in the *Voluspo* it is likewise intimated that the Volva has risen from the grave.

The poem, like most of the others in the collection, is essentially dramatic rather than narrative, summarizing a story which was doubtless familiar to every one who heard the poem recited.

---

1. Once were the gods together met,
And the goddesses came and council held,

---

1. Lines 1-3 are identical with *Thrymskvitha,* 13, 1-3. *Baldr:* concerning this best and noblest of the gods, the son of Othin and

And the far-famed ones the truth would find,
Why baleful dreams to Baldr had come.

2. Then Othin rose, the enchanter old,
And the saddle he laid on Sleipnir's back;
Thence rode he down to Niflhel deep,
And the hound he met that came from hell.

3. Bloody he was on his breast before,
At the father of magic he howled from afar;
Forward rode Othin, the earth resounded
Till the house so high of Hel he reached.

4. Then Othin rode to the eastern door,
There, he knew well, was the wise-woman's grave;
Magic he spoke and mighty charms,
Till spell-bound she rose, and in death she spoke:

Frigg, who comes again among the survivors after the final battle, cf. *Voluspo,* 32 and 62, and notes. He is almost never mentioned anywhere except in connection with the story of his death, though Snorri has one short passage praising his virtue and beauty. After stanza 1 two old editions, and one later one, insert four stanzas from late paper manuscripts.

2. *Sleipnir:* Othin's eight-legged horse, the son of Loki and the stallion Svathilfari; cf. *Lokasenna,* 23, and *Grimnismol,* 44, and notes. *Niflhel:* the murky ("nifl") dwelling of Hel, goddess of the dead. *The hound:* Garm; cf. *Voluspo,* 44.

3. *Father of magic:* Othin appears constantly as the god of magic. *Hel:* offspring of Loki and the giantess Angrbotha, as were the wolf Fenrir and Mithgarthsorm. She ruled the world of the unhappy dead, either those who had led evil lives or, according to another tradition, those who had not died in battle. The

5. "What is the man,   to me unknown,
That has made me travel   the troublous road?
I was snowed on with snow,   and smitten with rain,
And drenched with dew;   long was I dead."

Othin spake:

6. "Vegtam my name,   I am Valtam's son;
Speak thou of hell,   for of heaven I know:
For whom are the benches   bright with rings,
And the platforms gay   bedecked with gold?"

The Wise-Woman spake:

7. "Here for Baldr   the mead is brewed,
The shining drink,   and a shield lies o'er it;
But their hope is gone   from the mighty gods.
Unwilling I spake,   and now would be still."

---

manuscript marks line 3 as the beginning of a stanza, and thus the editions vary in their grouping of the lines of this and the succeeding stanzas.

6. The manuscript has no superscriptions indicating the speakers. *Vegtam* ("The Wanderer"): Othin, as usual, conceals his identity, calling himself the son of Valtam ("The Fighter"). In this instance he has unusual need to do so, for as the wise-woman belongs apparently to the race of the giants, she would be unwilling to answer a god's questions. *Heaven:* the word used includes all the upper worlds, in contrast to hell. *Benches,* etc.: the adornment of the benches and raised platforms, or elevated parts of the house, was a regular part of the preparation for a feast of welcome. The text of the two last lines is somewhat uncertain.

7. Grundtvig, followed by Edzardi, thinks a line has been lost between lines 3 and 4.

Othin spake:

8. "Wise-woman, cease not! I seek from thee
All to know that I fain would ask:
Who shall the bane of Baldr become,
And steal the life from Othin's son?"

The Wise-Woman spake:

9. "Hoth thither bears the far-famed branch,
He shall the bane of Baldr become,
And steal the life from Othin's son.
Unwilling I spake, and now would be still."

Othin spake:

10. "Wise-woman, cease not! I seek fiom thee
All to know that I fain would ask:
Who shall vengeance win for the evil work,
Or bring to the flames the slayer of Baldr?"

The Wise-Woman spake:

11. "Rind bears Vali in Vestrsalir,
And one night old fights Othin's son;

---

9. Concerning the blind Hoth, who, at Loki's instigation, cast the fatal mistletoe at Baldr, cf. *Voluspo*, 32-33 and notes. In the manuscript the last line is abbreviated, as also in stanza 11.

10. In the manuscript lines 1-2 are abbreviated, as also in stanza 12.

11. *Rind:* mentioned by Snorri as one of the goddesses. Concerning her son Vali, begotten by Othin for the express purpose of avenging Baldr's death, and his slaying of Hoth the day after his birth, cf. *Voluspo*, 33-34, where the lines of this stanza appear practically verbatim. *Vestrsalir* ("The Western Hall"): not elsewhere mentioned in the poems.

His hands he shall wash not, his hair he shall
comb not,
Till the slayer of Baldr he brings to the flames.
Unwilling I spake, and now would be still."

Othin spake:

12. "Wise-woman, cease not! I seek from thee
All to know that I fain would ask:
What maidens are they who then shall weep,
And toss to the sky the yards of the sails?"

The Wise-Woman spake:

13. "Vegtam thou art not, as erstwhile I thought;
Othin thou art, the enchanter old."

Othin spake:

"No wise-woman art thou, nor wisdom hast;
Of giants three the mother art thou."

The Wise-Woman spake:

14. "Home ride, Othin, be ever proud;
For no one of men shall seek me more

---

12. The manuscript marks the third line as the beginning of a stanza; something may have been lost. Lines 3-4 are thoroughly obscure. According to Bugge the maidens who are to weep for Baldr are the daughters of the sea-god Ægir, the waves, whose grief will be so tempestuous that they will toss the ships up to the very sky. "Yards of the sails" is a doubtfully accurate rendering; the two words, at any rate in later Norse nautical speech, meant respectively the "tack" and the "sheet" of the square sail.

13. Possibly two separate stanzas. *Enchanter:* the meaning of the original word is most uncertain.

Till Loki wanders loose from his bonds,
And to the last strife the destroyers come."

---

14. Concerning Loki's escape and his relation to the destruction of the gods, cf. *Voluspo,* 35 and 51, and notes. While the wise-woman probably means only that she will never speak again till the end of the world, it has been suggested, and is certainly possible, that she intends to give Loki her counsel, thus revenging herself on Othin.

RIGSTHULA

The Song of Rig

Introductory Note

The *Rigsthula* is found in neither of the principal codices. The only manuscript containing it is the so-called *Codex Wormanius,* a manuscript of Snorri's *Prose Edda.* The poem appears on the last sheet of this manuscript, which unluckily is incomplete, and thus the end of the poem is lacking. In the *Codex Wormanius* itself the poem has no title, but a fragmentary parchment included with it calls the poem the *Rigsthula.* Some late paper manuscripts give it the title of *Rigsmol.*

The *Rigsthula* is essentially unlike anything else which editors have agreed to include in the so-called *Edda.* It is a definitely cultural poem, explaining, on a mythological basis, the origin of the different castes of early society: the thralls, the peasants, and the warriors. From the warriors, finally, springs one who is destined to become a king, and thus the whole poem is a song in praise of the royal estate. This fact in itself would suffice to indicate that the *Rigsthula* was not composed in Iceland, where for centuries kings were regarded with profound disapproval.

Not only does the *Rigsthula* praise royalty, but it has many of the earmarks of a poem composed in praise of a particular king. The manuscript breaks off at a most exasperating point, just as the connection between the mythical "Young Kon" (Konr ungr, konungr, "king"; but cf. stanza 44, note) and the monarch in question is about to be established. Owing to the character of the Norse settlements in Iceland, Ireland, and the western islands generally, search for a specific king leads back to either Norway or Denmark; despite the arguments advanced by Edzardi, Vigfusson, Powell, and others, it seems most improbable that such a poem should have been produced elsewhere than on the Continent, the region where Scandinavian royalty most flourished. Finnur Jonsson's claim for Norway, with Harald the Fair-Haired as the probable king in question, is much less impressive than Mogk's ingenious demonstration that the poem was in all probability composed in Denmark, in honor of either Gorm the Old or Harald Blue-Tooth. His proof is based chiefly on the evidence provided by stanza 49, and is summarized in the note to that stanza.

The poet, however, was certainly not a Dane, but probably a wandering Norse singer, who may have had a dozen homes, and who clearly had spent much time in some part of the western island world chiefly inhabited by Celts. The extent of Celtic influence on the Eddic poems in general is a matter of sharp dispute. Powell, for example, claims almost all the poems for the "Western Isles," and attributes nearly all their good qualities to Celtic influence. Without here attempting to enter into the details of the argument, it may be said that the weight of authoritative opinion, while clearly recognizing the marks of Celtic influence in the poems, is against this view; contact between the roving Norsemen of Norway and Iceland and the Celts of Ireland and the "Western Isles," and particularly the Orkneys, was so extensive as to make the presumption of an actual Celtic home for the poems seem quite unnecessary.

In the case of the *Rigsthula* the poet unquestionably had not only picked up bits of the Celtic speech (the name Rig itself is almost certainly of Celtic origin, and there are various other Celtic words employed), but also had caught something of the Celtic literary spirit. This explains the cultural nature of the poem, quite foreign to Norse poetry in general. On the other hand, the style as a whole is vigorously Norse, and thus the explanation that the poem was composed by an itinerant Norse poet who had lived for some time in the Celtic islands, and who was on a visit to the court of a Danish king, fits the ascertainable facts exceedingly well. As Christianity was introduced into Denmark around 960, the *Rigsthula* is not likely to have been composed much after that date, and probably belongs to the first half of the tenth century. Gorm the Old died about the year 935, and was succeeded by Harald Blue-Tooth, who died about 985.

The fourteenth (or late thirteenth) century annotator identifies Rig with Heimdall, but there is nothing in the poem itself, and very little anywhere else, to warrant this, and it seems likely that the poet had Othin, and not Heimdall, in mind, his purpose being to trace the origin of the royal estate to the chief of the gods. The evidence bearing on this identification is briefly summed up in the note on the introductory prose passage, but the question involves complex and baffling problems in mythology, and from very early times the status of Heimdall was unquestionably confusing to the Norse mind.

Rigsthula

They tell in old stories that one of the gods, whose name was Heimdall, went on his way along a certain seashore, and came to a dwelling, where he called himself Rig. According to these stories is the following poem:

1. Men say there went by ways so green
Of old the god, the aged and wise,
Mighty and strong did Rig go striding.
. . . .

Prose. It would be interesting to know how much the annotator meant by the phrase *old stories.* Was he familiar with the tradition in forms other than that of the poem? If so, his introductory note was scanty, for, outside of identifying *Rig* as *Heimdall,* he provides no information not found in the poem. Probably he meant simply to refer to the poem itself as a relic of antiquity, and the identification of Rig as Heimdall may well have been an attempt at constructive criticism of his own. The note was presumably written somewhere about 1300, or even later, and there is no reason for crediting the annotator with any considerable knowledge of mythology. There is little to favor the identification of Rig with Heimdall, the watchman of the gods, beyond a few rather vague passages in the other poems. Thus in *Voluspo,* 1, the Volva asks hearing "from Heimdall's sons both high and low"; in *Grimnismol,* 13, there is a very doubtful line which may mean that Heimdall "o'er men holds sway, it is said," and in "the Short Voluspo" (*Hyndluljoth,* 40) he is called "the kinsman of men." On the other hand, everything in the *Rigsthula,* including the phrase "the aged and wise" in stanza 1, and the references to runes in stanzas 36, 44, and 46, fits Othin exceedingly well. It seems probable that the annotator was wrong, and that Rig is Othin, and not Heimdall. *Rig:* almost certainly based on the Old Irish word for "king," "ri" or "rig."

1. No gap is indicated, but editors have generally assumed one. Some editors, however, add line 1 of stanza 2 to stanza 1.

2. Forward he went on the midmost way,
He came to a dwelling, a door on its posts;
In did he fare, on the floor was a fire,
Two hoary ones by the hearth there sat,
Ai and Edda, in olden dress.

3. Rig knew well wise words to speak,
Soon in the midst of the room he sat,
And on either side the others were.

4. A loaf of bread did Edda bring,
Heavy and thick and swollen with husks;
Forth on the table she set the fare,
And broth for the meal in a bowl there was.
(Calf's flesh boiled was the best of the dainties.)

5. Rig knew well wise words to speak,
Thence did he rise, made ready to sleep;
Soon in the bed himself did he lay,
And on either side the others were.

---

2. Most editions make line 5 a part of the stanza, as here, but some indicate it as the sole remnant of one or more stanzas descriptive of Ai and Edda, just as Afi and Amma, Fathir and Mothir, are later described. *Ai and Edda:* Great-Grandfather and Great-Grandmother; the latter name was responsible for Jakob Grimm's famous guess at the meaning of the word "Edda" as applied to the whole collection (cf. Introduction).

3. A line may have been lost from this stanza.

4. Line 5 has generally been rejected as spurious.

5. The manuscript has lines 1-2 in inverse order, but marks the word "Rig" as the beginning of a stanza.

6. Thus was he there for three nights long,
Then forward he went on the midmost way,
And so nine months were soon passed by.

7. A son bore Edda, with water they sprinkled him,
With a cloth his hair so black they covered;
Thræll they named him, ...

8. The skin was wrinkled and rough on his hands,
Knotted his knuckles, ...
Thick his fingers, and ugly his face,
Twisted his back, and big his heels.

9. He began to grow, and to gain in strength,
Soon of his might good use he made;

---

6. The manuscript does not indicate that these lines form a separate stanza, and as only one line and a fragment of another are left of stanza 7, the editions have grouped the lines in all sorts of ways, with, of course, various conjectures as to where lines may have been lost.

7. After line 1 the manuscript has only four words: "cloth," "black," "named," and "Thræll." No gap is anywhere indicated. Editors have pieced out the passage in various ways. *Water,* etc.: concerning the custom of sprinkling water on children, which long antedated the introduction of Christianity, cf. *Hovamol,* 159 and note. *Black:* dark hair, among the blond Scandinavians, was the mark of a foreigner, hence of a slave. *Thræll:* Thrall or Slave.

8. In the manuscript line 1 of stanza 9 stands before stanza 8, neither line being capitalized as the beginning of a stanza. I have followed Bugge's rearrangement. The manuscript indicates no gap in line 2, but nearly all editors have assumed one, Grundtvig supplying "and rough his nails."

9. The manuscript marks line 2 as the beginning of a stanza.

With bast he bound, and burdens carried,
Home bore faggots the whole day long.

10. One came to their home, crooked her legs,
Stained were her feet, and sunburned her arms,
Flat was her nose; her name was Thir.

11. Soon in the midst of the room she sat,
By her side there sat the son of the house;
They whispered both, and the bed made ready,
Thræll and Thir, till the day was through.

12. Children they had, they lived and were happy,
Fjosnir and Klur they were called, methinks,
Hreim and Kleggi, Kefsir, Fulnir,
Drumb, Digraldi, Drott and Leggjaldi,
Lut and Hosvir; the house they cared for,
Ground they dunged, and swine they guarded,
Goats they tended, and turf they dug.

---

10. A line may well have dropped out, but the manuscript is too uncertain as to the stanza-divisions to make any guess safe. *Crooked:* the word in the original is obscure. *Stained:* literally, "water was on her soles." *Thir:* "Serving-Woman."

12. There is some confusion as to the arrangement of the lines and division into stanzas of 12 and 13. The names mean: *Fjosnir,* "Cattle-Man"; *Klur,* "The Coarse"; *Hreim,* "The Shouter"; *Kleggi,* "The Horse-Fly"; *Kefsir,* "Concubine-Keeper"; *Fulnir,* "The Stinking"; *Drumb,* "The Log"; *Digraldi,* "The Fat"; *Drott,* "The Sluggard"; *Leggjaldi,* "The Big-Legged"; *Lut,* "The Bent"; *Hosvir,* "The Grey."

13. Daughters had they, Drumba and Kumba,
Ökkvinkalfa, Arinnefja,
Ysja and Ambott, Eikintjasna,
Totrughypja and Tronubeina;
And thence has risen the race of thralls.

14. Forward went Rig, his road was straight,
To a hall he came, and a door there hung;
In did he fare, on the floor was a fire:
Afi and Amma owned the house.

15. There sat the twain, and worked at their tasks:
The man hewed wood for the weaver's beam;
His beard was trimmed, o'er his brow a curl,
His clothes fitted close; in the corner a chest.

16. The woman sat and the distaff wielded,
At the weaving with arms outstretched she worked;
On her head was a band, on her breast a smock;
On her shoulders a kerchief with clasps there was.

---

13. The names mean: *Drumba,* "The Log"; *Kumba,* "The Stumpy"; *Ökkvinkalfa,* "Fat-Legged"; *Arinnefja,* "Homely-Nosed"; *Ysja,* "The Noisy"; *Ambott,* "The Servant"; *Eikintjasna,* "The Oaken Peg" (?); *Totrughypja,* "Clothed in Rags"; *Tronubeina,* "Crane-Legged."

14. In the manuscript line 4 stands after line 4 of stanza 16, but several editors have rearranged the lines, as here. *Afi and Amma:* Grandfather and Grandmother.

15. There is considerable confusion among the editors as to where this stanza begins and ends.

16. The manuscript marks line 3 as the beginning of a stanza.

17. Rig knew well wise words to speak,
Soon in the midst of the room he sat,
And on either side the others were.

18. Then took Amma ....
The vessels full with the fare she set,
Calf's flesh boiled was the best of the dainties.

19. Rig knew well wise words to speak,
He rose from the board, made ready to sleep;
Soon in the bed himself did he lay,
And on either side the others were.

20. Thus was he there for three nights long,
Then forward he went on the midmost way,
And so nine months were soon passed by.

21. A son bore Amma, with water they sprinkled him,
Karl they named him; in a cloth she wrapped him,
He was ruddy of face, and flashing his eyes.

---

17. The manuscript jumps from stanza 17, line 1, to stanza 19, line 2. Bugge points out that the copyist's eye was presumably led astray by the fact that 17, 1, and 19, 1, were identical. Lines 2-3 of 17 are supplied from stanzas 3 and 29.

18. I have followed Bugge's conjectural construction of the missing stanza, taking lines 2 and 3 from stanzas 31 and 4.

19. The manuscript marks line 2 as the beginning of a stanza.

20. The manuscript omits line 2, supplied by analogy with stanza 6.

22. He began to grow, and to gain in strength,
Oxen he ruled, and plows made ready,
Houses he built, and barns he fashioned,
Carts he made, and the plow he managed.

23. Home did they bring the bride for Karl,
In goatskins clad, and keys she bore;
Snör was her name, 'neath the veil she sat;
A home they made ready, and rings exchanged,
The bed they decked, and a dwelling made.

24. Sons they had, they lived and were happy:
Hal and Dreng, Holth, Thegn and Smith,
Breith and Bondi, Bundinskeggi,
Bui and Boddi, Brattskegg and Segg.

---

21. Most editors assume a lacuna, after either line 2 or line 3. Sijmons assumes, on the analogy of stanza 8, that a complete stanza describing *Karl* ("Yeoman") has been lost between stanzas 21 and 22.

22. No line indicated in the manuscript as beginning a stanza. *Cart:* the word in the original, "kartr," is one of the clear signs of the Celtic influence noted in the introduction.

23. *Bring:* the word literally means "drove in a wagon"—a mark of the bride's social status. *Snör:* "Daughter-in-Law." Bugge, followed by several editors, maintains that line 4 was wrongly interpolated here from a missing stanza describing the marriage of Kon.

24. No line indicated in the manuscript as beginning a stanza. The names mean: *Hal,* "Man"; *Dreng,* "The Strong"; *Holth,* "The Holder of Land"; *Thegn,* "Freeman"; *Smith,* "Craftsman"; *Breith,* "The Broad-Shouldered"; *Bondi,* "Yeoman"; *Bundinskeggi,* "With Beard Bound" (i.e., not allowed to hang unkempt); *Bui,* "Dwelling-Owner"; *Boddi,* "Farm-Holder"; *Brattskegg,* "With Beard Carried High"; *Segg,* "Man."

25. Daughters they had, and their names are here:
Snot, Bruth, Svanni, Svarri, Sprakki,
Fljoth, Sprund and Vif, Feima, Ristil:
And thence has risen the yeomen's race.

26. Thence went Rig, his road was straight,
A hall he saw, the doors faced south;
The portal stood wide, on the posts was a ring,
Then in he fared; the floor was strewn.

27. Within two gazed in each other's eyes,
Fathir and Mothir, and played with their fingers;
There sat the house-lord, wound strings for the bow,
Shafts he fashioned, and bows he shaped.

28. The lady sat, at her arms she looked,
She smoothed the cloth, and fitted the sleeves;
Gay was her cap, on her breast were clasps,
Broad was her train, of blue was her gown,

---

25. No line indicated in the manuscript as beginning a stanza. The names mean: *Snot,* "Worthy Woman"; *Bruth,* "Bride"; *Svanni,* "The Slender"; *Svarri,* "The Proud"; *Sprakki,* "The Fair"; *Fljoth,* "Woman" (?); *Sprund,* "The Proud"; *Vif,* "Wife"; *Feima,* "The Bashful"; *Ristil,* "The Graceful."

26. Many editors make a stanza out of line 4 and lines 1-2 of the following stanza. *Strewn:* with fresh straw in preparation for a feast; cf. *Thrymskvitha, 22.*

27. *Fathir and Mothir:* Father and Mother. Perhaps lines 3-4 should form a stanza with 28, 1-2.

28. Bugge thinks lines 5-6, like 23, 4, got in here from the lost stanzas describing Kon's bride and his marriage.

Her brows were bright, her breast was shining,
Whiter her neck than new-fallen snow.

29. Rig knew well wise words to speak,
Soon in the midst of the room he sat,
And on either side the others were.

30. Then Mothir brought a broidered cloth,
Of linen bright, and the board she covered;
And then she took the loaves so thin,
And laid them, white from the wheat, on the cloth.

31. Then forth she brought the vessels full,
With silver covered, and set before them,
Meat all browned, and well-cooked birds;
In the pitcher was wine, of plate were the cups,
So drank they and talked till the day was gone.

32. Rig knew well wise words to speak,
Soon did he rise, made ready to sleep;
So in the bed himself did he lay,
And on either side the others were.

---

31. The manuscript of lines 1-3 is obviously defective, as there are too many words for two lines, and not enough for the full three. The meaning, however, is clearly very much as indicated in the translation. Gering's emendation, which I have followed, consists simply in shifting "set before them" from the first line to the second—where the manuscript has no verb,—and supplying the verb "brought" in line 1. The various editions contain all sorts of suggestions.

32. The manuscript begins both line 1 and line 2 with a cap-

33. Thus was he there for three nights long,
Then forward he went on the midmost way,
And so nine months were soon passed by.

34. A son had Mothir, in silk they wrapped him,
With water they sprinkled him, Jarl he was;
Blond was his hair, and bright his cheeks,
Grim as a snake's were his glowing eyes.

35. To grow in the house did Jarl begin,
Shields he brandished, and bow-strings wound,
Bows he shot, and shafts he fashioned,
Arrows he loosened, and lances wielded,
Horses he rode, and hounds unleashed,
Swords he handled, and sounds he swam.

36. Straight from the grove came striding Rig,
Rig came striding, and runes he taught him;
By his name he called him, as son he claimed him,

---

ital preceded by a period, which has led to all sorts of strange stanza-combinations and guesses at lost lines in the various editions. The confusion includes stanza 33, wherein no line is marked in the manuscript as beginning a stanza.

34. *Jarl:* "Nobly-Born."

35. Various lines have been regarded as interpolations, 3 and 6 being most often thus rejected.

36. Lines 1, 2, and 5 all begin with capitals preceded by periods, a fact which, taken in conjunction with the obviously defective state of the following stanza, has led to all sorts of conjectural emendations. The exact significance of Rig's giving his own name to Jarl (cf. stanza 46), and thus recognizing him, potentially at least, as a king, depends on the conditions under

And bade him hold his heritage wide,
His heritage wide, the ancient homes.

37. ....
Forward he rode through the forest dark,
O'er the frosty crags, till a hall he found.

38. His spear he shook, his shield he brandished,
His horse he spurred, with his sword he hewed;
Wars he raised, and reddened the field,
Warriors slew he, and land he won.

39. Eighteen halls ere long did he hold,
Wealth did he get, and gave to all,
Stones and jewels and slim-flanked steeds,
Rings he offered, and arm-rings shared.

40. His messengers went by the ways so wet,
And came to the hall where Hersir dwelt;
His daughter was fair and slender-fingered,
Erna the wise the maiden was.

---

which the poem was composed (cf. Introductory Note). The whole stanza, particularly the reference to the teaching of magic (runes), fits Othin far better than Heimdall.

37. Something—one or two lines, or a longer passage—has clearly been lost, describing the beginning of Jarl's journey. Yet many editors, relying on the manuscript punctuation, make 37 and 38 into a single stanza.

39. The manuscript marks both lines 1 and 2 as beginning stanzas.

40. *Hersir:* "Lord"; the hersir was, in the early days before the establishment of a kingdom in Norway, the local chief, and

41. Her hand they sought, and home they brought her,
Wedded to Jarl the veil she wore;
Together they dwelt, their joy was great,
Children they had, and happy they lived.

42. Bur was the eldest, and Barn the next,
Joth and Athal, Arfi, Mog,
Nith and Svein, soon they began—
Sun and Nithjung— to play and swim;
Kund was one, and the youngest Kon.

43. Soon grew up the sons of Jarl,
Beasts they tamed, and bucklers rounded,
Shafts they fashioned, and spears they shook.

44. But Kon the Young learned runes to use,
Runes everlasting, the runes of life;

---

hence the highest recognized authority. During and after the time of Harald the Fair-Haired the name lost something of its distinction, the hersir coming to take rank below the jarl. *Erna:* "The Capable."

42. The names mean: *Bur,* "Son"; *Barn,* "Child"; *Joth,* "Child"; *Athal,* "Offspring"; *Arfi,* "Heir"; *Mog,* "Son"; *Nith,* "Descendant"; *Svein,* "Boy"; *Sun,* "Son"; *Nithjung,* "Descendant"; *Kund,* "Kinsman"; *Kon,* "Son" (of noble birth). Concerning the use made of this last name, see note on stanza 44. It is curious that there is no list of the daughters of Jarl and Erna, and accordingly Vigfusson inserts here the names listed in stanza 25. Grundtvig rearranges the lines of stanzas 42 and 43.

44. The manuscript indicates no line as beginning a stanza. *Kon the Young:* a remarkable bit of fanciful etymology; the

Soon could he well the warriors shield,
Dull the swordblade, and still the seas.

45. Bird-chatter learned he, flames could he lessen,
Minds could quiet, and sorrows calm;
. . . .
The might and strength of twice four men.

46. With Rig-Jarl soon the runes he shared,
More crafty he was, and greater his wisdom;
The right he sought, and soon he won it,
Rig to be called, and runes to know.

47. Young Kon rode forth through forest and grove,
Shafts let loose, and birds he lured;
There spake a crow on a bough that sat:
"Why lurest thou, Kon, the birds to come?

---

phrase is 'Konr ungr," which could readily be contracted into "Konungr," the regular word meaning "king." The "kon" part is actually not far out, but the second syllable of "konungr" has nothing to do with "ungr" meaning "young." *Runes:* a long list of just such magic charms, dulling swordblades, quenching flames, and so on, is given in *Hovamol,* 147-163.

45. The manuscript indicates no line as beginning a stanza. *Minds:* possibly "seas," the word being doubtful. Most editors assume the gap as indicated.

46. The manuscript indicates no line as beginning a stanza. *Rig-Jarl:* Kon's father; cf. stanza 36.

47. This stanza has often been combined with 48, either as a whole or in part. *Crow:* birds frequently play the part of mentor in Norse literature; cf., for example, *Helgakvitha Hundingsbana* I, 5, and *Fafnismol,* 32.

48. " 'Twere better forth on thy steed to fare,
. . . . and the host to slay.

49. "The halls of Dan and Danp are noble,
Greater their wealth than thou hast gained;
Good are they at guiding the keel,
Trying of weapons, and giving of wounds.

* * *

---

48. This fragment is not indicated as a separate stanza in the manuscript. Perhaps half a line has disappeared, or, as seems more likely, the gap includes two lines and a half. Sijmons actually constructs these lines, largely on the basis of stanzas 35 and 38. Bugge fills in the half-line lacuna as indicated above with "The sword to wield."

49. *Dan and Danp:* These names are largely responsible for the theory that the *Rigsthula* was composed in Denmark. According to the Latin epitome of the *Skjöldungasaga* by Arngrimur Jonsson, "Rig (Rigus) was a man not the least among the great ones of his time. He married the daughter of a certain Danp, lord of Danpsted, whose name was Dana; and later, having won the royal title for his province, left as his heir his son by Dana, called Dan or Danum, all of whose subjects were called Danes." This may or may not be conclusive, and it is a great pity that the manuscript breaks off abruptly at this stanza.

HYNDLULJOTH

The Poem of Hyndla

Introductory Note

The *Hyndluljoth* is found in neither of the great manuscripts of the *Poetic Edda,* but is included in the so-called *Flateyjarbok* (Book of the Flat Island), an enormous compilation made somewhere about 1400. The lateness of this manuscript would of itself be enough to cast a doubt upon the condition in which the poem has been preserved, and there can be no question that what we have of it is in very poor shape. It is, in fact, two separate poems, or parts of them, clumsily put together. The longer one, the *Poem of Hyndla* proper, is chiefly a collection of names, not strictly mythological but belonging to the semi-historical hero-sagas of Norse tradition. The wise-woman, Hyndla, being asked by Freyja to trace the ancestry of her favorite, Ottar, for the purpose of deciding a wager, gives a complex genealogy including many of the heroes who appear in the popular sagas handed down from days long before the Icelandic settlements. The poet was learned, but without enthusiasm; it is not likely that he composed the *Hyndluljoth* much before the twelfth century, though the material of which it is compounded must have been very much older. Although the genealogies are essentially continental, the poem seems rather like a product of the archæological period of Iceland.

Inserted bodily in the *Hyndluljoth* proper is a fragment of fifty-one lines, taken from a poem of which, by a curious chance, we know the name. Snorri quotes one stanza of it, calling it "the short *Voluspo.*" The fragment preserved gives, of course, no indication of the length of the original poem, but it shows that it was a late and very inferior imitation of the great *Voluspo.* Like the *Hyndluljoth* proper, it apparently comes from the twelfth century; but there is nothing whatever to indicate that the two poems were the work of the same man, or were ever connected in any way until some blundering copyist mixed them up. Certainly the connection did not exist in the middle of the thirteenth century, when Snorri quoted "the short *Voluspo.*"

Neither poem is of any great value, either as mythology or as poetry. The author of "the short *Voluspo*" seems, indeed, to have been more or less confused as to his facts; and both poets were too late to feel anything of the enthusiasm of the earlier school. The names of Hyndla's heroes, of course, suggest an unlimited number of stories, but as most of these have no direct relation to the poems of the *Edda,* I have limited the notes to a mere record of who the persons mentioned were, and the saga-groups in which they appeared.

Freyja spake:

1. "Maiden, awake! wake thee, my friend,
My sister Hyndla, in thy hollow cave!
Already comes darkness, and ride must we
To Valhall to seek the sacred hall.

2. "The favor of Heerfather seek we to find,
To his followers gold he gladly gives;
To Hermoth gave he helm and mail-coat,
And to Sigmund he gave a sword as gift.

---

1. *Freyja:* The names of the speakers do not appear in the manuscripts. On Freyja cf. *Voluspo,* 21 and note; *Skirnismol,* introductory prose and note; *Lokasenna,* introductory prose and note. As stanzas 9-10 show, Ottar has made a wager of his entire inheritance with Angantyr regarding the relative loftiness of their ancestry, and by rich offerings (Hyndla hints at less commendable methods) has induced Freyja to assist him in establishing his genealogy. Freyja, having turned Ottar for purposes of disguise into a boar, calls on the giantess *Hyndla* ("She-Dog") to aid her. Hyndla does not appear elsewhere in the poems.

2. *Heerfather:* Othin; cf. *Voluspo,* 30. *Hermoth:* mentioned in the *Prose Edda* as a son of Othin who is sent to Hel to ask for the return of the slain Baldr. *Sigmund:* according to the *Volsungasaga* Sigmund was the son of Volsung, and hence Othin's great-great-grandson (note that Wagner eliminates all the intervening generations by the simple expedient of using

3. "Triumph to some, and treasure to others,
To many wisdom and skill in words,
Fair winds to the sailor, to the singer his art,
And a manly heart to many a hero.

4. "Thor shall I honor, and this shall I ask,
That his favor true mayst thou ever find;
. . . .
Though little the brides of the giants he loves.

5. "From the stall now one of thy wolves lead forth,
And along with my boar shalt thou let him run;
For slow my boar goes on the road of the gods,
And I would not weary my worthy steed."

Hyndla spake:

6. "Falsely thou askest me, Freyja, to go,
For so in the glance of thine eyes I see;

Volsung's name as one of Othin's many appellations). Sigmund alone was able to draw from the tree the sword which a mysterious stranger (Othin, of course) had thrust into it (compare the first act of Wagner's *Die Walküre*).

3. Sijmons suggests that this stanza may be an interpolation.

4. No lacuna after line 2 is indicated in the manuscript. Editors have attempted various experiments in rearranging this and the following stanza.

5. Some editors, following Simrock, assign this whole stanza to Hyndla; others assign to her lines 3-4. Giving the entire stanza to Freyja makes better sense than any other arrangement, but is dependent on changing the manuscript's "thy" in line 3 to "my," as suggested by Bugge. The boar on which Freyja rides ("my worthy steed") is, of course, Ottar.

6. Hyndla detects Ottar, and accuses Freyja of having her

On the way of the slain thy lover goes with thee,
Ottar the young, the son of Instein."

Freyja spake:

7. "Wild dreams, methinks, are thine when thou sayest
My lover is with me on the way of the slain;
There shines the boar with bristles of gold,
Hildisvini, he who was made
By Dain and Nabbi, the cunning dwarfs.

8. "Now let us down from our saddles leap,
And talk of the race of the heroes twain;
The men who were born of the gods above,
. . . .

9. "A wager have made in the foreign metal
Ottar the young and Angantyr;

---

lover with her. Unless Ottar is identical with Oth (cf. *Voluspo*, 25 and note), which seems most unlikely, there is no other reference to this love affair. *The way of the slain:* the road to Valhall.

7. Various experiments have been made in condensing the stanza into four lines, or in combining it with stanza 8. *Hildisvini* ("Battle-Swine"): perhaps Freyja refers to the boar with golden bristles given, according to Snorri, to her brother Freyr by the dwarfs. *Dain:* a dwarf; cf. *Voluspo*, 11. *Nabbi:* a dwarf nowhere else mentioned.

8. The first line is obviously corrupt in the manuscript, and has been variously emended. The general assumption is that in the interval between stanzas 7 and 8 Freyja and Hyndla have arrived at Valhall. No lacuna is indicated in the manuscript.

9. *Foreign metal:* gold. The word *valr,* meaning "foreign,"

We must guard, for the hero young to have,
His father's wealth, the fruits of his race.

10. "For me a shrine of stones he made,—
And now to glass the rock has grown;—
Oft with the blood of beasts was it red;
In the goddesses ever did Ottar trust.

11. "Tell to me now the ancient names,
And the races of all that were born of old:
Who are of the Skjoldungs, who of the Skilfings,
Who of the Othlings, who of the Ylfings,
Who are the free-born, who are the high-born,
The noblest of men that in Mithgarth dwell?"

---

and akin to "Welsh," is interesting in this connection, and some editors interpret it frankly as "Celtic," i.e., Irish.

10. *To glass:* i.e., the constant fires on the altar have fused the stone into glass. Glass beads, etc., were of very early use, though the use of glass for windows probably did not begin in Iceland much before 1200.

11. Possibly two stanzas, or perhaps one with interpolations. The manuscript omits the first half of line 4, here filled out from stanza 16, line 2. *Skjoldungs:* the descendants of Skjold, a mythical king who was Othin's son and the ancestor of the Danish kings; cf. Snorri's *Edda, Skaldskaparmal,* 43. *Skilfings:* mentioned by Snorri as descendants of King Skelfir, a mythical ruler in "the East." In *Grimnismol,* 54, the name Skilfing appears as one of Othin's many appellations. *Othlings:* Snorri derives this race from Authi, the son of Halfdan the Old (cf. stanza 14). *Ylfings:* some editors have changed this to "Ynglings," as in stanza 16, referring to the descendants of Yng or Yngvi, another son of Halfdan, but the reference may be to the same mythical family to which Helgi Hundingsbane belonged (cf. *Helgakvitha Hundingsbana* I, 5).

Hyndla spake:

12. "Thou art, Ottar, the son of Instein,
And Instein the son of Alf the Old,
Alf of Ulf, Ulf of Sæfari,
And Sæfari's father was Svan the Red.

13. "Thy mother, bright with bracelets fair,
Hight, methinks, the priestess Hledis;
Frothi her father, and Friaut her mother;—
Her race of the mightiest men must seem.

14. "Of old the noblest of all was Ali,
Before him Halfdan, foremost of Skjoldungs;
Famed were the battles the hero fought,
To the corners of heaven his deeds were carried.

15. "Strengthened by Eymund, the strongest of men,
Sigtrygg he slew with the ice-cold sword;
His bride was Almveig, the best of women,
And eighteen boys did Almveig bear him.

---

12. *Instein:* mentioned in the *Halfssaga* as one of the warriors of King Half of Horthaland (the so-called Halfsrekkar). The others mentioned in this stanza appear in one of the later mythical accounts of the settlement of Norway.

14. Stanzas 14-16 are clearly interpolated, as Friaut (stanza 13, line 3) is the daughter of Hildigun (stanza 17, line 1). *Halfdan* the Old, a mythical king of Denmark, called by Snorri "the most famous of all kings," of whom it was foretold that "for three hundred years there should be no woman and no man in his line who was not of great repute." After the slaying of Sigtrygg he married Almveig (or Alvig), daughter of King Eymund of Holmgarth (i.e., Russia), who bore him eighteen

16. "Hence come the Skjoldungs, hence the Skilfings,
Hence the Othlings, hence the Ynglings,
Hence come the free-born, hence the high-born,
The noblest of men that in Mithgarth dwell:
And all are thy kinsmen, Ottar, thou fool!

17. "Hildigun then her mother hight,
The daughter of Svava and Sækonung;
And all are thy kinsmen, Ottar, thou fool!
It is much to know,— wilt thou hear yet more?

18. "The mate of Dag was a mother of heroes,
Thora, who bore him the bravest of fighters,
Frathmar and Gyrth and the Frekis twain,
Am and Jofurmar, Alf the Old;
It is much to know,— wilt thou hear yet more?

19. "Her husband was Ketil, the heir of Klypp,
He was of thy mother the mother's-father;

---

sons, nine at one birth. These nine were all slain, but the other nine were traditionally the ancestors of the most famous families in Northern hero lore.

16. Compare stanza 11. All or part of this stanza may be interpolated.

17. *Hildigun* (or Hildiguth): with this the poem returns to Ottar's direct ancestry, Hildigun being Friaut's mother. *Line 4:* cf. the refrain-line in the *Voluspo* (stanzas 27, 29, etc.).

18. Another interpolation, as Ketil (stanza 19, line 1) is the husband of Hildigun (stanza 17). *Dag:* one of Halfdan's sons, and ancestor of the Döglings. Line 5 may be a late addition.

19. *Ketil:* the semi-mythical Ketil Hortha-Kari, from whom various Icelandic families traced their descent. *Hoalf:* probably King Half of Horthaland, hero of the *Halfssaga,* and son of Hjorleif and Hild (cf. stanza 12, note).

Before the days of Kari was Frothi,
And born of Hild was Hoalf then.

20. "Next was Nanna, daughter of Nokkvi,
Thy father's kinsman her son became;
Old is the line, and longer still,
And all are thy kinsmen, Ottar, thou fool!

21. "Isolf and Osolf, the sons of Olmoth,
Whose wife was Skurhild, the daughter of Skekkil,
Count them among the heroes mighty,
And all are thy kinsmen, Ottar, thou fool!

22. "Gunnar the Bulwark, Grim the Hardy,
Thorir the Iron-shield, Ulf the Gaper,
Brodd and Hörvir both did I know;
In the household they were of Hrolf the Old.

---

20. *Nanna:* the manuscript has "Manna." Of Nanna and her father, Nokkvi, we know nothing, but apparently Nanna's son married a sister of Instein, Ottar's father.

21. *Olmoth:* one of the sons of Ketil Hortha-Kari. *Line 4:* here, and generally hereafter when it appears in the poem, this refrain-line is abbreviated in the manuscript to the word "all."

22. An isolated stanza, which some editors place after stanza 24, others combining lines 1-2 with the fragmentary stanza 23. In the manuscript lines 3-4 stand after stanza 24, where they fail to connect clearly with anything. *Hrolf the Old:* probably King Hrolf Gautreksson of Gautland, in the saga relating to whom (*Fornaldar sögur* III, 57 ff.) appear the names of Thorir the Iron-shield and Grim Thorkelsson.

23. "Hervarth, Hjorvarth, Hrani, Angantyr,
Bui and Brami, Barri and Reifnir,
Tind and Tyrfing, the Haddings twain,—
And all are thy kinsmen, Ottar, thou fool!

24. "Eastward in Bolm were born of old
The sons of Arngrim and Eyfura;
With berserk-tumult and baleful deed
Like fire o'er land and sea they fared,—
And all are thy kinsmen, Ottar, thou fool!

25. "The sons of Jormunrek all of yore
To the gods in death were as offerings given;

---

23. Stanzas 23 and 24 name the twelve Berserkers, the sons of Arngrim and Eyfura, the story of whom is told in the *Hervararsaga* and the *Orvar-Oddssaga*. Saxo Grammaticus tells of the battle between them and Hjalmar and Orvar-Odd. Line 1 does not appear in the manuscript, but is added from the list of names given in the sagas. The Berserkers were wild warriors, distinguished above all by the fits of frenzy to which they were subject in battle; during these fits they howled like wild beasts, foamed at the mouth, and gnawed the iron rims of their shields. At such times they were proof against steel or fire, but when the fever abated they were weak. The etymology of the word *berserk* is disputed; probably, however, it means "bear-shirt."

24. The manuscript omits the first half of line 1, here supplied from the *Orvar-Oddssaga*. *Bolm:* probably the island of Bolmsö, in the Swedish province of Smaland. In the manuscript and in most editions stanza 24 is followed by lines 3-4 of stanza 22. Some editors reject line 5 as spurious.

25. In the manuscript line 1 stands after line 4 of stanza 29. Probably a stanza enumerating Jormunrek's sons has been lost. Many editors combine lines 3-4 of stanza 22 and lines 2-4 of

He was kinsman of Sigurth,— hear well what I say,—
The foe of hosts, and Fafnir's slayer.

26. "From Volsung's seed was the hero sprung,
And Hjordis was born of Hrauthung's race,
And Eylimi from the Othlings came,—
And all are thy kinsmen, Ottar, thou fool!

27. "Gunnar and Hogni, the heirs of Gjuki,
And Guthrun as well, who their sister was;
But Gotthorm was not of Gjuki's race,
Although the brother of both he was:
And all are thy kinsmen, Ottar, thou fool!

---

stanza 25 into one stanza. *Jormunrek:* the historical Ermanarich, king of the Goths, who died about 376. According to Norse tradition, in which Jormunrek played a large part, he slew his own sons (cf. *Guthrunarhvot* and *Hamthesmol*). In the saga Jormunrek married Sigurth's daughter, Svanhild. Stanzas 25-27 connect Ottar's descent with the whole Volsung-Sigurth-Jormunrek-Gjuki genealogy. The story of *Sigurth* is the basis for most of the heroic poems of the *Edda,* of the famous *Volsungasaga,* and, in Germany, of the *Nibelungenlied.* On his battle with the dragon *Fafnir* cf. *Fafnismol.*

26. *Volsung:* Sigurth's grandfather and Othin's great-grandson. *Hjordis:* daughter of King Eylimi, wife of Sigmund and mother of Sigurth. *Othlings:* cf. stanza 11.

27. *Gunnar, Hogni,* and *Guthrun:* the three children of the Burgundian king *Gjuki* and his wife Grimhild (Kriemhild); Guthrun was Sigurth's wife. *Gotthorm,* the third brother, who killed Sigurth at Brynhild's behest, was Grimhild's son, and thus a step-son of Gjuki. These four play an important part in the heroic cycle of Eddic poems. Cf. *Gripisspo,* introductory note.

28. "Of Hvethna's sons was Haki the best,
And Hjorvarth the father of Hvethna was;
. . . .

29. "Harald Battle-tooth of Auth was born,
Hrörek the Ring-giver her husband was;
Auth the Deep-minded was Ivar's daughter,
But Rathbarth the father of Randver was:
And all are thy kinsmen, Ottar, thou fool!"

* * *

Fragment of "The Short Voluspo"

30. Eleven in number the gods were known,
When Baldr o'er the hill of death was bowed;
And this to avenge was Vali swift,
When his brother's slayer soon he slew.

---

28. In the manuscript and in many editions these two lines stand between stanzas 33 and 34. The change here made follows Bugge. The manuscript indicates no gap between stanzas 27 and 29. *Hvethna:* wife of King Halfdan of Denmark.

29. The manuscript and many editions include line 1 of stanza 25 after line 4 of stanza 29. The story of *Harald Battle-tooth* is told in detail by Saxo Grammaticus. Harald's father was *Hrörek,* king of Denmark; his mother was *Auth,* daughter of *Ivar,* king of Sweden. After Ivar had treacherously detroyed Hrörek, Auth fled with Harald to Russia, where she married King *Rathbarth.* Harald's warlike career in Norway, and his death on the Bravalla-field at the hands of his nephew, Sigurth Ring, son of *Randver* and grandson of Rathbarth and Auth, were favorite saga themes.

30. At this point begins the fragmentary and interpolated "short *Voluspo*" identified by Snorri. The manuscript gives no indication of the break in the poem's continuity. *Eleven:* there

31. The father of Baldr was the heir of Bur,
. . . .

32. Freyr's wife was Gerth, the daughter of Gymir,
Of the giants' brood, and Aurbotha bore her;
To these as well was Thjazi kin,
The dark-loving giant; his daughter was Skathi.

33. Much have I told thee, and further will tell;
There is much that I know;— wilt thou hear yet more?

34. Heith and Hrossthjof, the children of Hrimnir.
. . . .

---

are various references to the "twelve" gods (including Baldr); Snorri (*Gylfaginning*, 20-33) lists the following twelve in addition to Othin: Thor, Baldr, Njorth, Freyr, Tyr, Bragi, Heimdall, Hoth, Vithar, Vali, Ull and Forseti; he adds Loki as of doubtful divinity. *Baldr* and *Vali:* cf. *Voluspo,* 32-33.

31. The fragmentary stanzas 31-34 have been regrouped in various ways, and with many conjectures as to omissions, none of which are indicated in the manuscript. The order here is as in the manuscript, except that lines 1-2 of stanza 28 have been transposed from after line 2 of stanza 33. *Bur's heir: Othin;* cf. *Voluspo,* 4.

32. *Freyr, Gerth, Gymir:* cf. *Skirnismol. Aurbotha:* a giantess, mother of Gerth. *Thjazi* and *Skathi:* cf. *Lokasenna,* 49, and *Harbarthsljoth,* 19.

33. Cf. *Voluspo,* 44 and 27.

34. *Heith* ("Witch") and *Hrossthjof* ("Horse-thief"): the only other reference to the giant *Hrimnir* (*Skirnismol,* 28) makes no mention of his children.

35. The sybils arose from Vitholf's race,
From Vilmeith all the seers are,
And the workers of charms are Svarthofthi's children,
And from Ymir sprang the giants all.

36. Much have I told thee, and further will tell;
There is much that I know;— wilt thou hear yet more?

37. One there was born in the bygone days,
Of the race of the gods, and great was his might;
Nine giant women, at the world's edge,
Once bore the man so mighty in arms.

38. Gjolp there bore him, Greip there bore him,
Eistla bore him, and Eyrgjafa,
Ulfrun bore him, and Angeyja,
Imth and Atla, and Jarnsaxa.

---

35. This stanza is quoted by Snorri (*Gylfaginning,* 5). Of *Vitholf* ("Forest Wolf"), *Vilmeith* ("Wish-Tree") and *Svarthofthi* ("Black Head") nothing further is known. *Ymir:* cf. *Voluspo,* 3.

37. According to Snorri (*Gylfaginning,* 27) Heimdall was the son of Othin and of nine sisters. As Heimdall was the watchman of the gods, this has given rise to much "solar myth" discussion. The names of his nine giantess mothers are frequently said to denote attributes of the sea.

38. The names of Heimdall's mothers may be rendered "Yelper," "Griper," "Foamer," "Sand-Strewer," "She-Wolf," "Sorrow-Whelmer," "Dusk," "Fury," and "Iron-Sword."

39. Strong was he made with the strength of earth,
With the ice-cold sea, and the blood of swine.

40. One there was born, the best of all,
And strong was he made with the strength of earth;
The proudest is called the kinsman of men
Of the rulers all throughout the world.

41. Much have I told thee, and further will tell;
There is much that I know;— wilt thou hear yet more?

42. The wolf did Loki with Angrbotha win,
And Sleipnir bore he to Svathilfari;
The worst of marvels seemed the one
That sprang from the brother of Byleist then.

---

39. It has been suggested that these lines were interpolated from *Guthrunarkvitha* II, 22. Some editors add the refrain of stanza 36. *Swine's blood:* to Heimdall's strength drawn from earth and sea was added that derived from sacrifice.

40. In the manuscript this stanza stands after stanza 44. Regarding Heimdall's kinship to the three great classes of men, cf. *Rigsthula,* introductory note, wherein the apparent confusion of his attributes with those of Othin is discussed.

42. Probably a lacuna before this stanza. Regarding the *wolf* Fenrir, born of *Loki* and the giantess *Angrbotha,* cf. *Voluspo,* 39 and note. *Sleipnir:* Othin's eight-legged horse, born of the stallion *Svathilfari* and of Loki in the guise of a mare (cf. *Grimnismol,* 44). *The worst:* doubtless referring to Mithgarthsorm, another child of Loki. *The brother of Byleist:* Loki; cf. *Voluspo,* 51.

43. A heart ate Loki,— in the embers it lay,
And half-cooked found he the woman's heart;—
With child from the woman Lopt soon was,
And thence among men came the monsters all.

44. The sea, storm-driven, seeks heaven itself,
O'er the earth it flows, the air grows sterile;
Then follow the snows and the furious winds,
For the gods are doomed, and the end is death.

45. Then comes another, a greater than all,
Though never I dare his name to speak;
Few are they now that farther can see
Than the moment when Othin shall meet the wolf.

* * *

Freyja spake:

46. "To my boar now bring the memory-beer,
So that all thy words, that well thou hast spoken,

---

43. Nothing further is known of the myth here referred to, wherein Loki (Lopt) eats the cooked heart of a woman and thus himself gives birth to a monster. The reference is not likely to be to the serpent, as, according to Snorri (*Gylfaginning*, 34), the wolf, the serpent, and Hel were all the children of Loki and Angrbotha.

44. Probably an omission, perhaps of considerable length, before this stanza. For the description of the destruction of the world, cf. *Voluspo*, 57.

45. Cf. *Voluspo*, 65, where the possible reference to Christianity is noted. With this stanza the fragmentary "short *Voluspo*" ends, and the dialogue between Freyja and Hyndla continues.

46. Freyja now admits the identity of her boar as Ottar, who

The third morn hence he may hold in mind,
When their races Ottar and Angantyr tell."

Hyndla spake:

47. "Hence shalt thou fare, for fain would I sleep,
From me thou gettest few favors good;
My noble one, out in the night thou leapest
As Heithrun goes the goats among.

48. "To Oth didst thou run, who loved thee ever,
And many under thy apron have crawled;
My noble one, out in the night thou leapest,
As Heithrun goes the goats among."

Freyja spake:

49. "Around the giantess flames shall I raise,
So that forth unburned thou mayst not fare."

---

with the help of the "memory-beer" is to recall the entire genealogy he has just heard, and thus win his wager with Angantyr.

47. *Heithrun:* the she-goat that stands by Valhall (cf. *Grimnismol,* 25), the name being here used simply of she-goats in general, in caustic comment on Freyja's morals. Of these Loki entertained a similar view; cf. *Lokasenna,* 30.

48. *Oth:* cf. stanza 6 and note, and *Voluspo,* 25 and note. Lines 3-4, abbreviated in the manuscript, are very likely repeated here by mistake.

49. The manuscript repeats once again lines 3-4 of stanza 47 as the last two lines of this stanza. It seems probable that two lines have been lost, to the effect that Freyja will burn the giantess alive "If swiftly now thou dost not seek, / And hither bring the memory-beer."

Hyndla spake:

50. "Flames I see burning, the earth is on fire,
And each for his life the price must lose;
Bring then to Ottar the draught of beer,
Of venom full for an evil fate."

Freyja spake:

51. "Thine evil words shall work no ill,
Though, giantess, bitter thy baleful threats;
A drink full fair shall Ottar find,
If of all the gods the favor I get."

SVIPDAGSMOL

The Ballad of Svipdag

Introductory Note

The two poems, *Grougaldr* (*Groa's Spell*) and *Fjolsvinnsmol* (the *Ballad of Fjolsvith*), which many editors have, very wisely, united under the single title of *Svipdagsmol*, are found only in paper manuscripts, none of them antedating the seventeenth century. Everything points to a relatively late origin for the poems: their extensive use of "kennings" or poetical circumlocutions, their romantic spirit, quite foreign to the character of the unquestionably older poems, the absence of any reference to them in the earlier documents, the frequent errors in mythology, and, finally, the fact that the poems appear to have been preserved in unusually good condition. Whether or not a connecting link of narrative verse joining the two parts has been lost is an open question; on the whole it seems likely that the story was sufficiently well known so that the reciter of the poem (or poems) merely filled in the gap with a brief prose summary in pretty much his own words. The general relationship between dialogue and narrative in the Eddic poems is discussed in the introductory note to the *Grimnismol*, in connection with the use of prose links.

The love story of Svipdag and Mengloth is not referred to elsewhere in the *Poetic Edda*, nor does Snorri mention it; however, Groa, who here appears as Svipdag's mother, is spoken of by Snorri as a wise woman, the wife of Orvandil, who helps Thor with her magic charms. On the other hand, the essence of the story, the hero's winning of a bride ringed about by flames, is strongly suggestive of parts of the Sigurth-Brynhild traditions. Whether or not it is to be regarded as a nature or solar myth depends entirely on one's view of the whole "solar myth" school of criticism, not so highly esteemed today as formerly; such an interpretation is certainly not necessary to explain what is, under any circumstances, a very charming romance told, in the main, with dramatic effectiveness.

In later years the story of Svipdag and Mengloth became popular throughout the North, and was made the subject of many Danish and Swedish as well as Norwegian ballads. These have greatly assisted in the reconstruction of the outlines of the narrative surrounding the dialogue poems here given.

Svipdagsmol

I. GROUGALDR

Groa's Spell

Svipdag spake:

1. "Wake thee, Groa! wake, mother good!
At the doors of the dead I call thee;
Thy son, bethink thee, thou badst to seek
Thy help at the hill of death."

Groa spake:

2. "What evil vexes mine only son,
What baleful fate hast thou found,
That thou callest thy mother, who lies in the mould,
And the world of the living has left?"

Svipdag spake:

3. "The woman false whom my father embraced
Has brought me a baleful game;
For she bade me go forth where none may fare,
And Mengloth the maid to seek."

Groa spake:

4. "Long is the way, long must thou wander,
But long is love as well;
Thou mayst find, perchance, what thou fain wouldst have,
If the fates their favor will give."

---

1. *Svipdag* ("Swift Day"): the names of the speakers are lacking in the manuscripts.

3. *The woman:* Svipdag's stepmother, who is responsible for

Svipdag spake:

5. "Charms full good then chant to me, mother,
And seek thy son to guard;
For death do I fear on the way I shall fare,
And in years am I young, methinks."

Groa spake:

6. "Then first I will chant thee the charm oft-tried,
That Rani taught to Rind;
From the shoulder whate'er mislikes thee shake,
For helper thyself shalt thou have.

7. "Then next I will chant thee, if needs thou must travel,
And wander a purposeless way:
The bolts of Urth shall on every side
Be thy guards on the road thou goest.

8. "Then third I will chant thee, if threatening streams
The danger of death shall bring:

---

his search for *Mengloth* ("Necklace-Glad"). This name has suggested that Mengloth is really Frigg, possessor of the famous Brisings' necklace, or else Freyja (cf. *Lokasenna,* 20, note).

6. For this catalogue of charms (stanzas 6-14) cf. the *Ljothatal* (*Hovamol,* 147-165). *Rani* and *Rind:* the manuscripts have these words in inverse relation; I have followed Neckel's emendation. Rind was the giantess who became the mother of Vali, Othin's son, the one-night-old avenger of Baldr (cf. *Voluspo,* 33-34, and *Baldrs Draumar,* 11 and note). Rani is presumably Othin, who, according to a skaldic poem, won Rind by magic.

7. *Urth:* one of the three Norns, or Fates; cf. *Voluspo,* 20.

Yet to Hel shall turn both Horn and Ruth,
And before thee the waters shall fail.

9. "Then fourth I will chant thee, if come thy foes
On the gallows-way against thee:
Into thine hands shall their hearts be given,
And peace shall the warriors wish.

10. "Then fifth I will chant thee, if fetters perchance
Shall bind thy bending limbs:
O'er thy thighs do I chant a loosening-charm,
And the lock is burst from the limbs,
And the fetters fall from the feet.

11. "Then sixth I will chant thee, if storms on the sea
Have might unknown to man:
Yet never shall wind or wave do harm,
And calm is the course of thy boat.

12. "Then seventh I chant thee, if frost shall seek
To kill thee on lofty crags:
The fatal cold shall not grip thy flesh,
And whole thy body shall be.

---

8. *Horn* and *Ruth:* these two rivers, here used merely to symbolize all dangerous streams, are not included in the catalogue of rivers given in *Grimnismol,* 27-29, for which reason some editors have changed the names to Hron and Hrith.

10. This stanza is a close parallel to *Hovamol,* 150, and the fifth line may well be an interpolation from line 4 of that stanza.

13. "Then eighth will I chant thee, if ever by night
Thou shalt wander on murky ways:
Yet never the curse of a Christian woman
From the dead shall do thee harm.

14. "Then ninth will I chant thee, if needs thou must strive
With a warlike giant in words:
Thy heart good store of wit shall have,
And thy mouth of words full wise.

15. "Now fare on the way where danger waits,
Let evils not lessen thy love!
I have stood at the door of the earth-fixed stones,
The while I chanted thee charms.

16. "Bear hence, my son, what thy mother hath said,
And let it live in thy breast;
Thine ever shall be the best of fortune,
So long as my words shall last."

---

13. *A dead Christian woman:* this passage has distressed many editors, who have sought to emend the text so as to make it mean simply "a dead witch." The fact seems to be, however, that this particular charm was composed at a time when Christians were regarded by all conservative pagans as emissaries of darkness. A dead woman's curse would naturally be more potent, whether she was Christian or otherwise, than a living one's. Presumably this charm is much older than the poem in which it here stands.

16. At this point Groa's song ends, and Svipdag, thus fortified, goes to seek Mengloth. All the link that is needed between the poems is approximately this: "Then Svipdag searched long for

Svipdagsmol

II. FJOLSVINNSMOL

The Lay of Fjolsvith

17. Before the house he beheld one coming
To the home of the giants high.

Svipdag spake:

"What giant is here, in front of the house,
And around him fires are flaming?"

Fjolsvith spake:

18. "What seekest thou here? for what is thy search?
What, friendless one, fain wouldst thou know?
By the ways so wet must thou wander hence,
For, weakling, no home hast thou here."

Svipdag spake:

19. "What giant is here, in front of the house,
To the wayfarer welcome denying?"

Mengloth, and at last he came to a great house set all about with flames. And before the house there was a giant."

17. Most editors have here begun a new series of stanza numbers, but if the *Grougaldr* and the *Fjolsvinnsmol* are to be considered as a single poem, it seems more reasonable to continue the stanza numbers consecutively. Bugge thinks a stanza has been lost before 17, including Fjolsvith's name, so that the "he" in line 1 might have something to refer to. However, just such a prose link as I have suggested in the note on stanza 16 would serve the purpose. Editors have suggested various rearrangements in the lines of stanzas 17-19. The substance, however, is clear enough. The giant *Fjolsvith* ("Much-Wise"), the warder of the house in which Mengloth dwells, sees Svipdag coming and stops him with the customary threats. The assignment of the

Fjolsvith spake:

"Greeting full fair thou never shalt find,
So hence shalt thou get thee home.

20\. "Fjolsvith am I, and wise am I found,
But miserly am I with meat;
Thou never shalt enter within the house,—
Go forth like a wolf on thy way!"

Svipdag spake:

21\. "Few from the joy of their eyes will go forth,
When the sight of their loves they seek;
Full bright are the gates of the golden hall,
And a home shall I here enjoy."

Fjolsvith spake:

22\. "Tell me now, fellow, what father thou hast,
And the kindred of whom thou camst."

Svipdag spake:

"Vindkald am I, and Varkald's son,
And Fjolkald his father was.

23\. "Now answer me, Fjolsvith, the question I ask,
For now the truth would I know:

---

speeches in stanzas 17-20, in the absence of any indications in the manuscripts, is more or less guesswork.

22\. *Vindkald* ("Wind-Cold"), *Varkald* ("Cold of Early Spring") and *Fjolkald* ("Much Cold"): Svipdag apparently seeks to persuade Fjolsvith that he belongs to the frost giants.

Who is it that holds and has for his own
The rule of the hall so rich?"

Fjolsvith spake:

24. "Mengloth is she, her mother bore her
To the son of Svafrthorin;
She is it that holds and has for her own
The rule of the hall so rich."

Svipdag spake:

25. "Now answer me, Fjolsvith, the question I ask,
For now the truth would I know:
What call they the gate? for among the gods
Ne'er saw man so grim a sight."

Fjolsvith spake:

26. "Thrymgjol they call it; 'twas made by the three,
The sons of Solblindi;
And fast as a fetter the farer it holds,
Whoever shall lift the latch."

Svipdag spake:

27. "Now answer me, Fjolsvith, the question I ask,
For now the truth would I know:

---

24. *Svafrthorin:* who he was, or what his name means, or who his son was, are all unknown.

26. *Thrymgjol* ("Loud-Clanging"): this gate, like the gate of the dead, shuts so fast as to trap those who attempt to use it (cf. *Sigurtharkvitha en skamma,* 68 and note). It was made by the dwarfs, sons of *Solblindi* ("Sun-Blinded"), the traditional craftsmen, who could not endure the light of day.

What call they the house? for no man beheld
'Mongst the gods so grim a sight."

Fjolsvith spake:

28. "Gastropnir is it, of old I made it
From the limbs of Leirbrimir;
I braced it so strongly that fast it shall stand
So long as the world shall last."

Svipdag spake:

29. "Now answer me, Fjolsvith, the question I ask,
For now the truth would I know:
What call they the tree that casts abroad
Its limbs o'er every land?"

Fjolsvith spake:

30. "Mimameith its name, and no man knows
What root beneath it runs;
And few can guess what shall fell the tree,
For fire nor iron shall fell it."

Svipdag spake:

31. "Now answer me, Fjolsvith, the question I ask,
For now the truth would I know:

---

28. *Gastropnir:* "Guest-Crusher." *Leirbrimir's* ("Clay-Giant's") *limbs:* a poetic circumlocution for "clay"; cf. the description of the making of earth from the body of the giant Ymir, *Vafthruthnismol,* 21.

30. *Mimameith* ("Mimir's Tree"): the ash Yggdrasil, that overshadows the whole world. The well of Mimir was situated at its base; cf. *Voluspo,* 27-29.

What grows from the seed of the tree so great,
That fire nor iron shall fell?"

Fjolsvith spake:

32. "Women, sick with child, shall seek
Its fruit to the flames to bear;
Then out shall come what within was hid,
And so is it mighty with men."

Svipdag spake:

33. "Now answer me, Fjolsvith, the question I ask,
For now the truth would I know:
What cock is he on the highest bough,
That glitters all with gold?"

Fjolsvith spake:

34. "Vithofnir his name, and now he shines
Like lightning on Mimameith's limbs;
And great is the trouble with which he grieves
Both Surt and Sinmora."

---

32. Gering suggests that two stanzas have been lost between stanzas 15 and 16, but the giant's answer fits the question quite well enough. The fruit of Yggdrasil, when cooked, is here assumed to have the power of assuring safe childbirth.

34. *Vithofnir* ("Tree-Snake"): apparently identical with either the cock Gollinkambi (cf. *Voluspo,* 43) or Fjalar (cf. *Voluspo,* 42), the former of which wakes the gods to battle, and the latter the giants. *Surt:* the giant mentioned in *Voluspo,* 52, as ruler of the fire-world; here used to represent the giants in general, who are constantly in terror of the cock's eternal watchfulness. *Sinmora:* presumably Surt's wife, the giantess who possesses the weapon by which alone the cock Vithofnir may be slain.

Svipdag spake:

35. "Now answer me, Fjolsvith, the question I ask,
For now the truth would I know:
What call they the hounds, that before the house
So fierce and angry are?"

Fjolsvith spake:

36. "Gif call they one, and Geri the other,
If now the truth thou wouldst know;
Great they are, and their might will grow,
Till the gods to death are doomed."

Svipdag spake:

37. "Now answer me, Fjolsvith, the question I ask,
For now the truth would I know:
May no man hope the house to enter,
While the hungry hounds are sleeping?"

Fjolsvith spake:

38. "Together they sleep not, for so was it fixed
When the guard to them was given;
One sleeps by night, the next by day,
So no man may enter ever."

Svipdag spake:

39. "Now answer me, Fjolsvith, the question I ask,
For now the truth would I know:

---

35. The last two lines have been variously emended.

36. *Gif* and *Geri:* both names signify "Greedy." The first part of line 3 is conjectural; the manuscripts indicate the word "eleven," which clearly fails to make sense.

Is there no meat that men may give them,
And leap within while they eat?"

Fjolsvith spake:

40. "Two wing-joints there be in Vithofnir's body,
If now the truth thou wouldst know;
That alone is the meat that men may give them,
And leap within while they eat."

Svipdag spake:

41. "Now answer me, Fjolsvith, the question I ask,
For now the truth would I know:
What weapon can send Vithofnir to seek
The house of Hel below?"

Fjolsvith spake:

42. "Lævatein is there, that Lopt with runes
Once made by the doors of death;
In Lægjarn's chest by Sinmora lies it,
And nine locks fasten it firm."

Svipdag spake:

43. "Now answer me, Fjolsvith, the question I ask,
For now the truth would I know:
May a man come thence who thither goes,
And tries the sword to take?"

---

42. *Lævctein* ("Wounding Wand"): the manuscripts differ as to the form of this name. The suggestion that the reference is to the mistletoe with which Baldr was killed seems hardly reasonable. *Lopt:* Loki. *Lægjarn* ("Lover of Ill"): Loki; cf. *Voluspo,* 35,

Fjolsvith spake:

44. "Thence may he come who thither goes,
And tries the sword to take,
If with him he carries what few can win,
To give to the goddess of gold."

Svipdag spake:

45. "Now answer me, Fjolsvith, the question I ask,
For now the truth would I know:
What treasure is there that men may take
To rejoice the giantess pale?"

Fjolsvith spake:

46. "The sickle bright in thy wallet bear,
Mid Vithofnir's feathers found;
To Sinmora give it, and then shall she grant
That the weapon by thee be won."

Svipdag spake:

47. "Now answer me, Fjolsvith, the question I ask,
For now the truth would I know:
What call they the hall, encompassed here
With flickering magic flames?"

---

where the term appears as an adjective applied to Loki. This is Falk's emendation for the manuscripts' "Sægjarn," meaning "Sea Lover." *Sinmora:* cf. stanza 34.

44 *Goddess of gold:* poetic circumlocution for "woman," here meaning Sinmora.

46. *Sickle:* i.e., tail feather. With this the circle of impossibilities is completed. To get past the dogs, they must be fed with the wing-joints of the cock Vithofnir; the cock can be killed only

Fjolsvith spake:

48. "Lyr is it called, and long it shall
On the tip of a spear-point tremble;
Of the noble house mankind has heard,
But more has it never known."

Svipdag spake:

49. "Now answer me, Fjolsvith, the question I ask,
For now the truth would I know:
What one of the gods has made so great
The hall I behold within?"

Fjolsvith spake:

50. "Uni and Iri, Bari and Jari,
Var and Vegdrasil,
Dori and Ori, Delling, and there
Was Loki, the fear of the folk."

---

with the sword in Sinmora's possession, and Sinmora will give up the sword only in return for the tail feather of the cock.

48. *Lyr* ("Heat-Holding"): just what the spear-point reference means is not altogether clear. Presumably it refers to the way in which the glowing brightness of the lofty hall makes it seem to quiver and turn in the air, but the tradition, never baffled by physical laws, may have actually balanced the whole building on a single point to add to the difficulties of entrance.

50. *Loki,* the one god named, was the builder of the hall, with the aid of the nine dwarfs. *Jari, Dori,* and *Ori* appear in the *Voluspo* catalogue of the dwarfs (stanzas 13 and 15); *Delling* appears in *Hovamol,* 161, and *Vafthruthnismol,* 25, in the latter case, however, the name quite possibly referring to some one else. The other dwarfs' names do not appear elsewhere. The manuscripts differ as to the forms of many of these names.

Svipdag spake:

51. "Now answer me, Fjolsvith, the question I ask,
For now the truth would I know:
What call they the mountain on which the maid
Is lying so lovely to see?"

Fjolsvith spake:

52. "Lyfjaberg is it, and long shall it be
A joy to the sick and the sore;
For well shall grow each woman who climbs it,
Though sick full long she has lain."

Svipdag spake:

53. "Now answer me, Fjolsvith, the question I ask,
For now the truth would I know:
What maidens are they that at Mengloth's knees
Are sitting so gladly together?"

Fjolsvith spake:

54. "Hlif is one named, Hlifthrasa another,
Thjothvara call they the third;

---

52. *Lyfjaberg* ("Hill of Healing"): the manuscripts vary as to this name; I have followed Bugge's suggestion. This stanza implies that Mengloth is a goddess of healing, and hence, perhaps, an hypostasis of Frigg, as already intimated by her name (cf. stanza 3, note). In stanza 54 Eir appears as one of Mengloth's handmaidens, and Eir, according to Snorri (*Gylfaginning,* 35) is herself the Norse Hygeia. Compare this stanza with stanza 32.

54. The manuscripts and editions show many variations in these names. They may be approximately rendered thus: Helper, Help-Breather, Folk-Guardian, Shining, White, Blithe, Peaceful, Kindly (?), and Gold-Giver.

Bjort and Bleik, Blith and Frith,
Eir and Aurbotha."

Svipdag spake:

55. "Now answer me, Fjolsvith, the question I ask,
For now the truth would I know:
Aid bring they to all who offerings give,
If need be found therefor?"

Fjolsvith spake:

56. "Soon aid they all who offerings give
On the holy altars high;
And if danger they see for the sons of men,
Then each from ill do they guard."

Svipdag spake:

57. "Now answer me, Fjolsvith, the question I ask,
For now the truth would I know:
Lives there the man who in Mengloth's arms
So fair may seek to sleep?"

Fjolsvith spake:

58. "No man there is who in Mengloth's arms
So fair may seek to sleep,
Save Svipdag alone, for the sun-bright maid
Is destined his bride to be."

---

55. One of the manuscripts omits stanzas 55 and 56.

56. The first line is based on a conjectural emendation.

Svipdag spake:

59. "Fling back the gates! make the gateway wide!
Here mayst thou Svipdag see!
Hence get thee to find if gladness soon
Mengloth to me will give."

Fjolsvith spake:

60. "Hearken, Mengloth, a man is come;
Go thou the guest to see!
The hounds are fawning, the house bursts open,—
Svipdag, methinks, is there."

Mengloth spake:

61. "On the gallows high shall hungry ravens
Soon thine eyes pluck out,
If thou liest in saying that here at last
The hero is come to my hall.

62. "Whence camest thou hither? how camest thou here?
What name do thy kinsmen call thee?
Thy race and thy name as a sign must I know,
That thy bride I am destined to be."

Svipdag spake:

63. "Svipdag am I, and Solbjart's son;
Thence came I by wind-cold ways;

---

63. *Solbjart* ("Sun-Bright"): not elsewhere mentioned. *The words of Urth:* i.e., the decrees of fate; cf. stanza 7.

With the words of Urth shall no man war,
Though unearned her gifts be given."

Mengloth spake:

64\. "Welcome thou art, for long have I waited;
The welcoming kiss shalt thou win!
For two who love is the longed-for meeting
The greatest gladness of all.

65\. "Long have I sat on Lyfjaberg here,
Awaiting thee day by day;
And now I have what I ever hoped,
For here thou art come to my hall.

66\. "Alike we yearned; I longed for thee,
And thou for my love hast longed;
But now henceforth together we know
Our lives to the end we shall live."

65\. *Lyfjaberg* cf. stanza 52 and note.

A CATALOG OF SELECTED DOVER BOOKS IN ALL FIELDS OF INTEREST

DRIED FLOWERS: How to Prepare Them, Sarah Whitlock and Martha Rankin. Complete instructions on how to use silica gel, meal and borax, perlite aggregate, sand and borax, glycerine and water to create attractive permanent flower arrangements. 12 illustrations. 32pp. $5\frac{3}{8}$ x $8\frac{1}{2}$. 0-486-21802-3

EASY-TO-MAKE BIRD FEEDERS FOR WOODWORKERS, Scott D. Campbell. Detailed, simple-to-use guide for designing, constructing, caring for and using feeders. Text, illustrations for 12 classic and contemporary designs. 96pp. $5\frac{3}{8}$ x $8\frac{1}{2}$. 0-486-25847-5

THE COMPLETE BOOK OF BIRDHOUSE CONSTRUCTION FOR WOODWORKERS, Scott D. Campbell. Detailed instructions, illustrations, tables. Also data on bird habitat and instinct patterns. Bibliography. 3 tables. 63 illustrations in 15 figures. 48pp. $5\frac{1}{4}$ x $8\frac{1}{2}$. 0-486-24407-5

SCOTTISH WONDER TALES FROM MYTH AND LEGEND, Donald A. Mackenzie. 16 lively tales tell of giants rumbling down mountainsides, of a magic wand that turns stone pillars into warriors, of gods and goddesses, evil hags, powerful forces and more. 240pp. $5\frac{3}{8}$ x $8\frac{1}{2}$. 0-486-29677-6

THE HISTORY OF UNDERCLOTHES, C. Willett Cunnington and Phyllis Cunnington. Fascinating, well-documented survey covering six centuries of English undergarments, enhanced with over 100 illustrations: 12th-century laced-up bodice, footed long drawers (1795), 19th-century bustles, 19th-century corsets for men, Victorian "bust improvers," much more. 272pp. $5\frac{5}{8}$ x $8\frac{1}{4}$. 0-486-27124-2

FIRST FRENCH READER: A Beginner's Dual-Language Book, edited and translated by Stanley Appelbaum. This anthology introduces fifty legendary writers–Voltaire, Balzac, Baudelaire, Proust, more–through passages from The Red and the Black, Les Misérables, Madame Bovary, and other classics. Original French text plus English translation on facing pages. 240pp. $5\frac{3}{8}$ x $8\frac{1}{2}$. 0-486-46178-5

WILBUR AND ORVILLE: A Biography of the Wright Brothers, Fred Howard. Definitive, crisply written study tells the full story of the brothers' lives and work. A vividly written biography, unparalleled in scope and color, that also captures the spirit of an extraordinary era. 560pp. $6\frac{1}{8}$ x $9\frac{1}{4}$. 0-486-40297-5

THE ARTS OF THE SAILOR: Knotting, Splicing and Ropework, Hervey Garrett Smith. Indispensable shipboard reference covers tools, basic knots and useful hitches; handsewing and canvas work, more. Over 100 illustrations. Delightful reading for sea lovers. 256pp. $5\frac{3}{8}$ x $8\frac{1}{2}$. 0-486-26440-8

FRANK LLOYD WRIGHT'S FALLINGWATER: The House and Its History, Second, Revised Edition, Donald Hoffmann. A total revision–both in text and illustrations–of the standard document on Fallingwater, the boldest, most personal architectural statement of Wright's mature years, updated with valuable new material from the recently opened Frank Lloyd Wright Archives. "Fascinating"–*The New York Times*. 116 illustrations. 128pp. $9\frac{1}{4}$ x $10\frac{3}{4}$. 0-486-27430-6

PHOTOGRAPHIC SKETCHBOOK OF THE CIVIL WAR, Alexander Gardner. 100 photos taken on field during the Civil War. Famous shots of Manassas Harper's Ferry, Lincoln, Richmond, slave pens, etc. 244pp. $10\frac{5}{8}$ x $8\frac{1}{4}$. 0-486-22731-6

FIVE ACRES AND INDEPENDENCE, Maurice G. Kains. Great back-to-the-land classic explains basics of self-sufficient farming. The one book to get. 95 illustrations. 397pp. $5\frac{3}{8}$ x $8\frac{1}{2}$. 0-486-20974-1